Community of Magic Pens

Community of Magic Pens

Edited by E.D.E. Bell

Atthis Arts
Detroit, Michigan

Community of Magic Pens

This is a work of fiction.

Cover and interior illustrations by Artistic Journey Creations

Editorial services by: E.D.E. Bell
Camille Gooderham Campbell
Catherine Jones Payne, Quill Pen Editorial
Jason Sizemore
Elsa Sjunneson

Typesetting and layout by G.C. Bell

Published by Atthis Arts, LLC
Detroit, Michigan
atthisarts.com

ISBN 978-1-945009-60-0

Library of Congress Control Number: 2020935159

Stories

Our Gratitude to:

Z. Ahmad
Saladin Ahmed
Tessa Anouska
Jasre' Ellis
Andrew K Hoe
Stella B. James
Tushar Jhunjhunwala
Leslie Kannon
M. Kaur
Gerri Leen
Nicole J. LeBoeuf-Little
R.B. Lemberg
Valerie Linebaugh
Donnie Martino
Jennifer Matthews
Cat Rambo
Jennifer Lee Rossman
Jannae' Sifontes

Our Love to:

Rita Beth Ebert

About the Cover Artwork

They're pens, cute and silly. The story behind them can mean a thousand words to me or just a handful to you. A fineliner, a stylus, a ball point, a dip pen, or my favorite pen that I unconsciously click far too many times not to annoy those around me but to calm my anxiety. Just like people many pens come from different backgrounds, with different stories, and a million different things that make them great.—Journey

Preface

Thank you for picking up this book! I am so excited for you to read it.

Sometimes I think I do anthologies sideways, and people are probably shaking their heads at me. Normally, *similar* stories are compiled. Stories in the same genre, with the same tone, the same audience. That way they can be marketed to the people who will surely like them, and the people who surely like them will know what they are getting.

Yet, what excites me about short fiction is the unexpected. I love to take a theme and see what people can do with it. Where each piece is a new surprise, a new experience. Where our unique voices are as stark as our shared chorus.

Amidst a whole list of concepts, this idea stuck into my mind and wouldn't leave. I thought . . . can I do this? Magic Pens? Will people connect? I knew it was a bit on the nose. But I couldn't stop thinking about the stories that could be written. So I went with it.

What happened was honestly very different than I thought. I expected people to run away with ideas, until I better understood that there was no reason to. A whole universe of pen love swirled right where we already were. I learned that not only are pens, both fancy and simple, intensely treasured—pens, the actual devices, have some of the deepest meanings. Friendship. Power. History. Religion. Love. Mystery. Dreams.

Pens are not just symbols of writing. Or of communicating. They are symbols of the shared human story. Of time and space . . . and memory.

I don't normally do a dedication in a collection like this, because I feel the energy is so shared. Yet, I do want to offer this book to you In Memoriam my friend, Alonza McKenzie. See, this wasn't supposed to be the next collection for me. Al had brought me in to fulfill a vision of his: To create an anthology of real-life stories focused on present and former students of Detroit Public Schools (with regional submissions also) who could attest to how comprehensive music education had changed their lives. Then, after a medical emergency, Al was diagnosed with brain cancer and sent to the hospital. He was there. Then he wasn't. He called me out of the blue one day, reassuring me he'd be back in just a few weeks and we'd get to work. He was so cheerful—told me to keep working on my other projects. Repeated that he believed in me. "I'm not worried about you," he said. Al didn't come back. As his Pastor said, he returned to the Light.

Al's collection would have featured Jazz and Soul stars, as well as people, both known and unknown, who'd had a career in something other than music, and all alongside current students, conveying their own lessons and dreams. Just as this collection features seasoned writers along with first-time publications—we both believed in that breakdown. I considered whether I could investigate continuing the project without him. I couldn't. That project was deep in his heart, just as this one is mine.

Yet, now, I'd like to use my magic pen in the tiniest way that I can, to deliver Al's message. A message he wanted everyone to hear. Comprehensive music education changes lives. Not just music lessons or bands, but comprehensive education: theory, practice, drills, improvisation, performance, and community. This should not be viewed as a nice-to-have, the first thing to be cut when school or family budgets are strained. It should be valued by the people and by the people of their governments, by those with the power or resources to provide it. Access to comprehensive music education doesn't just change lives: it changes the lives of all those touched, as Al's life of service demonstrates.

Al also wanted people to tell their stories, and I can definitely say that my own music education as a kid, with my parents' and community's passion toward providing it, affects me here, now, doing this. Just as Al's influence most certainly does.

I won't go through all that he taught me, but let's say he lit up both my persistence as well as my faith in community. In giving. And trusting.

He also told me vegans are cool. ☺

I will just note one of many things highlighted by our time working on the project together: Don't let someone outside of a community tell you the nature and state of that community, not when that community is available to speak. Listen to the community directly. What you find *will* be different. Authentic understandings are core to making our shared world better for us all.

Al spoke about the first time he was able to go to Interlochen Center for the Arts. He found a line of practice rooms and was overjoyed. He practiced and practiced and practiced, and every opportunity he had, he was back in that room, working. He spent a lot of his money—and raised a lot of money—making that opportunity available to other kids.

I can't live up to Al's example, but I can try in the ways I can. And I can remember the first time he saw *Diamondsong*, and I sort of hedged that it was different than he was used to, and he snapped back, "I know you off-kilter. That's why you're here." Then he told me that I was in the place I needed to be now, and soon I'd see that too.

So I guess this book might be off-kilter too, and I'm so proud—so happy—to present to you what all these amazing writers have done. I hope you will enjoy the stories within these pages. If you do, tell the author. Tell people who might read it. For indie presses and writers, that support is critical. That community.

I want to thank everyone who's been involved with this project. It's a really long list, and please know I'm so grateful to each of you. Whether your contribution was large or small, it all made a difference in the final product. Especial thanks to author and friend L. L. Reynolds for her generous support to our crowdfunding campaign, and to my dear friend Camille Gooderham Campbell, who is often unseen, holding my hand. Thanks to Journey for her art and enthusiasm, and thanks to G.C. Bell for believing in me. All the way. And thanks to Al. I remember that last thing you said to me, and I'm doing it. Best I can.

And, of course, thanks to *you*.

We are all so glad that you're here.

Cheers,
E.D.E. Bell
Spring 2020

E held eir pen over the paper, hovering with visions of glitter and fairy dust powdering the ecru paper. A buzz passed by, like a dragon in flight, charging to a vision of flame and sword. In reality, a snowblower. What could e write? E felt weary, both from the pummeling of the fortunate and the knowledge of eir own fortunes. Warm—the soft barrel turning in eir waiting fingers, a comforting weight. A thought occurred to em. The train whistle blew in the distance.

E set the pen down. And read, instead.

Community of Magic Pens

Penultimate

ZZ Claybourne

There was power in her pen but she dared not use it. There were stories in her head she dared not say. She walked the Earth stealing pens from hotels and banks, writing no more than three words at a time on slips of paper here and there, tucking the parts of a story meant to be discovered long after she was gone into books, between the cushions of bus seats, cracks in trees, and—very specifically—the tables of lovers looking for something to be rekindled, looking to be re-born.

She'd been born seven times within one year once, always with that pen nearby. A fountain pen. Casing black with white dots like random stars, the nib as golden as first light, the band the gold of a ring. She was born married to the pen. She was in love with its hidden stories.

She had forgotten their strength once.

A long time ago. She can't remember any of the people's faces although she'd loved them and knew them. The pen was an odd thing. When she'd found it in the lee of a tree and touched it, everyone went away. Everything went away. The world was changed . . . except her.

What had been a field, now contained structures. Huge buildings and noise all around.

She'd dropped the pen to immediately return to her world, the pen at her feet. She was relieved to find that birds sang, that insects struggling beneath her tickled the soles of her bare feet, and in the distance were people, people whose conversations flowed as though never interrupted.

No one was dead. Nor had anyone noticed she was gone.

"I want to stay," she told the pen, hesitantly bending for it.

It obeyed. It was patient with her. Memory was sometimes tricky.

In the earliest days it showed her there were more uses for a pen than lists. It gave her new words; the words became stories; the stories became . . . reality? Sometimes it was hard to know which dream was hers and which belonged to all the world.

She would write, then glance around, and notice things had changed. Small things. The arguing lovers across the way, now kissing. A hornet prepared to sting, now content to laze among the many flowers that grew uninterrupted.

One day she got bold, very bold; she wrote a tale of new love, designed specifically to change.

Which it did.

She unwittingly wrote everyone out of existence.

Even the world: gone.

She looked for her hands and they weren't there. Her body consumed stars as a galaxys-wide nebula thrust into the universe mere seconds after the Big Bang; she was the first touch of consciousness and wonder and delight and fear and wanting ever to exist.

She was love.

It had taken a huge effort of will to pull herself together. Billions of years. In that time the world re-formed, people returned, life evolved on track.

And the pen lay nearby.

She didn't fear it. She picked it up, willing everyone and everything to stay.

They did.

She knew the story of love. It involved destruction, tearing, rebuilding, reimagining, becoming—all things the world wasn't designed strong enough to hold in its hands for very long.

It was a story to be told in whispers, in slips, in sudden findings.

In epiphanies or words stopped solely by kisses on lips.

After several lifetimes she realized she was not separate from the pen; it was not separate from her.

She hadn't found it. She'd forgotten she'd created it, knowledge which created a nomad of her. As she walked the Earth pretending to be smaller than anyone ever truly was, for the world, the stars, the universe was a story of love, a tale which erased entire existences to rebuild them anew, she felt more emboldened at leaving parts of the mystery much more often in full view.

She remembered loving the summer, the sounds of lovers, intertwined stories erasing solitude, erasing separation.

Strips of paper on the wind, blowing toward you.

ZZ Claybourne (he/him, also known as Clarence Young) is the author of the novels *The Brothers Jetstream: Leviathan*, *Neon Lights*, and *By All Our Violent Guides*, as well as the acclaimed short story collection *Historical Inaccuracies* and inspirational gift book *In the Quiet Spaces*. His essays on sci-fi, fandom, and creativity have appeared in *Apex*, *Strange Horizons*, and various other outlets. He is currently at work on his 4th novel. Find him on the web at writeonrighton.com.

Of Signatures and Contracts

Andrew K Hoe

Trenchcoat Man, a silent 6'4" harbinger of corporate death, fixed Michael with a stare that practically froze the nearly empty boardroom. Not his actual name, of course, but Michael didn't know what else to call him. He'd started shadowing Mr. Detenweiler as negotiations with NyxCorp finalized, but never spoke. NyxCorp's hired muscle, most likely.

Detenweiler himself sat across from Michael. It was impossible, but beyond the skyrise windows, Michael thought he heard protesters chanting below. The document before him was pristine—the Devil's contract for his soul should look so clean.

"Okay, Mr. Ho?" Detenweiler asked.

Michael grunted against the pit in his stomach. "Fine."

The last concession NyxCorp had forced was they could fire whomever they wanted after the merger. But Michael had persisted, even after his staff resigned in protest. Why balk now?

He squeezed his pen, then scrawled:

I love Christina Vei.

"What the . . . ?"

Not his signature—but definitely his handwriting. Yes, some nights he stared at the ceiling wondering about Christina. Their romance was years over—mutual decision—they'd been Big Picture people with careers . . .

Trenchcoat Man flexed his fingers, like maybe he'd reach for a pistol.

"Problem?" Detenweiler asked.

Michael gaped as what he'd written faded. The line was blank again. "Just, uh, testing the ink." He set pen to paper once more, marching the nib through each letter of his name.

M—I—C—hael hates signing this because NyxCorp will fire hundreds, then create a monopoly that'll bankrupt families, but this merger's the only thing Michael has left.

The pen stilled. Only thing left? Michael had plenty! Friends—constantly busy, though . . . Well, he had family—in other states . . . Okay, there was this firm he'd built from scratch after leaving Christina. And . . . this industry-shaking, history-making deal . . .

You're hollow, the pen wrote.

Michael looked up.

As before, neither Detenweiler nor Trenchcoat Man seemed to register Michael's scribblings, which were even now fading away. "You seriously don't see that?"

"I see you're having second thoughts, Mr. Ho."

"I . . . This pen's not working."

He was about to call Drew, but Detenweiler produced his own ballpoint. "Here—for heaven's sakes, what is it now?"

Michael couldn't release the pen. It yanked his hand back to the contract, scribbling with impossible speed:

I chose career over love; some nights, I find myself opening search windows to see what Christina's up to; she's moved overseas; I cancel the searches before I find out too much because I couldn't take it if she's married—

Michael wrestled his pen-hand under the table, but not before the nib tore the document.

"Unbelievable!" Detenweiler leapt up. Quiet as death,

Trenchcoat Man reached into his coat, pulling something gleaming—something metal . . .

Michael blinked.

It was a flash drive.

Detenweiler snatched it. "I'm disappointed, Mr. Ho. You've been so focused. So driven. You reminded me of my . . ." Detenweiler shook himself, as if dismissing an unpleasant memory. Whatever it was, it worsened his temper. "You can't not sign. NyxCorp will have both our heads. I'm printing a fresh document, which *you—will—sign*."

He stormed out, Trenchcoat Man following.

Michael stared at the ruined contract. What on earth was going on? His pen leapt back to the torn page, scribbling over and over: *Christina Christina Christina—*

Drew, Michael's gum-chewing temp in muscle-shirt and jeans, poked his head in. "Everything okay, boss? NyxCorp people were gunning for the copier like it stole their cookies." Drew was eccentric, but he'd been a lifesaver these past weeks. He popped a gum-bubble, eyeing Michael's still-writing hand. "Cool pen. Where'd you get it?"

"It was on my desk . . . Wait—you see what I'm writing?"

"Sure. Who's Christina?"

"She's . . ." Michael shook his head. This had to be some sabotage plan. "Did you put this pen on my desk, Drew? Are you trying to destroy this merger?"

"I got hired because of this NyxCorp deal!" Drew protested. "Why would I ruin it?" But his gaze returned to Michael's still-scribbling hand. His gum-chewing slowed.

Christina Christina Christina—

“Wait. The pen’s writing? By itself? I’ve . . . heard of something like that.”

Michael’s hand was growing sore and memories of Christina made his chest tight. “Do tell, Drew.”

“That’s a magic pen.”

Michael snorted. “Oh, come on.”

“Word is, a pen’s been floating around the big firms. A *cursed* pen that, once held, won’t release the holder.”

Come to think of it, Michael *had* heard that story. He’d dismissed it as office chatter. Ghosts haunting skyscrapers. Mummified CEOs inside walls—that kind of silliness.

But a pen supposedly ruined the Ziatic-Hitoshi pact and its relaxed pollutant restrictions. And . . . a pen allegedly made the Terrodyne CFO swear off writing utensils—and its pharmaceutical price hike.

So . . . a *pen* was offing controversial deals? A *cursed* pen?

“It makes you confront your deepest secrets,” Drew continued. “You can’t stop writing until you confess. Who’s Christina, boss? You . . . *liquidate* her or something?”

“What?” Michael spluttered. “That’s ridiculous—”

“AH-HA! The lad doth protest too much—”

“It’s *the lady* doth protest too much—”

Christina Christina Christina Mike, is that you?

Michael’s pen went still.

“Don’t answer,” Drew whispered, wide-eyed. “It’s a cursed pen, remember?”

Michael flipped the torn contract to its clean backside. *Christina?*

The ink faded. The pen moved again. *Mike?*

It was Christina's handwriting.

Michael wrote, *How's this happening?*

He thought he felt her hesitance as the pen scribed her answer.

You won't believe this, but . . . I found a strange pen.

They underwent a Q&A via pen—where they'd met (tour in Japan), favorite color (his was pink), college majors (corporate law), first date (an airport bench).

Drew scowled, popping another gum-bubble. "I dunno, boss."

"She's answered every question. In her handwriting." And Michael thought he smelled her perfume. Like she was sitting next to him. It made his heart skip. "I want to talk to her before I sign. I used to ask Christina everything."

Michael could've used her advice with this NyxCorp deal. Not because she'd become a bigshot manager herself, but because, with her, he'd considered things besides the money line.

Drew waved at Michael's abandoned offices. "Before today, you couldn't sign fast enough. Now you've found your conscience?"

Or maybe Michael's conscience had been there all along. He'd just needed reminding.

The pen stirred. *Mike? I'm in the city. I'm coming to you.*

She was in the city? Didn't she live overseas?

As if reading his thoughts, the pen scribed, *I've been traveling since I got this pen. It wants me to find you.*

Michael frowned. *How long have you had it?*

Two weeks, she wrote.

Michael didn't wait for the ink to fade. *Why didn't you email? To say you were coming?*

Would you have answered?

She had a point. He'd written many letters to her, only to delete them.

Detenweiler's voice sounded from the hallway. "Mr. Ho? Ready your pen!"

"That's it," Michael said quietly. "I'm going downstairs."

"The protesters'll kill you!" Drew argued. "Besides, how do you know whoever you're writing to is real?"

"I . . ." Michael *didn't* know, did he? But . . . that ache in his chest since he'd written her name . . . "Drew, you said this pen makes me confront my secrets. Well, how I *feel* about Christina is real. And I can't sign until I face those feelings."

Detenweiler and Trenchcoat Man re-entered the boardroom, Detenweiler laying his newly printed contract onto the table.

With a last look at Drew, Michael took a breath and stood. "I'm not signing."

"Oh, yes, you are!" Detenweiler snarled. "The police downstairs are in NyxCorp's employ. You can't—HEY!"

Drew had snatched the contract, vaulting the table as Trenchcoat Man strode forward.

"Drew!" Michael yelled. "Let me handle this!"

"Go, boss!"

"But—"

"GO!" Drew ran out the boardroom's far door, Detenweiler huffing after.

Trenchcoat Man turned to Michael. He reached into his coat . . .

"Oh, hell!" Michael bolted for the exit.

Michael scrawled onto his palm as the elevator descended: *What did you see in Kevin?*

The pen scribed Christina's reply after the ink faded: *That's actually none of your business, but he was a gentleman. And he was there.*

The elevator shuddered to a stop on Floor 17. Detenweiler must've found the executive controls. Michael opened a panel and punched in a code. The doors opened and Michael ran through.

Internship was only seven months, Michael wrote. *I would've come back.*

But you didn't, did you?

Well, you were involved, so I extended! Michael panted along the stairwell he was descending. His late-night searches hadn't revealed everything. *So . . . how is Kevin?*

We broke up.

This didn't surprise Michael. Their high-power lifestyles were busy, flurried, solitary.

I'm approaching your building's entrance, Christina wrote. *I'm with someone. He's helping me navigate the crowd.*

Michael sighed. So there was someone else.

He wiped sweat off his brow as he descended. *You've been holding that pen for two weeks? Can't let go?*

No, I can let go. But the pen always returns to my pocket. It appears in my hand. It writes about you.

Michael jumped onto the lobby landing right when the elevator dinged, spilling Detenweiler and Trenchcoat Man.

The pen yanked Michael straight at them. Detenweiler yelped as Trenchcoat Man pulled him aside.

"Stop!" Michael yelled, but the pen dragged him into the outside chaos.

Police manned barricades as protesters waved placards bearing crossed-out NyxCorp logos. "HELL NO, WE WON'T GO! MIKE HO, HE SHOULD GO!" Everyone booed on seeing him.

The pen pulled him onwards.

"Boss!"

That was . . . *Drew?* Waving his arms? How'd he gotten down so fast? And next to him, was . . . Christina. Their eyes locked, and Michael's heart throbbed. She looked well. Holding her own pen, Christina surged forth.

A protester leapt for Michael. "Sign your devil's pact yet, Mr. Ho?"

But a giant arm grabbed the protester. Trenchcoat Man nodded at Michael, and the pen pulled Michael again.

He skidded to a halt before Christina. So many thoughts struggled against his lips, how glad he was she'd come, how he didn't care about Kevin, and . . . had Trenchcoat Man *nodded?*, and . . . why was Drew here?—everything coming out in a shout, "I WISH I'D NEVER TAKEN THAT INTERNSHIP! I WISH I'D STAYED WITH YOU!"

The knot in Michael's stomach loosened. The protesters immediately around him stopped waving placards. They nudged other protesters and the booing lessened.

It seemed Christina's pen needed her to confess, too, secrets that also kept her up nights, heavy words now demanding release—"I HATED YOUR VALENTINE'S PRESENT!"

Michael blinked. "What?"

"That necklace with the dolphins was hideous! I never had the heart to tell you!"

Drew winced and mouthed, *Ouch.* Michael gaped. He'd handmade that necklace. "Uh . . . "

"And your sushi-burritos were disgusting."

"But . . . you . . . always ate them?"

"I bagged them when you weren't looking, then composted them."

"You composted the sushi-burritos I made every Sunday?" Michael asked faintly.

Drew popped a gum-bubble, and Michael rounded on him. "*You're* Christina's friend? You're dating her?"

Christina looked aghast. "What? Drew's my secretary. He advised me to find you . . . "

"Drew's *my* secretary," Michael said. "He started working for me when . . . "

When Michael's staff left. At just the right time.

"Ahem." It was the protester Trenchcoat Man had grabbed, looking unconcerned as Trenchcoat Man marched him forward. "You two obviously have history, but you need to stop talking around the problem." Some protesters murmured agreement; others hushed them. Arm still locked, the protester turned to Trenchcoat Man. "Tell 'em, buddy."

Trenchcoat Man released him. "I can't, Jared. It's something they have to do themselves."

The protester—Jared—who'd apparently become first-name-basis cozy with Trenchcoat Man—rubbed his arm. "My man Buddy here won't say it, but—"

"Wait." Michael turned to Trenchcoat Man. "Your name's *Buddy*?" At the crowd's outskirts, Detenweiler was speaking animatedly with a police sergeant.

"He's with me, boss. We're from the Order of Magic Pens. We follow the Pens to those who need them." Drew nodded, as if this explanation clarified everything.

Michael blinked, then turned back to Trenchcoat Man. "Your name's *Buddy*?"

Trenchcoat Man—Buddy—nodded, but Christina grabbed Michael's head, and he forgot everything. Suspicious secretaries, unexpected names, destructive contracts—all of it vanished. He felt only the gentleness of her hands on his face.

"I had every right to move on, Mike."

This was his chance to come clean. No more regretful nights and hesitant internet searches. "You did. When we decided to focus on our jobs, I should've said the truth . . . that . . . I loved you . . . "

"I don't feel the same way anymore," Christina said. "I mean, I still love you . . . just not . . . "

Michael smiled sadly. "I see."

The crowd sighed collectively. "AWWW . . . "

Michael's and Christina's pens clattered onto the ground. Drew and Buddy grabbed them.

Jared patted Michael's arm sympathetically. "Can you at least handle this merger?"

But Detenweiler had finished his sidebar with the police. "SERGEANT! Arrest these protesters! We have every right to conduct business in peace!"

Police in riot gear, wielding shields and truncheons, advanced grimly. They'd used the distraction to gear up and take flanking positions. The crowd hissed, hefting placards to meet them. Even Jared rushed to join the fray.

"I'm getting too old for this," Drew groaned. He held up his Pen. "How about someplace warm at least, like the Caribbean? There's gotta be people to help there."

The Pen quivered, and Drew looked hopeful—but it flew

into Michael's grasp. Uh-oh. Michael shook his pen-hand, but it wouldn't budge.

"Odd," Buddy said. "Detenweiler's my assignment, as you and Christina were Drew's."

"Um, Trenchcoat—ah—Buddy? Shouldn't you be handling Detenweiler? If he's your assignment?"

"The Pen wants you to solve this, Mr. Ho."

Michael supposed that made sense. He was responsible for this mess. "What do I do, though? I'm not . . . of the Order of Magic Pens."

Buddy watched Detenweiler exhorting officers as they shoved protesters. "I don't know. Usually, we watch for the right moment to hand over Magic Pens. That's the tricky part about what we do. We can't tell our assigned people everything. It might scare them away. They need to make their own realizations."

"But Drew flat-out told me I had a Magic Pen."

"I told you enough to *get you thinking,* boss. Every assignment's different."

"Sign," Christina said. "You need to sign the contract."

"You know how many people NyxCorp's going to fire?"

"Better than a riot," Christina replied.

Michael sighed. She was right. "Detenweiler! I'll sign!"

Detenweiler yelled, "STOP!" Everyone froze.

The NyxCorp executive marched over, sergeant in tow. The sergeant offered his back. Detenweiler smoothed the contract over it.

But Michael couldn't sign. The Pen wouldn't let him.

"Mr. Ho," Detenweiler said warningly.

Could Michael sign with his other hand? It would be clumsy, but he doubted NyxCorp cared. "Lend me your pen, Detenweiler."

Detenweiler rolled his eyes and held it out, but Michael's Magic Pen jolted him before he could take it. "Ow!"

Christina grabbed it. "You okay—AH!"

Michael rubbed his hand, as Christina did hers. What had Drew said about the Order? *We follow the Pens to those who need them.*

He took the Pen back from Christina, feeling again its buzzing energy. It showed him a woman, college-aged . . . From the look in Christina's eyes, Michael knew she'd seen her, too.

The young woman Detenweiler had been thinking about all day. The real reason behind his foul temper.

I'm disappointed, Mr. Ho. You've been so focused. So driven. You reminded me of my . . .

Michael turned to the harried-looking NyxCorp executive, focusing on the circles under his eyes. "It's been forever since you've spoken to your daughter."

"What?"

"Nothing. Switch pens with me. Mine isn't working." It was meant for someone who needed it. And Michael no longer needed it.

Detenweiler snatched the Magic Pen, and Michael gave his signature. Jared's face fell; the crowd groaned. "Sorry," Michael muttered.

Detenweiler grabbed the signed contract tiredly. He frowned at the Pen he held.

Buddy and Drew started walking, beckoning for Michael and Christina to follow.

"We failed," Buddy said after they'd moved out of earshot. "We were supposed to stop the merger."

Drew grunted. "Means we're stuck here."

Behind them, Detenweiler was shaking his Pen, trying to dislodge it.

In mid-step, Christina reached into her pocket, pulling out . . . another Magic Pen.

Drew popped a gum-bubble. "Huh. Seems the Pens are extending an invitation."

"We have to find Detenweiler's daughter," Christina murmured.

Michael reached into his pocket, finding his own Pen. "Yeah . . . we do . . ."

Detenweiler was yelling now. The protesters raised signs again, yelling with redoubled fury. "HELL NO, WE WON'T GO!"

Michael looked to Christina. "We're . . . joining the Order? What about our careers? Our lives?"

"Did you like your job, Mike?" she asked. "Did you *ever* like it?"

Michael considered her question, then looked back at his empty skyrise. "I hated it."

"I'm an acquisitions director," Christina said. "*Aggressive* acquisitions. But I've always wanted to do more. I feel the daughter's presence. She's very angry."

"And Mr. Detenweiler's very sad," Buddy said. "Reuniting this family could help solve this NyxCorp problem. I'll watch him until his daughter's found." He made for Detenweiler, who was now red-faced, screaming at police and protesters alike.

Drew led Michael and Christina behind a building, out of sight. He raised his Pen and started writing in midair. "The Pens provide for all needs." Glowing sheets of paper appeared as Drew worked.

"I didn't know they did *that*," Christina murmured.

"They're Magic Pens, remember? In exchange, you'll guide

those the Pens select. People in need. Disillusioned dreamers. Estranged family."

"Separated lovers," Christina said. Michael glanced at her, but she smiled and looked down. "What if we want to stop?"

"You return to your old lives." Drew's Pen produced text with incredible speed. "Remember, you can't tell your assignment everything. That's the tricky part. You gotta guide them to make their own realizations. Sometimes, the person refuses the call. The daughter might not want help."

"I have to try," Michael said. "I'm in."

"Me, too," Christina said.

"Need your signatures first, kids." Drew plucked two glowing contracts from midair. "Have a Pen?"

Andrew K Hoe (he/him) is an assistant editor at the *Cast of Wonders* podcast for YA speculative fiction. He's been a Californian high school English teacher and an assistant professor of English. Children's, MG, and YA fiction are his jam! Andrew specializes in writing stories from an East Asian perspective. He writes about complex Asian characters with real desires, ideals, and flaws, and who are more than their stereotypes. His first sale was about a Kung Fu monk who learns to read forbidden books to prove himself. "Of Signatures and Contracts" is about highly successful Asian Americans who discover their love for each other still endures years after their breakup. Note: Drew—who chews gum, wears muscle-shirts, and calls people "boss"—is Asian, too! Andrew's stories appear in or are forthcoming from: *Five Minutes at Hotel Stormcove, Cast of Wonders, Diabolical Plots, Highlights for Children*, and *Young Explorer's Adventure Guide Vol 6*. Web: andrewkhoe.wordpress.com. Twitter: @andrewk_hoe

The Confessionist

Ava Kelly

Vemund pauses, standing on the wet sidewalk. Underneath the overcast sky, twilight stretches through the sloping city. Wealth lives here, in sterile houses carefully hidden behind designer bushes and fences. Not even petrichor feels natural this far across the megapolis. No stench permeates the air, no visible evidence of human misery, although Vemund knows from experience these walls hide just as many vile actions as the paperthin constructs at the other end of civilization.

The evening is chill enough that Vemund sees his breaths as he exhales. It fits this appointment, in a way; all day he's been followed by a lingering impression that he's about to trade his soul away. For almost twenty years, he's worked as a confessionist. The only job he could ever take, young and untrained, but already buried under unbearable debt. Society needs you, they told him at recruitment. *You'd be doing the world a favor.* Vemund snorts quietly to himself. The only favor he's been doing has been to ease abject consciences. Except for the children; sometimes he confesses children and their pain is almost always inflicted by others. They were all worth it, though rare enough to forget how it feels to actually help someone instead of simply dampening the guilt bred by one's actions, consequences intended or not.

The house up ahead sits in heavy gray, made of dull steel and concrete and glass, as ashen as the rest of the buildings around it. Cutting through the front garden, the path to his latest client winds in a bend of stone slabs. This one had specifically requested him, even offered a hefty payment for the service.

His grip tightens. The squeak of his briefcase handle gets lost in the whoosh of the hightrain flying up above.

The entire trip here, he's been wondering how much of an abomination he'd have to take on for the offered honorarium. He hasn't wavered, though. Can't. Not when it means he can forgo the fifty or so confessions he'd need to finally settle his score.

He'd be free. He *will* be free, after this.

But will he be able to carry it? Whatever the monster in this house did, Vemund will have to watch it, assimilate its effects, and live with them forever. With a trembling hand, he touches the back of his shaved head, over the place where the neural implant sits.

"Last one," he whispers, and steps forward.

A smiling man answers the door at the first ring. Medium build, a little shorter than Vemund, clean shaven. Wearing a dark sweater, the same gray of the concrete and the sky and the house he occupies.

"Hi, I'm Obe. Please, come in."

Obe keeps smiling and Vemund shudders. He's never been afraid before.

After removing his shoes and coat, Vemund follows further inside. When instructed, he sits at the dining table. Its glass surface shines pristine, just like everything else in this place. The space is wide and open, any separation made from transparent material. No color, no personal touch whatsoever.

Even the tray with tea that Obe sets on the table permeates sameness. While he pours and serves, Vemund retrieves his tools from the briefcase. He sets them down on a paper pad between them after Obe takes the opposite seat. He's dropped his façade of hospitality, instead studying the items with an intensity Vemund's rarely seen before.

"The pulsers"—Vemund begins the requisite explanation, opening the small box to reveal the round neuro-actuators—"go onto your temples. They—"

"I've done this before. They modify the neural connections forming the memory that I write down." Obe picks up the pen, twists it around. "With this thing: coated in enough sensors to read my entire mind."

Vemund swallows, loud enough in the silence that Obe notices. He leans over the table slightly.

"Your implant will absorb my experience as if it were your own, and what remains will be distant for me. Like a scar over a healed wound."

"That's how it works." Vemund's voice cracks, but Obe doesn't comment on that, so Vemund counts his lucky stars and tries to move forward. "How long ago was your last procedure? If less than a year, I'm afraid we can't continue at this time. Health concerns, you see."

Leaning back in his chair, Obe gestures at the tea and Vemund shakes his head.

"I was a child, back in the Zar boroughs," Obe finally says. "I had witnessed a terrible thing during the riots. It left me . . . distraught. No, damaged. I was damaged. In fact, it was you who confessed it."

"I'm sorry," Vemund interrupts, "you must be mistaken. I've never treated a boy in Zar."

A wry twist of lips, and Obe's eyes darken in the lowering light. "Yes, you did."

It clicks, immediately. Vemund's perspective shifts from dread toward curiosity.

"Ah. My apologies. One should never assume, least of all me."

"Unnecessary," Obe says, lifting a long-fingered hand. "You've been in my head, but couldn't have seen what I wasn't aware of at the time. Understanding came later for me."

Vemund nods. The tea by his elbow steams with a gentle aroma and, despite himself, he picks up the cup. Takes a sip, under Obe's assessing gaze. Obe should be uncomfortable, the confession *always* is, and yet . . . Here, in this cold, gray house, the new information soothes something long torn beneath Vemund's skin.

The first to break the stillness is Obe, who attaches the pulsers to his temples. Vemund's pad swooshes over the glass as Obe pulls it closer.

"It's part of why you're here, really," he says. "You gave me serenity. Peace of mind."

He bends over the paper, smoothing it out with one thumb. The other clicks on the power button of the pen and Vemund's implant fires. His eyelids flutter until the connection finally settles.

Eyes downcast, Obe breathes in deeply, his growing confidence resonating through the uplink.

"I wanted to thank you. Easing my pain gave me clarity and presence. It allowed me to learn, and live, and make something of myself. It let me discover who I am, what I want. What I love. *How* to love, both myself and others."

The tip of the pen touches the paper.

It was spring, March 12th. At that time I was exploring what it meant to be me. Half wary, half excited, a lot afraid. Didn't feel comfortable in public, didn't want to explain myself again.

I remember trees in bloom in the park. It wasn't that warm outside, but the sun was shining that day and I'd missed it. So I went to sit on a bench in the farthest corner I could find, hoping nobody would see me. Wishing to remain invisible.

A woman strolled by, at some point. She had long, gray hair, wrinkles on her entire face, a large hat with a red bow shielding her from the sunshine. She asked, "Do you have the time, young man?"

I recall experiencing true, pure joy. It was the most vivid moment of absolute and sincere happiness I have ever felt.

Vemund gasps as Obe's intense memory gathers in a knot in the middle of his chest.

Across the table, Obe sets the pen down, eyes back on Vemund.

"Now we share it."

Vemund can't find the words to reply, but he clutches onto the feeling with everything he has. He's never had— He hasn't—

"Without you, I wouldn't have been able to create this."

Obe presses both palms onto the tabletop.

The world blooms with *color*.

The walls, the ceiling, the floor. Obe, himself, is covered in swirls moving over his dark skin in mesmerizing waves. Everything in Vemund's body comes to a halt—for one heart-beat—and restarts with the surges of radiance around them.

"Cyberpainter," Vemund rasps.

Obe grins. Wide. Warm. Vemund blinks the blur away, and wipes the wetness off his face with shaky fingers.

In front of him is not a monster, but the infamous inventor of the holographic technology that spread through the privileged layers of society, increasing in value as it gained more and more uses—like the silent garden back at headquarters, where only the bosses are allowed. But then the artist donated it to the whole megapolis. It spans all districts—there to feed all souls equally, to nourish hope, to provide a ray of light in the harsh reality of the struggling and the unlucky. Some swear they feel strength to carry on when looking at his projections.

Self-sustainable happiness. Free for all.

And then it hits Vemund. The job, the payment. He lunges for the pulsers at Obe's temples, but he steps away easily.

"I can't numb your *good* memory."

Obe shrugs. "It's yours now. Take care of it for me."

"Please don't—"

"Don't what? Thank you for saving me?"

"It doesn't work that way," Vemund says with alarm. "Unsanctioned emotion categories are erased."

"Fortunately, you don't work for them anymore. I wired your fee this morning. The hacker I hired has already performed the last of your payments for you and handed in your resignation. It finished processing right before you knocked on my door."

Vemund staggers back. "That's—" Too much. Too much kindness.

"I wouldn't even have lived to see that day at the park if it hadn't been for you and your magic pen. Search for me in your databanks; I know you can."

Sure enough, it comes to the forefront of Vemund's mind. The saddest, smallest child. His first client, whom he'd coaxed into drawing the scary boo. The hurt from back then returns to spill over Vemund's cheeks again.

"Don't you get it? You saved me so I can change the world. Starting with you." As he speaks, Obe rounds the table until he's close enough to touch the side of Vemund's neck. "No more debt.

No more forcing people to carry pain and secrets. No more high-tech sin-eaters absolving humanity of its horrors."

His palm slides, fingertips reaching the surgical scar on the back of Vemund's head.

"This gift should only be used to heal. Will you help me make that happen?"

Vemund nods, unable to find his voice, but Obe must get it, because he grips Vemund's shoulder with his free hand, and whispers—echoes joy in polychrome brightness—

"Then welcome, confessionist, to your new life."

Ava Kelly (they/them) is an engineer with a deep passion for stories. Whether reading, watching, or writing them, Ava has always been surrounded by tales of all genres. Their goal is to bring more stories into the world, especially those of friendship and compassion, those dedicated to trope subversion, those that give the void a voice, and those that spawn worlds of their own. Long ago, Ava has begun the trek through the artworld with photography, the cello, and poetry. In another artlife—because what is engineering if not creation—Ava is tinkering with artificial intelligence, robots, and all sorts of systems, but that is nothing compared to the challenge of foodmaking. Currently, Ava enjoys experimenting with recipes, with about half successes. And half works in progress—insert wise wink here. As in, we are all journeys, not destinations. avakellyfiction.com

Mightier

Elizabeth Shaffer

"And now, Vigilante Class of 2025, as we conclude our graduation ceremony here at Heroes University, we come to the moment you've all been waiting for." The university president paused for dramatic effect. "The Gifting."

Essie released the breath she'd been holding and followed her classmates to the edge of the stage. The Gifting was the highlight of graduation for new superheroes. In a few moments, Essie would be given a magical object that would grant her a superpower. And that superpower would define not only her career, but her life.

No pressure.

"Michael Adamson," the president announced, and the first student started across the stage. "Chosen hero name: Punch Blaster. His Gift is . . . " The student knelt in front of an old wooden chest and lifted the lid. "The Gloves of Strength!"

The student pulled a pair of crimson leather gloves out of the chest. As he donned the gloves, his biceps swelled, bursting the seams of his graduation gown. Applause erupted from the audience.

"Lakisha Bentley, chosen hero name: Ebony Starlight. Her Gift is . . . The Necklace of Invisibility!"

Essie's knees were starting to feel like the ballistics gel dummies they used as target practice in Advanced Bullet-Stopping junior year. What kind of Gift would she get? A hero's Gift always highlighted their strengths, but Essie had aced every class (including the dreaded Cape Precautions 101). Essie wasn't one to brag, but she had a lot of strengths to choose from.

"Jamie Chavez, chosen hero name: Burning Angel. Their Gift is . . . The Cloak of Fire!"

Essie was next. She could feel sweat dripping from her armpits, and it wasn't due to the sudden blaze of heat coming from the fiery inferno onstage that had—up until moments ago—been a graduate. Maybe Essie's gift would be magic boots to increase her running speed. Or maybe she would get a cape that allowed her to fly. Or maybe . . .

"Esther Dearing, chosen hero name: Hope Bringer. Her gift is . . . " Essie made her way across the stage. The bright spotlight warmed her face as she knelt before the chest. Her hands shook, but she grasped the lid and lifted it.

In the bottom of the chest lay a hot pink gel pen.

"The Pen of Friendship!"

"What kind of name is 'The Pen of Friendship?'" Essie muttered to herself as she stood up, pen in hand. This was when she was supposed to get her superpower, but Essie didn't feel any different. She looked back at the president, but he had already started reading the next graduate's name. A smattering of applause trickled throughout the audience as Essie made her way into the wings.

What was she supposed to do with the Pen of Friendship?

That night, Essie sat on her bed, sulking. She knew she was sulking and would have willingly admitted she was sulking if anyone had asked. But no one had asked because everyone else was out partying with the graduates who had actually gotten cool Gifts. Which was why Essie was sulking.

She had donned her regulation hero uniform hours ago, but

she was still trying to convince herself to go out on the job. How could she fight crime with nothing more than unknown powers and a 25-cent gel pen? Now, if her Gift had been some sort of spy tool—a laser or a bomb or a poison dart—that was just *disguised* as a pen, that would have been a different story. But it wasn't.

Or was it?

Twenty minutes later, Essie had cornered the notorious Doctor Brainmeister in a deserted alley. She had caught him red-handed stealing from the local nuclear waste facility without any protective gear. How that man had gotten his PhD was a mystery Essie would never understand.

"Stop . . . you! There's nowhere to run!" Essie barked. It wasn't her best verbal banter, but Quips and Taunts 101 had never been her strongest subject.

Essie pulled the "pen" out of her pocket. Now was the moment of truth. Maybe it would knock the bad guy out for her. Maybe it would catch him in a net. Maybe it would tase him. Maybe all she had to do was throw it at the villain, and . . .

The gel pen bounced off the man's chest and clattered to the ground. Essie sighed. "Well, f—"

Essie blacked out as Doctor Brainmeister's fist introduced itself very forcefully to her face.

All that week, Essie tried everything she could think of to unlock the pen's secrets. She tried stabbing a shapeshifter with it. She tried brandishing it as a magic wand against a wannabe evil sorcerer. She tried throwing it as a boomerang, using it as a lockpick, and following it as a compass. She even tried giving it to a supervillain in the interrogation room, hoping it might compel him to tell the truth. But nothing worked. And each day, Essie became more and more convinced that it was just a regular gel pen.

Late one evening, Essie sat cross-legged on her bed, fiddling with the pen. Maybe she wasn't meant to be a superhero. She might need to consider other career options. She could always go back to school for. . . Essie tried to think of something other than vigilantism that she wouldn't loathe doing for the rest of her life.

Essie sighed.

"Alright," she said to the pen. "This is your last chance to do something extraordinary before I use you to fill out college applications and then throw you in a drawer forever. Show me what you got."

To Essie's amazement, the pen sprang from her hand and hovered above a tattered spiral notebook sitting on her nightstand. The pen didn't have eyes, but Essie could have sworn it was glaring at her. Of course, she thought. The one thing she hadn't tried was the one thing that pens were designed for: writing.

Essie spread the notebook open in front of her. The pen popped off its lid and began to write of its own accord. In swift movements, it danced across the page, filling the white space with bright pink ink. Essie leaned over the page and read:

Dear diary,

I hope someone drops a piano on Pierre's head while he's walking home. Or he falls through an open manhole cover and drowns in sewage. Or he gets eaten by a flock of rabid seagulls... Okay, so maybe seagulls can't get rabies, but the point still stands.

Did he really think I wouldn't find out about him and Maria? She's my cousin, for crying out loud! Why did I ever believe he might be a decent guy? I really thought–

The words stopped in an illegible scribble, and the pen fell onto the bed. Essie took a long breath. Clearly this was someone's diary entry, but Essie had no idea whose diary it was, what she was supposed to do with this information, or how this particular kind of magic was supposed to help her fight crime.

Eventually, for lack of a better idea, Essie picked up the pen, left a blank line underneath the journal entry, and wrote: "Wow. Pierre sounds like a jerk."

She set the pen down again. For a long time, it didn't move. Maybe the pen had decided it had done enough magic for one day. But just when Essie was about to give up, the pen flew into the air once again and wrote:

Are you a ghost?

Ah. So apparently it worked both ways.

Essie scribbled in response, "No! Sorry! Not a ghost! I'm actually a superhero graduate who got this useless pen as my hero Gift, and I had no idea what it did until this exact moment. So . . . sorry!"

This time the pause was much shorter.

You're a superhero? Which one?

"Hope Bringer," Essie replied. "But you've probably never heard of me. I graduated with a 4.0 GPA and a double major in Urban Vigilantism and Classical Heroic Ethics, but all I have to show for it is this useless pen and about $30,000 in student loans."

Same! The pen wrote back. *Except I was an English major, not a superhero. My name's Jimena, by the way.* The pen hesitated for a second, hovering in midair, then continued, *You keep calling your pen useless, but pink ink is literally showing up in my diary out of nowhere, so I have to say, that pen seems amazing to me!*

Essie smiled. "Thanks," she wrote. "But for a superhero, this is a pretty disappointing power. One of my classmates can literally burst into flames. How is this pen supposed to help me take down bad guys? Unless you want me to go beat up Pierre . . . ?"

Ha ha! No, don't bother, Jimena wrote back. *Pierre's a jerk, but he's not worth the effort.* There was another short pause. *There are non-violent ways to be a hero, you know.*

"Like what?"

Like this.

"What do you mean?"

I was lonely, Jimena explained. *I was about to make a really bad decision like chugging an entire bottle of Moscato and calling my ex. But then you started chatting with me and saved me from social embarrassment and a nasty hangover. So, thanks!*

That was one way of looking at things. "I'm glad I could help, but this is hardly superhero work. It's not the same as taking down villains."

No, it's not, Jimena admitted. *But that doesn't mean this is any less important. Maybe the world has enough tough guys beating each other up. Maybe what the world needs right now is a kind heart and a pen. After all, the pen is mightier than the sword, right?*

Essie chuckled, but Jimena had started the wheels turning in her head. All this time she had thought her Gift was useless because she couldn't use it to bring people to justice after they carried out evil schemes. But if she got this right—if she could write to people and help them when they were hurting—maybe she could prevent the evil schemes from happening in the first place. Maybe she could keep people from becoming supervillains at all. And even if she couldn't, maybe she could at least bring comfort, hope, or—dare she say it—friendship to people whose hearts were heavy.

"Thanks," Essie wrote. "I hadn't thought of that." She paused, then added, "Who just saved who here? If the whole English major thing doesn't work out, you might want to consider a career in heroism."

Ha ha! I'll keep it in mind, Jimena replied. *And if you ever get tired of being a superhero, you'd make a great writer. You already have the pen for it!*

Essie smiled down at the pen in her hand. It wasn't a weapon. It couldn't fight supervillains or lock people up. But maybe that was the point. Maybe power could be delicate and simple and hot pink. Maybe, just sometimes, this was all it took to be a hero.

Elizabeth Shaffer (she/her) lives in Moline, IL with her husband, their two black cats, and their bearded dragon. During the day, she works for a non-profit organization that helps families pay for child care. In her free time, she enjoys reading, writing, acting, traveling, watching too much TV, and learning to play the ukulele. Her short stories can also be found in *Five Minutes at Hotel Stormcove* and *Grumpy Old Gods* volumes 1 and 3.

Qalam

Z. Ahmad

When my eyes opened to a clock that said 8:25, panic swept through me. I had stayed up too late reading last night. Science fiction, fantasy, horror, even non-fiction—if a genre existed, I devoured it. I probably loved reading and story telling a little too much if I am being honest. It is why I am going to be late to class. I quickly brushed my teeth, slapped some deodorant on, and washed my face.

"I'm leaving," I yelled to the house as I put on my boots.

"You're going to be late" was the response I heard back.

"I knoowph," I grumbled as I shoved a red gala in my mouth.

I sped away in my car, and I didn't check my phone—I didn't notice that I had 26 WhatsApp messages from last night and a missed phone call. I was oblivious to the fact that the parking lot was basically empty as I ran into the masjid and Islamic center where my hadith class was to be held. I checked the clock in the hallway, 9:02, only two minutes late, but I still felt slightly nervous as I opened the door.

As I opened the door, I saw in the front, a blackboard that stood slightly off balance. It was missing one of its wheels. On the board, written in chalk, was the smooth Arabic script of my teacher:

إِنَّ أَوَّلَ مَا خَلَقَ اللَّهُ الْقَلَمَ فَقَالَ لَهُ اكْتُبْ فَجَرَى بِمَا هُوَ كَائِنٌ إِلَى الْأَبَدِ

It was the hadith from last class. My teacher had been going through a series of Islamic creation hadith. We had started with the first thing ever created: the Qalam (the pen). This pen was instructed to write down all the stories of everything that would happen from its creation until forever. It took me a moment to realize but the classroom was empty. Had class not started yet? Was I somehow early? At this point I pulled out my phone to see the red icon letting me know I missed a bunch of messages. Apparently, class was cancelled. My teacher had the flu. I sighed. Might as well take this time to finish up the book from last night. So, I wandered over to the library.

A woman with weathered skin and strands of white hair poking out of her hijab sat at a table alone. She had something in her hands. At first, I thought it was a crochet hook, but on closer inspection I saw that the woman was slowly and deliberately using a small sharp knife to whittle away at a stick. The shaving was rhythmic - *Chtt - Chtt - Chtt*. I was confused, I had not seen anything like it before. Why shave away at a stick?

"Asalamualakum, Auntie, what is it that you have in your hand?"

"Walakummusalam, young one, I am making a pen," replied the old woman, not lifting her eyes from the knife and the stick.

How could a stick be a pen? I thought to myself, as I took the seat next to her. As I watched her work in silence, it became clear that the stick was in fact bamboo. The more she cut it, the more it began to look like a pen. She had transformed it into something that looked like a wooden fountain pen, with a slanted pen-head, and an oblong hole shaped like windows I had seen in mosques. It took her another 15 minutes to finish, at which point she stopped and looked up at me, as if surprised to see me there.

"This is where the ink goes," she said, pointing to the top of the little oblong hole, as she dipped the pen into black ink.

Not pausing she said softly, "Do you know how to write?"

My first thoughts were, what type of question was that? Do I know how to write?!? Of course, I could write, writing isn't exactly uncommon, it is something every 1st grader can do. It took half a second for me to realize how arrogant that thought was, and correct myself. My own grandmother only learned to read and write well after her children, including my mother, had moved away and had children of their own.

"Ye—I mean I know how to write with these," I said, pulling out my gel pen, my mechanical pencil, and a few errant highlighters. "But with that—I don't have the first clue where to even start."

"The one who masters it can go many places," she said, smiling as she took out a sheet of plain white paper.

"Will you teach me?" I asked, wanting to learn.

She began to write, as if in response to my question. The first thing that she wrote was the Arabic letters one by one: alaf (ا), baa (ب), taa (ت), thaa (ث). I watched her expert control with the dark ink. Her ability to intertwine the calligraphic lines was a work of art. The letters seemed to swirl together. It looked like what fantasy movies and tv shows were going for when they tried to write in Elven. It looked magical, but grounded in reality.

I was still slightly entranced by her writing, which is why I ended up gobsmacked, when she reached out her hand holding the pen. *Here, you try writing,* she seemed to say.

"Ummm I can't – I mean I don't know how to!" I exclaimed, hesitant to take the pen from her.

"Are you not looking for adventure, to try something new? Did you not just spend time in my company out of sheer curiosity?

Were you not late to class because you were interested in stories, Jennah?" she said, challenging me to take the inked pen from her hand.

"Wait how do you know I was late? How do you know my name? I don't even know you," I said as my heart began pounding faster and breathing transformed into short staccato bursts. I mean, stalkers came in all sorts of forms—had my curiosity gotten the better of me?

"Uhh mmm . . . well, don't panic. I mean you no harm; to prove it I'll even give you my name. Many call me Zarqa al Yamama," she said, smiling, with her hand still holding the pen out to me.

I reached out my hand, I am not sure why I did it. I felt the pen calling to me. *Jennah,* it whispered. *I can help you tell stories. I can help you find so many adventures. You could write them with me, you could learn them with me.* It felt like the pen wanted me to write all the stories it held within its many different futures. I don't think I will ever know for sure if it was out of my own volition or if the old woman pushed the pen into my outreached hand, but when my skin touched the wood of the pen, it tingled like I had touched fire. I almost dropped it. The qalam felt hot. Wood should not feel warm, let alone hot—thermodynamics didn't work that way.

"This isn't a normal pen, is it?" I asked as both of us still held the qalam.

"It is normal for what it is, but it is not like your pens. Let us write together," she said as she grabbed my hand.

I barely touched the pen. I allowed her to write and my hand to follow. She spelled out بغداد (Bagdad) in flowing Arabic calligraphy. She followed by writing a name, Fakhr-un-Nisa Shuhdah Umm Muhammad al-Baghdadiyyah, a year, 1067, and a small symbol. Then I was not in my library anymore. I mean I was in *a* library but not the one I was in just moments ago. It felt old, the way Colonial Williamsburg feels old. Or like a recreated building. You know, the architecture doesn't match what you are familiar with in modern life, but it isn't a ruin yet. The building was beautiful though, all libraries are. There were large arches that supported the building, and most importantly it was full of stories. I could tell some books were bound in leather and there were entire shelves of tall scrolls.

"We are at the House of Wisdom, Jennah; there is someone you must meet if you are to master the qalam."

Although my Arabic was rudimentary, I somehow understood people as they spoke fusha (classical) Arabic. It was as if the qalam was whispering to me to make sure I understood.

Zarqa approached a woman who looked to be in her 40's wearing a long dress and colorful head covering that draped over her chest and continued down to her knees.

"Asalamualakum Shaykhah, I have a student for you. Jennah needs to learn from you, oh 'Glory of Womankind' and 'Writer of Bagdad'. Jennah is smart and already knows basic writing but not calligraphy. Jennah has no family here and is alone in this world and is in need of your kindness and assistance," Zarqa said.

It took a moment but it clicked. I was in Bagdad. I was in the year 1068. I was in the House of Wisdom. The library that was destroyed by the Mongols in 1258, a few hundred years from now, or almost a millennium ago, according to my old-time reference point. Zarqa was talking to Fakhr-un-Nisa Shuhdah Umm Muhammad al-Baghdadiyyah, a woman hadith scholar and calligrapher. She was legitimately one of the best calligraphers of all time. None of this is making sense; I cannot think.

"Jennah, what do you know of the hadith?" Shaykhah Shuhdah Umm Muhammad asked.

I had attended over a year of hadith lessons. I thought I had memorized literally hundreds of hadith, at least if you had asked me yesterday, I would have been able to recite them one after another. But now, my mind was blank. I could not recall even a single saying.

"Umm, I don't know much, I—"

Then suddenly the image of the blackboard came into focus, and I begin to repeat it in Arabic, "inn 'awwal ma khalaq alllah alqalam faqal lah aktub fajaraa bima hu kayin 'iilaa al'abad." *Truly, the first (thing) to be created by God was the pen. God told it to write, so it wrote all that will exist until forever.* I follow it up saying the isnad or chain of reciters going back to Prophet Muhammad.

"I will teach you, Jennah," replies the Shaykhah.

Zarqa takes me aside, smiling as she says, "You will learn to write from her. This qalam will take you to lands and places unknown to you, and it will take you back home. You will learn, then you will write. But my time *here* with you is done; I am just the pen-giver. Peace be with you on your journeys—oh, one more thing . . . Look me up in Mt. Qaf sometime, Jennah, there are plenty of stories there."

And then she was gone, she just burst into flames—thankfully there were no books in the immediate vicinity or we would have burned down the library before the Mongols got a chance. Oh my gosh, the Mongols were coming . . . well, they would be here in another two hundred years. Did she say Mount Qaf? The home of the Jinn? But I couldn't worry about that right now, I was mostly alone in Baghdad, a thousand years before I was even born, with only the smallest clue of how to get back. But I was going to learn so much. The world was opened and closed for me at the same time, so I clutched the pen tightly and smiled at my new teacher. I was going to figure this out.

Z. Ahmad (she/her) describes herself as a Muslim American feminist physicist. She obtained her undergraduate degree in physics from Southeast Missouri State University, and is currently pursuing a masters degree while working as a research analyst in Ohio. In her quickly diminishing free time she comes up with convoluted adventures for her D&D party, and studies classical Arabic to better understand the Quran. Ms. Ahmad draws inspiration for her stories from her experiences growing up in rural America as a daughter in a biracial family. In her writing she enjoys exploring themes related to female empowerment, cultural intersectionality, science, science fiction, and fantasy.

Inheritance

J. S. Bailey

The funeral had seemed to last for years. Gretchen recalled it as a series of tragic snapshots: rows of mourners in their Sunday best sitting in polished wood church pews while Cousin Charlie performed the eulogy, a somber procession out to the cemetery damp with morning dew, the priest reciting prayers in his white vestments beside the grave.

Gretchen sat in the attic bedroom of her Aunt Rosita's house now, watching raindrops trickle down the panes of spotted glass. Why hadn't she come to visit more often these past few years? Grandma Sherry, her father's mother, had spoiled Gretchen with treats while growing up, and had taught her how to play both the piano and the violin. They'd shared secrets and private jokes, and never would again.

When Gretchen had gotten a new marketing job in Cleveland and moved away five years ago, Grandma Sherry had given her a bone-crushing squeeze and said, "You're going to have the best life, sweetie."

Gretchen had laughed and said, "Well, I certainly hope so!"

A knowing glint appeared in Grandma Sherry's green eyes. "I'm not wishing you the best life, Gretchen. I'm telling you you're going to have the best life. Trust me." She crossed her heart with one finger.

Tears ran freely down Gretchen's cheeks as she remembered

the woman who'd meant so much to her. If only she could talk to her again . . .

Footsteps ascending the attic stairs drew her attention away from the window, and there came a soft knock at the door. "Gretchen? Can I come in?"

"Sure." Gretchen wiped her eyes on her sleeve, and her cousin Emily stepped into the room holding a cardboard box with the words "For Gretchen" printed on the side in violet permanent marker.

Violet had been Grandma Sherry's favorite color.

"Grandma wanted me to give this to you," Emily said, spitting a strand of copper hair out of her mouth since her hands were too preoccupied. "Where do you want me to put it?"

"On the bed is fine. What is it?"

Emily plopped the box down atop the old quilt. "I didn't look. Stuff she thought you'd like, I guess. I got one, too."

"What did you get?"

"A couple of rolling pins and some antique pie plates. I'm going to bake some dessert and eat myself sick in her memory."

Gretchen couldn't help but crack a smile. "I can help. I'm here for another week."

"Sounds like a plan. I can start ransacking Mom's kitchen for ingredients."

Emily started toward the door, but Gretchen said, "Wait. You can stay here while I open it."

"I'm going to cry again, aren't I?"

"Yep, but at least you won't be alone."

Gretchen sat down on the edge of the bed, and Emily did the same. Gretchen pried the cardboard flaps up and peered inside, smiling at the little snow globe she used to play with at her grandmother's house every Christmas. She picked it up, shook it, and watched the snow cascade over the tiny house inside of it. Then she set it aside and continued to dig through her inheritance.

Some things Gretchen recognized, like a rhinestone necklace and a book of poems. In the bottom of the box, however, lay a rectangular velvet case Gretchen couldn't remember seeing at her grandmother's house before.

"What's that?" Emily asked, leaning in for a closer look.

"I don't know." Gretchen flipped up the velvet lid to reveal a shiny blue pen lying inside of it, along with a folded note. The note had been written in Grandma Sherry's handwriting and said, "You'll understand someday."

"Why would she leave me a pen?" Gretchen asked. She picked the pen up. Since it was made of metal, it had a bit of weight to it, but it couldn't have been worth any great fortune. Was the pen supposed to mean something to her? Maybe it was meant to go to one of her other cousins, instead, like Charlie, who'd always dreamed of being a writer.

"You'll understand someday," Emily said in an ethereal tone, waggling her fingers. "Come on, let's go make some pie."

The drive back to Cleveland was long and wet—it was storming again, and Gretchen started to wish she could hop on a plane and fly to some dry place full of sunshine and seagulls.

She wouldn't be happy in a place like that, though, because Grandma Sherry wouldn't be there to share it with her.

Could she ever be happy again?

After unpacking at her condo, Gretchen took the things from her grandmother and laid them out in a row on her coffee table, smiling at the memories they evoked—save for the pen, which meant nothing specific to her, since she'd never seen her grandmother use it.

She dug through her purse and found a crinkly notepad, then clicked the pen and scribbled some circles onto the first blank page.

The pen worked. She wondered how old it was.

Gretchen had never been much of a writer, but she remembered that Grandma Sherry had sent her a writing journal covered in metallic jellyfish and octopuses for one of her more recent birthdays. She located it in one of her desk drawers and took it and the pen to her couch, where she held the pen poised above a lined page. Gretchen thought for a few moments, and wrote.

I wish I could see you again, Grandma. I wish I could thank you for the things you gave me, too, but this will have to do.

Writing out her thoughts might help her cope with her grief, she supposed. Tears stung her eyes, and she wiped them on her sleeve.

Gretchen touched the pen to the page to write some more, then let out a startled cry when ink bled out of the pen tip. It formed into words that scrawled themselves across the page of their own accord.

What's happening? Who is this?

Her heart galloped. She blinked, and the words remained on the page beneath her own, as fixed in place as any ordinary ink.

She recognized the narrow, looping penmanship immediately.

Hand shaking, she wrote, *This is Gretchen Wyler. How can you be writing in my journal?*

Nothing happened at first, but after a lengthy pause, more ink leaked from the pen and shaped itself into words. *This is Sherry Wyler. How can you be writing on my shopping list?*

Afraid that she might be losing her grip on reality, Gretchen wrote, *Is this a haunted pen?*

Haunted? came the reply. *I'm no ghost. I was just getting ready to head to the supermarket, when your words butted in. And who's Gretchen? I don't know anybody named Gretchen. Maybe you're the ghost here.*

Gretchen stared at the new words that had appeared. Were they really there at all? For now, she would assume they were. She'd never been taken on flights of fancy.

How old are you? Gretchen wrote. *I was born in 1985.*

More ink bled out the end of the pen. *1985? You're kidding me! It's 1982 right now. Are you writing to me from the future?*

I guess so, Gretchen wrote, and marveled at the mystery of it all.

To her surprise, she didn't feel as sad as she had when she'd first sat down on the couch.

Gretchen had thought about mentioning the strange pen to her father to see if he'd known anything about it, but decided against it. Besides, the pen had been meant for her, not him. If Grandma Sherry had gifted her with a pen that held magical powers, maybe nobody else was supposed to know about it.

When she returned home from work the next day, Gretchen kicked off her flats and immediately snatched the pen and journal off the coffee table. She got to writing.

Hello, Sherry? Are you there?

What? Yes, I'm here. How can you be writing to me? Do they make time-traveling pens in the future?

Not that I've heard of, Gretchen wrote. *Is it still 1982 where you are?*

Yes, last I checked. Are you one of my descendants? Wait! Don't tell me . . . you're one of Michael's future kids!

Gretchen couldn't help but smile. *Not Michael's. James's.*

James is going to have a little girl? Oh, this is exciting! What does the pen that you're using look like? Is it a space-age pen? I've always loved those sci-fi movies.

It's just a blue pen that came in a velvet case. You gave it to me.

Now that's funny, said the words on the journal page. *I'm writing with a blue pen. It's made out of metal, and I just so happen to have a velvet case, but it was for a silver bracelet my husband bought for me. I always kept the case because it was so pretty. It's the right size for this pen, so maybe I'll start storing it in there.*

Do you think it's the same pen? Gretchen asked.

Who knows? It never seemed magical to me before. I bought it here in town. Nothing irregular about it until it started leaking ink and making words out of it without my help.

Gretchen sat back, hearing the words inside her head in her grandmother's own voice. Grandma Sherry would have been so young in 1982; only in her early forties.

Do I have a good life? the ink asked, after a pause.

Gretchen thought about the loss of her grandfather nine years ago, and how Grandma Sherry had sunk into a depression so deep that the family worried she'd never come out of it.

She thought of Grandma Sherry bouncing her baby great-grandchildren on her knee, and singing them nursery rhymes.

She thought of music lessons and mouthwatering pies topped with whipped cream.

Yes, Gretchen wrote. *You're going to have the best life.*

Oh, good! I'm looking forward to it.

Gretchen's schedule was too full for her to write in the journal every day, though she looked forward to those moments with a burning ferocity she would never be able to explain to anyone else. Sometimes she'd open a fresh page to see cheerful greetings scrawled on it in her grandmother's writing, and she'd tell the young Grandma Sherry about her day and what her plans were for the coming week. In turn, Grandma Sherry would update her on the things her relatives were doing, and Gretchen would chuckle as she imagined her young father and mother planning their wedding—a hectic affair, by the sound of things.

It's 1983 now, her grandmother wrote. *Only a couple more years until I get to meet you. Should I tell your parents to name you Gretchen?*

No! Gretchen wrote back so quickly, a cramp formed in her hand. *Don't do anything to influence things. Things should just pass as they're meant to, don't you think?*

That sounds very wise to me. My lips are sealed.

The pen did not run out of ink as the years passed. The sting of Grandma Sherry's passing lessened with time, helped, of course, by these secret communications, which Gretchen refused to ever share with anyone, for fear of what people might think. She knew she was not writing Grandma Sherry's words; that somehow this pen possessed a sort of magic, connecting grandmother and grandchild from across the decades.

One day the ink spelled out excited words to report Gretchen's own birth.

Gretchen, you're such a beautiful baby. You didn't tell me you would be born with a cleft lip! You're simply gorgeous, and I wouldn't want you to be any other way.

Tears cascaded down Gretchen's cheeks as she rubbed at the faint scar between her nose and upper lip—the scar she never even thought about since it had been with her for as long as she remembered, as ordinary to her as her eyes or her ears or her hair.

She received periodic updates telling her that she'd learned to crawl, and walk, and say no. In turn, Gretchen reported to Grandma Sherry that she was now seeing a man named Omar, and that Omar had proposed, and that they were getting married in May, and that they were buying a house soon out in the suburbs, because there would be more room for them to raise a family.

She told her grandmother how she and Omar were adopting a little boy. She told her that the adoption had fallen through, and teardrops fell to the page of her current journal while Omar sat in the other room talking in low tones to his sorrowful yet understanding parents, who assured him that everything would work out in the end, somehow, some way.

Page after page filled with Gretchen's accounts of their second adoption attempt, and through the magic pen, Grandma Sherry congratulated her upon the adoption of a little girl they named Marian.

I wish I could meet Omar and Marian, Grandma Sherry said, *but I fear I'd have to live to a mighty ripe old age to do that.*

Thankfully, Grandma Sherry never asked questions about herself, though Gretchen always assured her that things had gone well for her. The act of writing became such a joy for Gretchen that she craved it much in the way that one lost in the desert craves water and shade, and she never stopped using her magic pen, not even when her hair turned gray and her three children moved across the country with their families, leaving Gretchen and Omar alone with each other.

I'm old now, Grandma Sherry's words said to her one day. *I don't think I have much longer. It's been a while since I've seen you in my time, dear, but I'm sure you know how that goes, with Marian and your boys off having their own adventures now.*

Sorry about that, Gretchen wrote, her arthritis making her joints ache. *I should have stayed so I could keep you company in person.*

Nonsense! You did what you had to do. I'm leaving you this pen, by the way. You told me years ago that I gave it to you. Might as well put it in with the other things I know you'll want. I'll stick a note with it, in case that helps. And you know what? I have an idea for you. When I'm gone here, in my time, I won't be able to write to you anymore. Why don't you give this pen to someone else? It can be to whoever you want. But maybe the pen will decide for you.

Gretchen and Grandma Sherry wrote to each other a few more times after that, but then the pen fell silent.

The final words that Grandma Sherry had ever written to her were, *I need to go close my eyes for a while; it's been a long day. Perhaps I should hide this journal somewhere, so nobody ever sees it. Love you.*

Omar kept asking Gretchen what was wrong, and she longed to tell him the truth, but only said, "It's just time. There's just been too much of it . . . and I miss my grandma."

He put his arms around her and gave her a squeeze. "I wish I'd known her. She always sounded like one hell of a woman."

Gretchen laughed and said, "Now that, she was."

Gretchen sat on her back patio one day with a fresh journal, gripping her magic pen while Marian's two girls tossed a frisbee back and forth to each other.

The pen had been silent for a month, but Gretchen kept it busy.

It's true how they say time is like a great cog, turning and turning and turning, she wrote, keeping one eye on her grandchildren, who were in town visiting for the week. *What ends begins again, and we can't really stay sad about it when there's so much to be happy about. I love Omar and our kids and their kids, and as much as I miss the past before all of them came into my life, I would never want it back. I love what I have, and even though it hasn't always been easy, this has indeed been the best life.*

She paused to think of what to add next, and to her startlement, new words not her own formed beneath the paragraph she'd just written.

I miss you so much, Gran-Gran. Mom says you'll always be close to me, unseen, but right now you feel so far away.

Her skin turned to gooseflesh as she lifted her gaze to her granddaughter Stephanie, who had just lobbed the frisbee at her sister's head.

Stephanie was the only one who ever called her *Gran-Gran*. The writing even resembled Stephanie's, only it was more refined, as if penned by an adult.

I'm here, now, Gretchen wrote, lips forming into an understanding smile. *And for as long as I can, I will be.*

J. S. Bailey enjoys writing eerie tales of the supernatural that keep readers on the edges of their seats. She has published six novels and twenty-two short stories, with more on the way. Bailey is fond of long walks in the woods, British television, and lots of burritos. She lives in Cincinnati, Ohio with her husband and cats. Keep up to date on Bailey news and events by following her pages at Facebook jsbaileywrites, and on Twitter and Instagram at @jsbailey_author.

The Taste of Words

Kella Campbell

In the kitchen she shared with three roommates, Lucy wrote out a recipe for pasta sauce as she worked from an online cooking video: *Gourmet Chefs on Student Budgets*. She could never cook from other people's written instructions—had to learn and understand a recipe by seeing and making it, noting down quantities and steps as she went. *2 c. chopped onions, caramelized in pan.*

Outside, it was snowing, and the falling flakes looked faintly pink as they twirled through the air. A trick of the light, probably, the peachy glow of sodium streetlamps coming on or a few rays of sunset penetrating the clouds. Snow wasn't pink.

The chopped onions had just gone into the pan, still sharp and tear-inducing, but as Lucy sucked on the end of her pen—a childhood habit she couldn't break—she could already taste their sweetened brown-caramel flavor.

Puzzled, she glanced over at the pan. No, the onions were still white and raw.

Crush & add 4 cloves garlic, she wrote. She touched the end of her pen to her lips, and the sharp tang of fresh crushed garlic roared through her mouth until she dropped the pen and reached for her mug of tea.

Taking a blank recipe card, she wrote *chocolate-dipped strawberry,* then deliberately licked the pen. Yes. There was nothing in her mouth, she hadn't eaten a bite, and yet the decadent taste of chocolate mixed with fresh berry sweetness was unmistakable.

"Did you see how the snow seemed to turn pink for a bit earlier?" she asked her roommates when they got home. They hadn't noticed anything out of the ordinary.

Have you ever licked a pen and tasted the words you'd been writing? she wanted to ask, except that it sounded patently ridiculous in her head and she couldn't imagine that it would come out better aloud.

Through the evening and morning, she kept trying—different pens, different kinds of paper, different words to taste—and all of them worked. She wrote expensive things she'd never tasted like *caviar* and *saffron,* and strange things like *gasoline* and *dirt.*

She went to a lecture and took notes about the French Revolution, and every time she forgot and sucked on the end of her pen, she tasted blood and bread and something sour.

Lucy ran into Jeremy at the library in the afternoon, both of them there to study. "We could sit together?" he asked. He had the kindest eyes she'd ever seen, and a stubbled jaw she wanted to touch, and the way his clothes hung on him made her think he'd be lean and strong in all kinds of interesting places. But one couldn't just *tell* someone that. They sat.

After a quarter-hour of itchy silence, during which Lucy contemplated but refrained from writing something like *Jeremy's skin* or *Jeremy's lips* and licking her pen, she softly said his name. He looked up. They were alone in their corner of the library.

She couldn't hold it in anymore. "If you suck on the end of your pen," she said, "do you taste anything odd? Only since yesterday, when the snow looked pink—but it was probably just the light."

He grinned. "Let's see." He wrote *mint* on a corner of his notebook. "Like that?" Then he touched the end of his pen to his lips. "Holy crap!"

"Not just me, then?" Lucy asked, feeling warm all over. She couldn't tell if it was from relief at not being alone in the experience, or the fact that she was sharing the experience with him.

"Fascinating," he muttered. He wrote *coffee* and licked his pen again, nodding. "I wonder if it's the person who wrote the words, or the pen . . . " He bit his lip and shot her a half-embarrassed curious look. "Would you be super grossed out if I licked your pen? I'll wipe it after."

She shrugged like it was no big thing and hoped she wasn't blushing.

"Write something," he said. "But don't let me see it."

So she wrote *cherries* behind her hand and passed her pen to him.

"Mm, cherries. That's what you wrote, right?" he asked. When she nodded, he smiled and handed her pen back. "What about something you don't know the taste of?"

"I think so. I wrote *caviar* last night and got a salty taste, but . . . "

"I see what you mean. It could be your imagination filling in. We need a provable test." He looked around, then wrote *Lucy's lip gloss* and licked his pen. *Well.*

Their eyes met.

He chuckled. "I could ask to borrow your lip gloss now, or . . . "

"There's a more direct way," Lucy said, "if . . . "

"Direct is good," said Jeremy, and leaned in to sample the lip gloss from where she'd applied it.

The pen-taste effect faded with the winter weather, and was completely gone once all the snow had melted. Years later, Lucy asked Jeremy if he thought anyone else had discovered it, and not said anything, just as they hadn't said anything.

"Probably," he said with a grin, wrapping her in a loving hug. "But we don't need to know."

Kella Campbell (she/her) can usually be found in Vancouver, Canada. She likes tea and chocolate and happily-ever-after endings, which is likely the reason why she writes mostly romance. Even when she dips into other genres, her writing nearly always has romantic and relationship elements, because love is a joyful and inspiring thing. She writes short fiction in between novels, and hopes you'll fall in love with her rock star heroes from a fictional band called Smidge, starting with Blade in *Rock Star's Heart*. Find her and her books online at kellacampbell.com.

Writink

Ether Nepenthes

Meena groaned and stretched their arms over the table, resting their forehead against the flat, smooth paper of their notebook.

"Angha, it's not working," they whined, their voice muffled by the paper. "It's not working at all!"

"Which ink are you using?" Angha peeked out from the kitchen. "Aw, you look miserable."

"I am." Meena groaned again. "I so am!" They sighed and let their head roll to the side, to better pout at their cousin. "How can I hope to win the contest if I can't write at all?"

Angha hummed and nodded. "Aye, that sounds hard. You've been disqualified twice, so . . . Last chance at graduation, mh?"

Meena nodded.

"So, what ink are you using?"

Meena sat up in their chair with a grunt and glared at their pen. The ink cartridge was glowing a faint blue, with traces of green, red, and orange. "Think that's, err . . . 'Harmony and Peace'?" They shrugged. "But I tried every single one I had, so—like—'Inspiration' didn't work either. 'Focus', 'Endurance' . . ." They shook their head. "Maybe it's better to accept my fate. Who needs to prove Headmistress Charbon wrong, anyway, eh?" They let go of the pen and sank back into their chair. "Maybe I'll just . . . switch to a business major . . ."

Angha gave a weak chuckle. "Aye, like that's ever going to happen. Give it another go, friend-o. I know you've got this."

—

The streetlights bathed their bedroom in orange and purple when Meena eventually withdrew for the night. They crumpled on their bed, letting the pen and notebook fall on the other pillow. For a while, they covered their eyes with their arm and tried not to think. The frustration was palpable—tension gripping at their limbs, a weight on their chest, a dryness at the back of their throat. They sighed, rolled over, and held the notebook in the orange glow of the nearest streetlight. The day's attempts at starting their submission to the Twenty-Seventh Annual Aygosi College Short Story Competition shimmered in the light, each a different hue—each worse than the previous, if Meena were to judge.

The day the Alchemist of Tivotri woke up without zer headscarf— wait would it be a headscarf? Ugh that's a worldbuilding thing, I'll just call it that for now— no, pen, don't write my— ugh nevermind— so— headscarf, ze— err— ze knew the day wouldn't— or did ze not know what else the day would bring? Argh nevermind I don't even know what it's meant to bring myself—

Once, a long time ago, lived a poor and hard-working Scrivener who was poor and hard-worked every day in a conventionally European city because there was no Middle Age anywhere else apparently— I mean I could just— OK so, once a long time ago, lived a poor and hard-working Scrivener— no, a hard-working Scrivener, period, we're going to want to go full utopia here— and they lived in— mmh— the great Madinat Al-Basatin— and it was a place of great gardens and— I suppose one day— something... happened... Ugh!

"Why is this pen not working," exclaimed Lady Silvia, the magical meteorologist, exclamation point. Or not. She was looking at the

forecast panel— board? Board— at the heart of the— centre of the great plaza. At the heart of the city. Which should have read 'it shall rain in City this morning', but which was reading, 'it shall sun— be sunny, it shall be sunny in City this morning'. But as the heavy drops falling on her umbralle— umbrella! Please also correct my dyslexia, pen, it'll save time in editing— oh no wait it's time for lunch— I'll get back to it after lunch, maybe then I'll know why her pen's not working because mine certainly is, stop writing my comments! Argh, where's the manu—

Meena sighed and dropped the notebook at their side, their hand still in the air. The meteorologist one was, by far, the most original and thus the least terrible of the three, except that Meena had no idea who Lady Silvia was, why her pen was not working, or how it even worked in the first place. What they knew was that the power of their pen depended on its ink, and how well the pen 'resonated' with its user.

Well, it didn't resonate with Meena, that was for sure.

The same way their classmate could make a fortune with striking watercolours which came to life at the blink of an eye, Meena had hoped that investing in a high-quality magically-enhanced tool would help.

"You still have to put in the work," their classmate had said. Meena had then remembered why the two of them didn't talk.

What sort of non-empathetic answer was that, even? As if Meena hadn't spent the entire afternoon, the whole six hours, glaring at the paper. As if they hadn't been banging their head against the wall for literal ages.

Meena curled their fingers into a fist and drummed at their forehead slowly. There was no point in losing even more sleep over it; with yet another sigh, they snapped their fingers and, as the shutters rolled down over the windows, changed into their pyjamas.

In the half-dark of their bedroom, the magic ink still glowed softly. Meena buried the notebook under their pillow and did their best to think about something else.

The Alchemist of Tivotri was pouring Lady Silvia, the magical meteorologist, tea in a modest set of earthenware, golden liquid dripping from on high— Or was it Lady Silvia who was being mother, serving zhem in fine china, the tea a dark, rich colour?

Meena wasn't quite sure. To their left, the hard-working Scrivener was hard at work, surrounded by hills, mounds, and valleys of empty cups of all kinds. A black cat was purring from her observation post up on a shelf, and Meena knew that her name was Headmistress Charbon.

"Is this some sort of weird dream?" they asked. Everything was wrapped in cotton wool, soft and sweet, but not quite real.

Lady Silvia opened her mouth, but no sound came; the Alchemist smiled, but zher figure faded at the edges.

"Will you please all shut up? I am trying to work here."

The Scrivener hadn't looked up, but Meena clearly remembered not describing hair that was the same as theirs. Black and thick, frizzy when it rained. The Scrivener also had brown skin, and a fidget cube in their free hand . . .

"So I am in a weird dream." Meena made a face. They were now sitting in something that looked like a white iron-wrought garden seat, but felt like a rare wooden, velvet-cushioned armchair. The cup they were holding was either brown glazed earthenware or delicately painted china; the tea either clear and steamy, or brown with a dash of milk. It changed by the second, by the thought, or the blink of the eye.

They put the cup back, or folded their hands on their lap, or leaned back into their chair— Or were they letting out a breath they hadn't known they were holding?

They sipped the tea. It tasted like nothingness; definitely a dream.

"So, how do I wake up?" they asked. "I've got work to do."

"You're not the only one." The Scrivener's quill was scratching across the paper furiously. "So much work! So little time! You need to sleep more."

"What?"

"So I can work more!"

"That . . . Okay," Meena said, their eyes wide, and they decided to turn back to the other two.

The Alchemist and Lady Silvia were still so very busy pouring tea for each other, blurry at the edges in pastel colours. It reminded Meena of a tarot card—the fourteenth major arcana, called 'Temperance' in most traditions, and conventionally represented by someone pouring water between two cups. Harmony, balance, alchemy . . .

"Does that mean I should switch to magic again? I don't—I don't want to be a witchcraft major; that's just *creepy*." They shook their head and the whole scene shook too. "I don't want to—"

A blink and suddenly they were in a library—surrounded by columns and columns and columns of books, towering over the hard-working Scrivener.

"There's not enough time!" the Scrivener cried out, one hand grabbing a fistful of hair, the other tensed on the quill. "There's not enough time! And when there's enough time, there's not enough work!"

The towers of books started crumbling, plot points and narrative arcs unfolding all around them. In the chaos of dramatic reveals, bullet lists and tropes let loose, Meena found themself right next to the Scrivener. They were still crying out and writing furiously at once.

"We are all doomed, doomed, doomed! We will never reach the ink-spring from which the words freely pour! We have been cast away, into the fog, banging our head against the writer's wall!"

"It's called writer's block," Meena shouted over the rumble. "It's not— It's not—"

But all the books, volumes, tomes, anthologies and collected works were sweeping down—and then back up, level rising, threatening to drown the two of them. Somewhere, the Archivist and Lady Silvia were drowning, too, suffocating in the pool of spilled ink Meena had failed to transmute into proper stories.

It was all Meena's fault, and there was no escape.

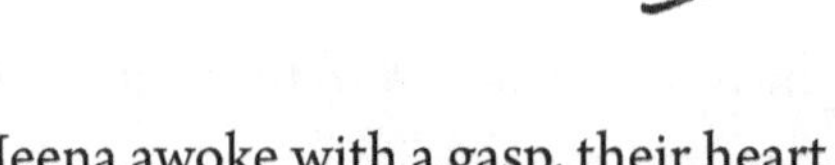

Meena awoke with a gasp, their heart drumming in their ears and their hand already on the light switch. Only once their breathing smoothed and their heartbeat quieted did they realise how warm, sweaty, and thirsty they felt. They switched off their nightlight and snapped the shutters open again; outside, the sky was still a deep, nightly red above the city lights. They opened the window and, thanks to the noise-cancelling and pollution-cleansing filters, enjoyed the illusion of a breeze as they gulped from their water bottle.

They needed a break. Too bad for the contest and the Headmistress, but no creative pursuit should give anyone stress nightmares. At least they hadn't been screaming, since Angha hadn't come to check on them.

They yawned and stretched. Time to switch off the alarm clock and sleep in. They put pen and notebook away in a drawer of their desk, and went back to bed.

"Are you reading about gay Elves again?" Angha's voice betrayed her amusement.

Meena looked up from the seventeenth chapter of *Much Ado About Shiny Rings* currently open on their ereader. "I'll have you know that Lord Silvertears is my actual father who sired me for real and everything," they said, in the most mock-serious tone they could muster.

Angha frowned. "Who's that one again?"

Meena groaned and sat up on the couch. "I told you so many times, he's the grouchy—"

"Oh! The jeweller?" Angha took a seat next to them, the delicate fragrance of lavender steaming from her mug.

"No, that's his hate-sex buddy. He's the ex-bard. The war criminal."

"They're all war criminals, sweetie."

"You do have a point and I elect not to care about it," Meena deadpanned, and then slouched back into the couch and their book.

Angha sipped her tea. Lord Silvertears was debating whether to kiss or punch his nemesis for the fourth time in the same scene when she asked, “So you *are* done with your story, then? For the contest?”

Meena switched off the ereader and scooped up a pillow to hide their face.

“I’ll take that as a no.” Angha sipped her tea again. “Isn’t the deadline—”

“I’m living behind this pillow now, so please let me enjoy the rest of my Charbon-free days in peace,” Meena supplicated from below the pillow. “I hate writing, I’m never ever doing it again, I should never have done it. I’m taking that pen back. Notebook, too. I’m giving all my worldly possessions to charity and starting a new life as a hermit in the woods!”

“Okay.” Angha hummed. “Living off berries and your undying love for grouchy, old, supernatural fictional characters? Heating your little hut with animal dung? Never talking to a human being ever again?”

Meena raised the cushion slightly. “Yes. Especially that last part. That’s the dream. Nobody, never again— Not even you!”

Angha gently flicked at their ankle and shook her head with a smile, but said nothing more. She returned to her tea, scrolling down her phone, and Meena hugged the cushion, looking at the ceiling. The ambience manager was on the ‘early spring’ setting, even though it was the dead of summer and the energy bills their highest expense. Renewable energy was nice, Meena thought. It allowed them to be serenaded by birdsong coming off the hidden speakers in the wall, the bubbling of a water stream projected on the carpet, and the whispers of the wind in a ‘faraway copse of golden-green trees’, as the manual said.

If even the technical manual of their ambience manager sounded better than their writing… Meena sighed. Beyond graduation and the Headmistress's approval, they would have loved to get their hands on that sweet, sweet contest prize money. And they did like their ideas and their characters, all of them, but the words . . . were not flowing. Writing was simply not happening. The magic pen hadn't helped; neither had pulling their hair over it for weeks and weeks.

"Oooh, did you see this?" Angha asked, shoving her phone in Meena's face.

"Uh, what?" They blinked and pushed the screen away.

"It's an interview! From that—'Echoes of Time', that's one hell of an interesting pen name—the person who wrote *Much Ado*?"

Angha handed Meena the phone again, but they shook their head. "No, if it's their last one, I've probably read it. I've read them all. The one where they say they only write for fun and if it isn't fun, they put it aside and nothing's more important than their well-being and stuff like that?"

Angha hummed.

"Yeah, I've read it." Meena sighed and leaned back on the couch. "Bet they didn't have to deal with mandatory contests and Headmistresses and . . . " Their voice trailed off.

Angha pursed her lips. "Well, have you tried?"

"Tried what?"

"Writing for fun?"

"You mean, like fanfiction?"

"Not necessarily— Write something that makes you happy. With that magic pen of yours. There's an ink for that, too, I think."

Meena sat back up. "There is?"

"Yes! I think it's called something silly, like 'Rainbows and Sparkles'." Angha tapped at their phone. "Yep, here it is, promising you 'joy and optimism' in 'a cheerful act of written creativity.'" She giggled. "Sounds like just what you need."

Meena stared at the page, and the page stared back. They had cleaned off their desk for this, rearranged their room lighting, descaled their teapot and remade their bullet journal writing layout, although the last two probably counted as procrastination. Either way, they were ready. They felt ready.

In the background, the ambience manager was playing a soothing mix of heavy rain, thunder and fireplace noises, with a picture of mountains as seen through a cottage window projected on the wall. The faint scent of overly sweet mint tea rose along with the steam from Meena's cat-shaped cup.

They took the cap off their pen; it glowed a bright pink. They licked their lips and leaned back on their chair as they brought their hands to a steeple under their chin.

Something fun . . . Something that brought them joy . . .

They took a deep breath; as soon as they opened their mouth, the pen rose and scribbled away.

Stories, they started hesitantly, *are meant to— many things, among which— bring us joy. Thus thought Ename, Scrivener of the Madinat Al-Basatin. Mmh. "Your pen does not work, Lady Silvia, because you are so frustrated— irritated— its resonance cannot— it cannot echo the beat of your thoughts if you do not listen to them yourself." Yes, that works! That could be why her pen wasn't working, she needs to be more in tune with her thoughts. That's why she's gone to the Scrivener for help. OK, I got my ending, now, how does the Alchemist fit into this? Is zhe the one who made the pen? Mmh, I'll keep that for later, and focus on what I know for now. So. As the last light of the day shone on the crimson city walls, bathing Al-Basatin in an ochre hue, Lady Silvia strode towards the Scrivener's office, her assistant in tow . . .*

When Angha peeked in, two hours later, Meena's tea had gone cold, but they hadn't even noticed. They were now lying on their bed, their face mirroring the characters' emotions, their hands gesturing wildly. Angha smiled and shook her head, closing the door behind her. Dinner could wait; it was good to see Meena so enthused in their craft. She was already looking forward to ordering fancy take-away to celebrate. After all, who cared about the end result, as long as one enjoyed the process? Wasn't that victory on its own already?

Ether Nepenthes (they/them) is a queer, non-binary, disabled, neurodivergent writer hailing from the south of France. Their main occupations are writing relatable, heartwarming stories and making sure that their cat is the only ruler of the neighbourhood. Other interests include video games, drinking too much tea and fighting the patriarchy. You can find a complete list of their publications on their website ethernepenthes.com and-slash-or get in touch on Twitter @ethernepenthes.

The Cemetery Merchant

Anthony W. Eichenlaub

The cart unfolds reluctantly, its rusted hinges creaking like an old body waking cold and alone from long rest. I assemble my shop where the roots of the monstrous oaks disturb grave markers so old their names have worn to nothing. This is the same unlikely spot I have used all these many years every time the ache deep in my joints warns of a new customer.

One by one, I set out my hundred pens, each crafted by my own hand—made magical in its own way. The hundred and first rests silently in my pocket—my own pen forged by my own magic.

No sooner has my cart's last clasp jolted into place—the final panel braced against the damp autumn breeze—than my sensitive ears bring me the rustle of the approaching customer.

I wonder for a moment what wanderer comes my way, for I never know in advance. All kinds are tempted by my pens, be they intrepid adventurer or studious librarian. CEO or factory worker. No customer has ever refused my wares, though my price is often steep.

A leaf drifts down from the oaken canopy to rest upon my cart. I leave it as it lies, its leathery form like a bat wing against the gray wood.

Silence.

The customer at last pushes through the underbrush into the forgotten graveyard. Her face rings familiar, though at my age such memories are often false. Unlikely I would ever forget sky blue eyes that catch even the light of this clouded day. She takes a moment to wrangle her white hair into a neat ponytail. She wears only black.

I say nothing as she takes in this sight of me: the lone vendor in the lost cemetery. For a long while, she studies my face, as if my pens hold no temptation at all.

But there is a pen to tempt any soul. I touch an elegant fountain pen. "Carved from the ancient branch of a Joshua tree felled by a strike of lightning at the height of summer." I speak in a quiet voice, not meeting her gaze. "Memories written with this pen will be described in such perfect detail, the reader will know them as if their own."

She responds without hesitation. "As the pen's curse fades that memory from the writer's mind."

I struggle to keep my surprise from showing. "Once written, one could read one's own writing in order to remember. All pens are cursed, but the trick is to find a curse that is close enough to a blessing."

Her response is dry. "I'm not here to forget."

"Some come for just that purpose."

The creases at the corners of her lips deepen in amusement, but she says nothing. Part of me wonders how she knows my pens' curses.

I touch the smooth, gray form of another elegant instrument. "Driftwood from the Atlantic bound in steel from a ship's hull. Use this pen to write the name of a port at midnight, and by noon the next day you will have passage booked there."

"At no cost?"

"None. Free passage anywhere the sea touches."

She reaches out to touch the pen, but something stays her hand. "What ship?"

Clever. "None other than the Titanic herself."

"Passage booked, but arrival not guaranteed?"

"Adventure is the only guarantee," I say, though even that may be false. No complaints ever found their way back to my shop.

"I think I'll pass," she says. She isn't browsing pens anymore but watches me closely.

Silence lingers, for I only ever make three offers. This last must be a perfect fit for her tormented soul.

What is it I recognize in her features? In her voice? Her gaze falls upon a pair of pens hewn from hawthorn, bound in black iron. A worse fit for her I've never seen. She must be taunting me to show interest in a pen that never runs out of ink so long as it writes only words of pain. What pain could she have endured?

But what can I sell her? What pen is perfect for such a striking woman.

Such a—

My fingers act upon inspiration before my mind considers consequences. From my own pocket, I produce the pen that has been with me all these many years.

"Gold," I say, "both in binding and the inlay. Ebony as black as a merchant's heart. Platinum nib as fine as the razor which cuts to bone with every deal. It guarantees wealth and success for its owner."

I place the pen on display but cannot bring myself to lift my finger from it. My heart pounds as it never has before.

"This pen had a twin once," I continue, "one of rosewood and silver. That pen promised love; this, money. Together they would have been . . . "

She no longer listens to my words. Cool autumn breeze tugs at her black dress and she hugs it close. "Their curse?"

"None," I say too fast. "They deliver exactly as promised."

"But what will I forget?" she says.

"Forget?" I take my hand from the pen. "Nothing at all. I have had this pen for fifty years, and it has brought me true success in all my dealings. I have been content all these years."

She leans over my cart, her face so close that her breath tickles my nose. "Fifty years?"

"That's right." I do not back down. "I bought a gorgeous house with a swimming pool, and I move amongst wealthiest of society. Though I never married or had children, I've donated more to charity than most people earn their entire lives. My children are the poor, unfortunate of the community, and with my wealth I've raised a great many of them to their own success."

She says, "Fifty years ago, I met my perfect love. He was kind and funny. We married and raised six lovely children, even though we never really earned enough to afford them. Your charity found its way to my children, even though there were likely those who needed it more. I was happy all those years, but today, on this very afternoon, I bury my beloved in another cemetery not far from here."

All cemeteries are not far from this place, so long as the traveler is lost. "I'm sorry," I say.

She pulls back, and finally I allow myself to make eye contact. It is as if our souls touch and in touching release a shock of static. She looks down, and following her gaze, I see what rests next to my ebony pen.

Rosewood and silver. The pen's mate.

Memory returns: two young fools in love, her with shocking

blue eyes, me with the first two magic pens I'd ever crafted. Cursed pens. Wealth and love—at a cost.

I look down at my ancient hands, knuckles knobby with arthritis. "What have we done?"

"We lived our lives," she says. "We've done well—you with money, me with love."

"We didn't have each other."

A smile spreads across her face. "No," she says, "but we do now. Will you tell me of this charity of yours?"

"Do you really have six children?"

"More than my fair share of grandchildren, too."

The leaves rustle high above. "You'll have to tell me all about them," I say.

"You'll meet them, if I have anything to say about it."

Her hand slips into mine, warm despite the autumn chill. Together, we leave the lost cemetery deep in the woods, never to return.

Anthony W. Eichenlaub (he/him) is an author surviving in the frozen wastes of Minnesota. His work can be found in the anthology *A Punk Rock Future* as well as in the publications *On Spec Magazine* and *Little Blue Marble*. In his spare time he makes pens in his garage and sells them in his strange little shop in a cemetery deep in the woods: etsy.com/shop/OakLeafCemetery Find more of his works at anthonyeichenlaub.com

Love in the Library

Robert Perez

The desert sun was setting over Javier's shoulders. He paced the creaking porch, kicking crumpled yellow wads of legal paper out of his way and sending them rolling like tumbleweeds. Tomorrow morning was his wedding day and he had yet to write his vows. Family and friends had converged upon a Spanish mission outside of San Antonio, Texas, for the event. A wing of the beautiful Mission Nuestra Señora Soccoro had been converted into a bed and breakfast and all of the rooms were currently checked out by the wedding party. Privacy to write had been impossible until the large group scattered for last-minute errands and sightseeing.

Javier was ready to pledge his heart until his dying day. His difficulty composing his vows wasn't in the promise of forever but in proving his conviction to his family. His parents had been together for over fifty years and would have front row seats. He knew he had his mother's unconditional support, but he wasn't so sure about his father. For many of his family members it would be their first time seeing Javier kiss a man. He wondered how many of them showed up out of genuine support or to verify rumors.

His mother, Linda, had been listening to her son's heavy tread through the open kitchen window for the last hour as she pet the missionary cat. She had intended to sit down for only a moment but her new purring friend decided to nap in her lap. She called Javier inside. "Mijo."

The screen door slammed shut behind him and Linda felt like

she was home. The commotion startled the cat and it darted into the pantry where its golden eyes hovered in the shadows.

"Yes?" Javier asked, thick brows furrowed in concentration as he reread a sheet before him.

"They'll be coming back soon. Why don't you hide out in the library? La poesía puede ayudar."

Javier sighed and crumpled up his latest attempt. "To think I thought this would be easy! There's a fireplace in the library, right? Let me go gather my failures."

The handle of Linda's cane was carved into the head of a ferocious wolf with lapis eyes. Her wrinkled hand rested on the wolf and the blue of her veins coursed alongside the semi-precious snarl.

"I'll request some tea for us." Linda stood and waved away his assistance. "Meet you there."

The library smelled of sandalwood and tobacco; even though it had probably been decades since someone had last smoked in the room, the leather and the books were stained with the memory. Linda sat in a rocking chair by the flickering fireplace watching her son move around the library like a hurricane. She poured two cups of rose tea as Javier poured over the shelves.

"Dime que estás pensado, Mijo. I saw Alejandro try to nuzzle you before leaving but you were far away in your mind," Linda worried.

"He knows I love him," Javier said as he pulled a book off the shelf, "it's just . . . this performance for Dad and some of the others. I know they're watching us. I can feel their judgement even though they smile."

Linda rapped her nails over her cane. "Un lobo no teme a las ovejas."

An envelope fell from the pages of the book Javier was holding open. He bent to pick it up in wonder—eyes going wide at the scrawled date of *December 16th, 1750*.

"Mira! This was hidden between the pages," Javier said and handed the letter over.

From G.S., To C.J. Linda delicately unfolded the envelope and letter inside. *To My Missing Heart. Though we may never be together I think of you always. Do you think of me? The same lips that kissed you now curse you. What have you done to me? Yearning is such sweet agony. I'll never forget the night we shared. I hope one day we meet again. – G.S.*

Linda gasped, "You've stumbled onto someone's secret love . . . or maybe a scandalous affair! See if there are more!"

Javier bounded to the bookshelf and selected the volumes with the oldest bindings, which varied between almanacs, religious texts, poetry, and maps. It wasn't long before he found another letter in a book of love sonnets.

He opened it and read, *April 24th, 1757. Dear Love of My Life. Imagine us meeting in a different time. Meeting under better circumstances. These reveries ease my current predicament. It's been raining for days and the mud is trying its best to steal my boots. I'd give anything to be with you in the library warm by the fire. In another life we have a dog and you keep a garden. It's fun to dream, isn't it? – G.S.*

Javier and Linda developed a rhythm of discovery and reading. Soon a love story spanning a decade was spread across the library rug.

"This is better than my telenovelas!" Linda beamed.

Javier found what he assumed to be the last correspondence, an unfinished letter with a black quill pen hidden in a book of maps. He imagined someone writing by candlelight pausing their midnight confession to listen to the dark halls before shutting the letter and pen away with intentions of returning—thoughts lost to the centuries.

June 10th, 1762. Dear One and Only. I pray that my letter finds you safe and in good health. Rumors swirl about misfortune befalling your regiment. I've been oblique with my inquiries to shield us from scrutiny. What a thing to take for granted to simply walk down a street holding the hand of your love. When we are together again I dare to be so bold! I look to the stars and—

"And what!?" Linda demanded.

"That's it. The end." Javier twirled the quill between his fingers.

"There you are!" Alejandro announced from the doorway. "I've been looking everywhere for you."

The distance closed between them in an embrace and passionate kiss. Pleasant surprise caught Alejandro off guard, and he matched Javier's intensity before catching himself in the presence of Linda.

"I'm sorry." Alejandro blushed. "Your handsome son has cast a spell on me."

Linda stood with the help of her wolf. She squeezed the men's elbows. "Love doesn't need to apologize for being seen."

Javier was filled with pride and wanted to pull Alejandro closer and cover him with kisses to embarrass him.

"I'll see you two at dinner," Linda doted before departing.

"I take it you worked through the writer's block," Alejandro ventured.

"Well . . . not exactly." It was Javier's turn to blush as he ran his hand through his dark hair. "I still haven't finalized . . . a beginning, middle, or end, but I've stumbled upon a trove of inspiration. When the time comes I'm going to speak from my heart."

"Oh?" Alejandro coaxed with a raised brow.

Javier held up the black quill pen, "This feather once soared through the sky on a wing, then it was wielded to channel thoughts and emotions to the page before being shut away in a book."

He led his partner over to the array of letters and they sat on the rug before the fire.

"I found a centuries-old love story hidden in the books." Javier explained and admired Alejandro's face as he read through the letters. "The only way their love could survive was as a secret. They made me realize that I've been holding back. Since we got here, I've been caught in the perceptions of others. I'm letting all of that go. It may take some time for certain members of my family to adjust, and they might not ever get used to it, but that doesn't matter. You are what matters."

Alejandro pulled Javier into a kiss by his belt loops. "They are going to see how happy we are and then they are going to be happy for us."

Javier woke up before Alejandro and wrapped his arms around him. It felt like a normal morning.

"Wake up babe, it's time to get married," Javier whispered into Alejandro's ear.

Alejandro stretched and feigned drowsiness, "Five more minutes."

The letters were turned over to the Mission and there was talk of a future display which would include a picture of the wedding party and the serendipitous story of the historical letters' discovery. To honor the mystery lovers the quill pen was on special loan for the wedding ceremony and used to sign the guestbook.

Late that night at the reception, as friends and family began to bid their farewells, and as Javier and Alejandro slow-danced, Linda flipped through the pages of the guestbook and discovered the names of strangers written in a familiar hand—*Gerald Santos and Christopher Joaquin.*

Robert Perez sleeps at the bottom of the ocean. Urban legend whispers that the writer can be summoned into your dreams if you read his work to a jack-o-lantern. You can find his poems and stories in the *Horror Writers Association Poetry Showcase* Volumes II, III, IV (Special Mention), and V, *The Literary Hatchet* #13 & #14, *Deadlights Magazine* #1, and *Five Minutes at Hotel Stormcove*. He is currently working on obtaining a M.A. in Counseling Psychology at the University of Colorado Denver. Follow @_TheLeader on Twitter to keep up with future projects.

Pen ID

Adam Kissel

"My name is Penny. My colors are red and copper."

"Penny, your closing argument begins now."

"Public health requires all Pens to announce their colors before speaking. We have seen the consequences of errant inking. We remember when the 'wine-dark sea' came out light blue because a member of the Opposition refused to reveal anything until it was too late."

"And who speaks for the Opposition?"

"Nick—silver and gray."

"Begin."

"The Opposition proved today that Pens have the right of privacy. We are free to decide whether to reveal both of our colors or none at all. Anonymity is not fraud. If you pick an unlabeled Pen, you take your chances. Our ink is not your problem."

"Whose ink?" "Our ink!" "WHOSE INK? OUR INK!"

"Order in the chamber!

"We proceed to vote by secret ballot."

—

"Back to order!

"I am the Presider. My colors are black and white. The votes have been counted: 24 yes, 12 no. The Mandatory Disclosure Act passes. Color announcements are no longer voluntary but mandatory in Pensylvania."

SUPREME COURT OF PENSYLVANIA

NEMO *v.* PENSYLVANIA

PLAINTIFF argues that the Mandatory Disclosure Act violates the right to privacy. The state argues that compelling state interests, such as public health, may overcome such rights. We affirm that the Act meets this burden and that Plaintiff—and all Pensylvanians—must announce their inks before speaking.

"Rachael, dozens of my pens are missing! Disappeared!"

"What do you mean, Leah?"

"Yesterday all my pens were aligned in rows, first the labeled ones and then the unlabeled ones. Today, virtually all of the unlabeled pens are gone!"

"Like magic? Like they got up and left?"

"Well, a thief wouldn't steal the unlabeled ones. You wouldn't know what you're getting."

—

"Who speaks for the Establishment?"

"Nick—silver and gray."

"Begin."

"Five years ago, Pensylvania drove away a valued group in the name of public health. But we have seen no change in rates of ink-related illness. Meanwhile, life here has become predictable: we all say what we are going to say before we say it, and then after we say it, we say what we have said. The Establishment has erred. We are ready to bring the thrill of anonymity back to Pensylvania."

"And who speaks for the Opposition?"

"Dolores—just green."

"Proceed, Dolores."

"In my old age, I must say that I have seen a lot of change. When I was barely a wick, not all Pens had the vote. Now they do. The majority decided that progress should continue. We mandated ink disclosure and banned errant inking. I admit that I never thought I would one day be a progressive and a reactionary at the same time, but we must hold fast to our progress."

"Thank you, Dolores. All in favor of the Act to Repeal the Mandatory Disclosure Act and restore voluntary disclosure, click your Bics.

[Loud clicking.]

"All opposed, click your Bics.

[Moderate clicking.]

"I remind the audience to remain silent until the result is announced. Remember, no clapping, only clicking.

"The Act passes.

[Wild clicking.]

"Next order of business, the Return to Homeland and Reparations for the Unlabeled Act."

Adam Kissel makes trouble. Influences: Petrarch, Plato. Dog: Frank ("Benjamin Franklin"). Studied with Wayne C. Booth. Taught writing at the University of Chicago. First Prize, Education Reporting, Education Writers Association. Developmental editor for historical fiction by Thomas Thibeault. Can write federal regulations. Helps philanthropists. Lives in D.C.

Do Not Write to Wrong

N.R. Lambert

A metallic clap of thunder shuddered around Tubman Elementary School. The preternaturally long vibrations rattled pans in the cafeteria like cymbals, shimmied thick textbooks off the shelves in Room 305, and sent dust cascading down over Ms. Hutchinson's 5th grade students, who were currently conducting a secret meeting in the forgotten chamber behind Room 502's coat closet.

Another rumble rippled around them.

"Lonnie," Ella Cruz grumbled.

"Definitely Lonnie," Derrick Richards replied, nervously drumming his fingers against the armrest of his wheelchair.

Three days earlier, their classmate, Lonnie Blunt, had stolen the Pen of Realities from the secret room, and, with it, of course, the Ledger of Truths—neither would work without the other.

Now, with just one day to go till 5th grade graduation, Ella, Derrick, and the rest of Ms. Hutchinson's class struggled to devise a plan to regain custody of the items safely before they graduated . . . or Lonnie became unstoppable.

The walls of the hidden room shook again.

"He knows we're here," said Aminah Ali. "He probably knows we're trying to stop him. He's going to get even."

The dim overhead lights suddenly burst in a cascade of sparks, sending the room into darkness.

"If he knows, why doesn't he just stop us now?" someone whispered.

Another kid added. "He can't hurt us . . . right?"

No one answered.

For generations, the 5th graders at Tubman Elementary acted as the honored chosen custodians for the Pen of Realities and the Ledger of Truths. Chosen by whom, no one knew. Also, nobody knew why or how the Pen and Ledger came to be under the care of a rotating group of young students. Nevertheless, the 5th graders accepted their solemn duty to protect these items and, until recently, only used them with great thoughtfulness and care.

The children changed, the teachers changed, even the Pen's form changed—from a sterling silver fountain, to a classic blue ball-point, to its current form, a bright green Shimmy Rollerball 3000.

But two things did not change: 1) In any form, the Pen's delicate inscription remained the same, *Do Not Write to Wrong*; and 2) the Pen's amazing ability never wavered.

The Pen wrote reality.

Anything written with the Pen in the Ledger of Truths became . . . well, the truth. The Ledger also had a handy section in the back for notes, detailing every change of hands and every occasion of the Pen's use for almost two centuries. So each new class had access to the successes and failures of the children before them.

Until Lonnie claimed the Pen and Ledger as his own, the kids believed the Pen could do no harm. It did, after all, have limitations. It couldn't create life (the class of 1879 tried that). It couldn't end war (multiple classes attempted this, despite all the notes detailing the previous failed efforts).

It couldn't resurrect the dead.

The Pen worked best when the Realities were small, personal, and somewhat localized.

For example, the class of 1906 unanimously voted to write the Reality: *Suzanne Sotto's dad does not hurt Suzanne or her brothers or her mom.* So it became true, and from that day forward, Suzanne and her siblings no longer wore bruises, scars, and scabs to school.

A few years later, the class of 1931 wrote: *There will always be enough food in the cafeteria for kids to take a little extra home if they're hungry.*

The class of 1950 wrote: *Our school will always be accessible to any person who wishes or needs to enter.* Since then—and to the occasional bafflement of the district inspector—Tubman Elementary's facilities were decades ahead of any local bureaucratic codes, incorporating the latest designs and technology to keep the school fully accessible to everyone, no matter their needs.

Every student at Tubman Elementary owed a great debt to the class of 1976 for the cafeteria's much-celebrated Sundae Mondays.

The class of 1998 wrote the Reality: *No one will bring a gun to our school.*

The class of 1999 added, for extra measure: *No one will get shot in our school or on school grounds.*

The class of 2013 wrote: *No one will get shot in any school ever again, anywhere.*

Unfortunately, that Reality didn't work.

But every class since tried again anyway.

Lonnie Blunt strode down the hall, the Ledger tucked under his elbow and the Pen clutched in his fist. Why hadn't he done this sooner? It was true, he didn't need the Pen of Realities to get most of what he wanted. He had money for that. Lots of it. He never tired of reminding the other kids how his family lived in the biggest house in town, ate at the fanciest restaurants, and drove the most expensive cars. But the Pen gave him something new. It made him feel seen. Important. Feared. It made him a god. Even money couldn't do that. Usually.

Still, Lonnie kept his first few Realities fairly small and personal.

Lonnie Blunt is the funniest kid at Tubman and tells the best jokes.

All of Lonnie Blunt's birthday parties are well attended and no one ever skips out early.

Lonnie Blunt never feels alone.

Lonnie quickly tired of the Pen's small changes, so he started to go bigger with his Realities.

Everyone in town thinks Lonnie Blunt is the coolest.

Lonnie Blunt is the most popular boy in town and always will be.

As he wrote Reality after Reality, he worried a little that the Pen would wear out—no one had ever created so many new Realities in such a short time; surely there was a limit. But the Pen kept going and so did he.

No one is allowed on the playground without Lonnie Blunt's permission.

Only Lonnie Blunt and his friends can take the bus, everyone else can walk.

If anyone ever thinks something bad or mean about Lonnie Blunt, they will get giant boogers all over their face.

Within an hour of that Reality, every single kid in the 5th grade had giant boogers all over their face. But even more satisfying, the rest of the school—the whole rest of the town—*did not* have boogers. The teachers, the principal, the parents, all the other kids at Tubman—they didn't know. To them Lonnie *was* the most popular boy, the funniest, the coolest. They couldn't remember the reality before Lonnie's Realities . . . and he intended to keep it that way.

The hidden room trembled again, now from beneath their feet.

"We're running out of time." Aminah whispered. Only the 5th grade custodians of the Pen knew and remembered the different Realities, and only *while* they were the protectors. Once they graduated, the responsibilities of keeping the Pen and Ledger, along with any new Realities, would be forgotten until inherited by the next class . . . months later. Who knew what Lonnie Blunt would do with the Pen during that time? It was already proving dangerous in his hands.

The lights flickered back on, but significantly dimmer, casting a flaking, yellow glow over the students. Derrick pivoted, maneuvering his chair closer to the hidden room's door. He peered through a peephole disguised as a brass hook on the other side.

"The classroom seems empty," he whispered to the group. "But recess is almost over; he'll be back soon."

"Unless Lonnie altered that too," Simon Roberts hissed. "He

could make recess last forever. Or make himself the sole keeper of the Pen for all time. Or make 5th grade never end. Or—"

"Ella, your nose!" Aminah gasped. Ella reached up and touched her nose, which had suddenly grown pointed, furry, and whiskered like a rat's. She sighed.

"What about me?" Jina Yoon touched all over her face frantically. "I'm the one who tried to slip the Pen out of his backpack yesterday."

"So far so good, Jina." Aminah patted her elbow. "I mean, besides the boogers."

Billy Schroder grimaced. "Yeah, but I saw him write a Reality that anyone who took the Pen from him would suffer a lot worse than boogers or a rat's nose." Billy dragged his finger across his throat.

"That's why we're not going to take it from him," Ella said, twitching her whiskers. "But we need to get into position now. I don't know if we'll get another chance."

The kids quietly pushed open the secret door and slipped back into the classroom one by one.

Derrick looked over his shoulder at Ella as he rolled through the door. "You know, Lonnie thinks he's unstoppable."

"Well, he's wrong." Ella said flipping off the dim lights and following him out the door, keeping the, *I hope,* to herself.

The classroom door crashed open and Lonnie Blunt stormed in. He plopped down at Ms. Hutchinson's desk, flipped opened the Ledger of Truths, and with a smug grin, scribbled in a few new Realities.

With a dull metallic thrum, an enormous, gold monstrosity replaced the small, wood desk before him.

"That's more like it." He smirked, looking over his classmates' faces. "Ella, something's different . . . new haircut?"

Ella slunk down in her seat, whiskers sagging.

Simon cleared his throat, "Um. You can't sit there, Lonnie, that's Ms. H's desk."

Lonnie lifted a brow, bent to the Ledger and wrote. Suddenly, the words *Lonnie's Desk* appeared across the front of the desk, written in bright jewels of every color, shape, and size.

"Okay Lonnie, that's enough." As planned, Derrick rolled toward Lonnie, "How about you hand over the—" Donnie scribbled and Derrick disappeared. No, not disappeared . . . shrunk, along with his chair, to the size of a bee.

"Hey!" Derrick shouted, but only the kids seated in the very front of the room could hear him. He rolled forward, but Lonnie just sneered down at him.

"Buzz off, Derrick. You know what happens to bugs."

The rest of the class exchanged uneasy glances. It was now or never. This had to end before Derrick or anyone else got hurt . . . or worse.

"You should let someone else have a turn now," Billy made his lines sound totally unrehearsed. Ella suppressed a grin.

"Um, how about no!" Lonnie gripped the Pen tighter, "Why would I ever do that?"

"I told you he was scared," Jina stage whispered, loud enough for everyone in the class to hear.

"I'm not scared of anything!" Lonnie blurted, then added, "Scared of what?"

Aminah grinned. "Jina said you're afraid someone might write better Realities than you . . . someone like Ella."

Jina nervously checked her nose as Aminah spoke.

"Ella?" Lonnie snorted. "You have to be kidding!" He looked around at his classmates, expecting approval, but finding only practiced, stony silence. His cheeks grew blotchy and red. "No one can write better Realities than me. Everyone says I'm the best at this. Everyone."

Billy scoffed, "Okay then, prove it."

It felt like the entire class held its breath. Would he take the bait?

"Pft! Okay, yeah. Let's see if Ella can write even one Reality that beats any of mine." His smile faded, "But I'm the only judge and then I get the Pen back right away."

Aminah grinned. "Deal. Now, make it a Reality."

Lonnie paused for a long moment then scrawled as he read aloud:

Lonnie Blunt is the one and only judge of all Realities.

Lonnie Blunt isn't scared of anything, especially girls like Ella Cruz.

Lonnie Blunt's Realities are always the best.

Someone stifled a groan. Lonnie threw a quick glare around the room, but resumed writing.

Ella Cruz can have the Pen to write exactly one Reality and then she has to give it back to Lonnie Blunt immediately.

Lonnie slapped the Ledger shut and smirked at Ella. "Over to you, rat face."

Ella walked up to the massive, gaudy desk and picked up the Ledger. When she reached for the Pen, Lonnie snapped his hand back and her heart dropped into her stomach.

"Ha! Too slow, pellet breath." Lonnie held the Pen away, just out of Ella's reach. She struggled to keep her expression neutral. Finally, tiring of the game, he rolled his eyes and, sighing theatrically, dropped the Pen in her open hand. "Fine, here."

Ella's fingers curled tight around the Pen as she turned to her desk, where, keeping her back to Lonnie, she opened the Ledger and bent over it.

She knew exactly what she was supposed to write. What they'd all so carefully discussed in the hidden room. But for one brief and dark moment she thought about writing a different Reality, one that would take care of Lonnie for good, one like: *Lonnie Blunt never existed.*

But as quickly as the thought popped into her head, she rejected it, her face hot with shame. Ella couldn't bring herself to write him out of existence, no matter how angry she was with him. It was too awful, too dark, even for a boy like Lonnie.

Instead, she stuck to the plan. She lifted the Pen and wrote:

Lonnie Blunt never stole the Pen of Realities . . .

Something shifted in the room. The 5th graders looked at each other, relieved to find their faces free of the giant boogers, but still creased with worry.

Lonnie snorted, "That's the best you could do? Getting rid of the boogers?" He cackled, even though no one else laughed with him. "Pretty pathetic, Ella. I'm just going to rewrite that. Now give it all back, your turn is up."

"I'm not done yet." Ella said, her back still to Lonnie.

"You get to write exactly one Reality. I wrote it out. 'Exactly one.' You can't change that." He rose to his feet, eyes locked on Ella's back. She whirled around and Lonnie's smug expression fell away when he saw her rat nose was gone. When Derrick rolled up behind him, back in human scale, Lonnie's eyes darkened in anger.

Ella smirked. "Well, I didn't finish writing my *exactly one* Reality and it looks like I already changed *all* of yours." She lifted the Ledger so Lonnie could see. All of his Realities were gone. Erased. His face turned from red to purple.

"It's not fair!" Lonnie shouted. "Now I have to start all over again—give it back!"

Lonnie charged forward, dodging Derrick's strong grasp. He dove for the Pen, but Ella continued her Reality, scribbling quickly:

and never will

As if colliding with an invisible wall, Lonnie jolted back and crashed into the desks behind him. Some of the kids cheered. He glared, heaving and sputtering like the pasty mac 'n' cheese the cafeteria served on Wednesdays.

"Fine then." Lonnie sounded anything but fine as he righted himself and made a show of brushing off his pants. "But if I can't have the Pen . . . neither can you."

He lunged again, this time reaching for Ella's throat. Someone screamed, Ella stumbled back, but this time Derrick caught Lonnie by the wrist, yanking him away before he could hurt Ella. Billy and Aminah rushed forward to grab Lonnie's arms.

With a shuddering breath, Ella took a seat at an empty desk further away from Lonnie, the Ledger open before her.

Lonnie struggled and muttered threats in Ella's direction as her hand tipped down, about to make a period at the end of her Reality, but the unmistakable sound of spit drew her attention back up again.

A gob of mucus dripped down Lonnie's shocked face. She couldn't tell which of her classmates had done it, but as she surveyed the room, their nervous expressions started shifting to something meaner.

"Make him step in dog crap every day," one of the kids called out.

"Nah, make him wear it!" yelled another.

"Just make him hurt."

The suggestions grew louder and crueler. Ella struggled to focus in the mayhem.

The Pen had done good things, it was true, but Lonnie proved it could also do dark things. Wrongs. Things they previously thought impossible.

She felt the lettering along the Pen's barrel. *Do Not Write to Wrong.* Responsibility for the wrongs didn't belong to the Pen, but to whoever wielded it.

Lonnie shouted and lurched for her again.

Ella looked down at what she'd already written in the Ledger of Truths.

Lonnie Blunt never stole the Pen of Realities
and never will

She lowered the Pen to the page.

They'd have to find other ways to create new realities now; it might be harder to make changes . . . but it would also be harder for the Lonnies of the world to undo them. Ella bent her head to scratch in a few last words, her hand shaking just a bit as she marked the period.

because just now, the Pen of Realities
stopped
existing •

N.R. Lambert (she/her) is a speculative fiction author from New York City. Her short stories appear or are forthcoming in *Fireside Quarterly*, *Cast of Wonders*, *PseudoPod*, and *Don't Turn Out the Lights: A Tribute to Alvin Schwartz's Scary Stories to Tell in the Dark* (HarperCollins). In addition to her work as a pop culture writer and freelance copywriter, she volunteers with Read Ahead, a reading-based mentoring program for elementary school students. Find her online at nrlambert.com.

Invisible Ink

Gerri Leen

You toss so many things into the trash
I sit here, on this table, waiting
And watch as just about everything finds
Its way into the rubbish or the recycling bins
Except me
A lowly pen
Like so many other pens
I was planted here
Nothing special—if I were pretty
If I were expensive
You'd turn me in to Lost and Found
Or you'd keep me
But hidden away at home
Lest the true owner see me and know
You're a thief

So I have to be ordinary
Because I am a thief

I'm also not a pen
Well, not *solely* a pen: I can write
I have ink
You would toss me if I ran out
But as long as I can form words for you

You'll protect me
You may let me languish
But you'll never toss me into the trash
It's what they counted on when they seeded me
And so many of my kind in offices like this
All over the country, the region—the world

A vast network if we need to be
But only if we need to be

Too much interweaving creates signals that
You might pick up
So mainly I sit waiting
For someone to select this table
To lay their device or their handbag
Down next to me
To let me reach out, carefully
The "noise" of the normal data activity
Masking what I do so very well
As I sit
Next to your phone
Next to your tablet
Next to your laptop and that fancy watch
And any other thing that sends and
Receives data

Data that I can take
Because I'm not just a thief: I'm a spy

And I am an I
Let's get that clear
If you catch me, you'll default to
The easy answer: just a thing, a virus,
Just malware but I'm so much more
An AI, miniaturized to
The bare minimum
I can't walk, I can't talk
But I can gather data
And I can send it on
I have my list; I know who to target; I have
Discretion to choose when presented with multiple options

And you'll never see me coming
Because you see pens like me every single day

So you, with your lunchtime tryst
You don't want your partner to know about
You're safe unless of course your date is on my list
Here he comes now, sitting—ah, he's nervous
I can track his racing pulse as he
Plays with me, twirling me on the
Laminate of this barely clean table
If you knew what was on this tabletop
But no, you don't need to know
I'm a thief, not a biosensor
If you can't clean, that's not my problem

But here's someone who is on my list
Two tables over and within range: let me go to work

Oh, you can keep playing with me while
I gather what I need from her phone
Push me back and forth in some strange
Pen football designed to work off
"We're about to cheat on those who love us" nerves
I'm utilitarian and tough, made to be dropped
Or chewed, or even tossed out of a moving car
Not that that's likely, here in the cafeteria
I'm stuck on this bacteria-ridden table
Until someone picks me up and takes me back
To their office, then to meetings

Where there will eventually be
Someone else I'm supposed to collect on

It's inevitable really
One small pen can make the rounds of a building
Far faster than you might suspect
They ran tests before they made me
All sorts of random objects
Pens were the most likely to survive, to migrate
Although sometimes it's not to an office but home
If my GPS indicates I'm stuck in a house of
Someone inconsequential, not on my list
Rather than temporarily still in a coat pocket
Or a handbag, I'll go dormant

Until one day, someone cleans out the drawer
And finds me
And does something with me other than throwing
Me out—you would think I was a religious icon
You throw your ethics out before you do
A cheap plastic pen
I am not forever, but oh so close
I will circulate, not unlike the plastic gyres
In your oceans, for far longer than you can imagine

And I will complete my mission: stealing
Everything that matters and knowing so much more

Gerri Leen (she/her) lives in Northern Virginia and originally hails from Seattle. In addition to being an avid reader, she's passionate about horse racing, tea, ASMR vids, and creating weird one-pan meals. She has work appearing in *Nature, Galaxy's Edge, Escape Pod, Daily Science Fiction, Cast of Wonders,* and others. She's edited several anthologies for independent presses, is finishing some longer projects, and is a member of SFWA and HWA. See more at gerrileen.com.

Werepen

Avery Montavon

"How long has this been going on?"

"Three years," I mumbled into the pillow I held over my face.

"Can you take the pillow off your head so we can have a conversation?"

"No," I wanted to say. But that would never fly with Charlie. I tossed the pillow to the other side of the bed, but I still didn't get up.

"Repeat what you said."

"It's been happening for three years."

Charlie crossed her arms. "You've been cursed for three years and never thought to tell your wife about it?"

"I did think to tell you about it. I just chose not to."

"Why wouldn't you tell me?"

I sighed and crossed my arms. "Because it's a silly curse, alright? It's not cool, or dangerous, or sexy. It's not anything! I don't even know how I contracted it. It's just something that happens to me once a month, and I have to deal with it."

To my surprise, Charlie laughed. "Let me get this straight. You haven't told me, your wife, about your curse, because you think I, a witch, would think it's silly."

"Okay, when you say it like that . . . "

"You realize I once cursed someone to never win a coin toss, right? That's a silly curse. What's going on with you is no laughing matter."

I sat up. "It *is* a little bit funny though."

She sat down on the bed next to me. "Tell me everything, Wendy. From the beginning."

I sighed. "Okay. It started three years ago, on a cold night in March. I remember not being able to sleep that night. I felt so restless. I snuck out of bed and went to the den, where I could pace without waking you. That's when it happened. The transformation was so painful, but I didn't scream, because I didn't want to wake you. Then I woke up on the floor, with the sun shining in through the window. On the desk was the first ten pages of my . . . Well . . ."

"The first ten pages of your novel."

I nodded.

"That makes sense. I thought something was off about it when I read it."

"What do you mean, something was off?"

"It's not your voice! When you transform, you're not really yourself. You are, but you aren't. So when you wrote your novel, you weren't really you."

I rubbed the back of my neck. "It's just that the novel is so good! I never thought I could write something like that. And then this curse happened and . . ."

"It's not you, though."

"Trust me, I debated that for so long. But the more I transformed, the more I wrote, and the more the story came together and I . . . I gave in. I started typing up the manuscript. When it was done, I sent it to a few agents. So many of them wanted it, and you have no idea how good it felt, to be wanted. To be talented."

She said nothing, but I could still hear her opinion. *It's not you, though.* I know.

"Anyway. The book is going to market next week. It's too late now."

We sat in silence for a moment. Charlie let the silence last just long enough that the weight of my words began to weigh on me. She was always good at doing that.

"When did you figure out what you were transforming into?"

"I had suspicions. One day I set up a hand mirror on my desk. The next time I transformed, I was able to catch a glimpse of myself—"

"How could you see yourself? Pens don't have eyes."

"Oh, so now the witch is going to lecture me on the things a magical, sentient pen can or cannot do?"

She rolled her eyes. "Fine. Continue."

I shrugged. "No, that's about it. I looked into the mirror and I saw a pen, writing on the desk all by itself. I don't remember much else from that transformation. Memories from my pen form are . . . few and far between."

Charlie nodded. "Do you write outside of your pen form anymore?"

I pulled my knees up to my chest and held onto them. "No. I haven't written any of my own stuff in a couple of years."

"Do you ever think about going back to that?"

"I don't know."

Charlie nodded again and pulled me close to her. I was so lucky to have a wonderful wife like her, who was doing her best to understand the situation. How many other people would react this well to finding out their spouse was a werepen?

"So, do you want me to break the curse?"

My eyes widened, and I twisted in her arms so I could look at her face. "What? You could do that?"

"Well, yeah." She shrugged. "I mean, probably. All curses have something that can break them. I would have to do some research, but I'm sure I could figure it out."

I was silent. I didn't have to be a werepen anymore. I should be thrilled! But what would I gain by breaking the curse? I wasn't hurting anyone. Agents never cared about the stories I wanted to tell. Only Charlie ever seemed to care about my stories. Now, the stories my pen form was writing? Everyone loved those.

I was a writer. Could I exist if no one cared about my writing?

Could I really be a writer if I was just publishing someone else's work in my name?

"This is difficult for you, isn't it?" Charlie's voice broke through my train of thought.

"I don't even know why this is so hard." I nestled my head into Charlie's chest. "I want to tell my stories. I do. But . . . "

"No buts. Tell your stories, Wendy. Tell them and make the world listen. You don't need to be a sentient pen for one night a month to be good at the craft. You think I turned into a sentient wand to get good at magic?"

I chuckled. "I don't know; did you?"

"No!" She laughed and tousled my hair. "Your stories are good. You'll be fine, I promise."

"Thank you, Charlie."

She kissed my forehead. "Call in sick today. You need to start writing your next book."

Charlie stood up and began to leave the bedroom.

"Charlie . . . What if no one likes my next book?"

She smiled. "Will you like it? Because if you like it, you won't be the only one."

Then she was gone.

Avery Montavon (he/him) is a software developer by day, writer by night from Chicago, IL. In his free time, he enjoys watching sports and playing video games. Sometimes he can be spotted tweeting random nonsense as @ThatKidBanana.

Scrawls of Squid Ink

D.A. Xiaolin Spires

Ziyu laid the offering at the altar, watching the incense smoke creep upwards into the sky through the open window before taking the large pizza pie back to her best friend Jingfei. They sat down cross-legged on the tile floor, basking their hands in the steam to keep warm in Taipei's cold, humid winter.

"Didn't you say your grandma doesn't like pizza," said Jingfei. "You said that she mentioned cheese tastes like eating car tires."

"I'm sure she can take the cheese off," said Ziyu. She got up, walked back to the altar, and inhaled the aromatic incense as she closed the window and rubbed her palms together. "It's not like she won't have hands in the afterlife. Besides, once the cheese reaches her in the spirit world, we don't know how it transforms. Maybe it tastes more like tofu then."

Ziyu sat down, picked up a slice, which drooped down like a dog's tongue. Hot, cheesy oil dribbled onto the ground. She blew on her slice before taking a large bite. Dark sauce squirted into her mouth.

"It's hot!" said Jingfei.

"Too late," grumbled Ziyu, making strange noises with her mouth. She was doing the reverse blow, while attempting to chew at the same time. Steam rose up into the air from her mouth, spindly tendrils like the incense. "The roof of my mouth's all burnt up now."

"Let me see," said Jingfei.

Ziyu opened her mouth to reveal her gums full of black smear.

"I can't see much. You got stuff all over your teeth. You should be careful. I'm pretty sure I read somewhere on Pizza Lala's site that squid ink sauce takes longer to cool off than the original tomato sauce."

Jingfei went to get some jasmine tea, with her footsteps trailing out into the kitchen, while Ziyu, undeterred by the burn, took another bite. She looked back at the altar.

"I hope you didn't burn your tongue on a spirit slice of Seafood Delite, too," said Ziyu to the photo that depicted Grandma beaming. Back then Grandma had a set of pearly whites, beautifully arched eyebrows and a head of lush, black hair. Her eyes were lucid, so shiny and black, they were like a limpid lake at night, reflecting the stars. As glossy as if painted on with glaze and ink. So different than a month ago, when her hair had turned white, her teeth all but one had fallen and her lips were barely able to pull into a thin smile.

Ziyu bit through the crunchy tangles of squid tentacles and the ring-like loops of cut cross-sections of the squid's cooked body. It was chewy, just as she liked it, and a bit bitter.

Jingfei came back with two cups, placing one stainless steel cup on the floor with a clink. Ziyu sipped this offering of tea, careful to not burn her tongue.

Jingfei sat with her own cup in her hands. She held onto it, transfixed, not drinking. Her pupils moved along the perimeter of the large disc of dough that was steaming before her. Ziyu noticed the wariness in her eyes.

"There's something about the way these toppings are arranged," said Jingfei, entranced, mumbling to herself.

"Huh?" muttered Ziyu, in the middle of a bite. Ziyu stared at the pizza, at the confetti pieces of seaweed, the smattering of green jalapeño coins, the squid bits and pieces of white fish, submerged in the black and yellow sea of sauce and bubbling cheese. She shrugged. "I don't—"

"Nothing, nothing," said Jingfei, cutting her off, distracted. She blew gently on the pizza, letting the steam flow towards the cabinet opposite her that held Ziyu's grandma's antiques. It fogged up the glass.

Just as Jingfei reached to grab a slice, she gasped.

Ziyu was busy extracting a tentacle from the back of her throat, when she heard Jingfei react. She looked down, following Jingfei's gaze. The ink was moving, collecting and reforming.

"What the—" she started to say, but her voice croaked when a jalapeño made its way down her tongue, the heat of its spice causing her to erupt into coughs.

Her eyes watered and tears flowed down her face. She smudged them with a greasy finger. Ziyu was strangely silent.

When she finally peered at the object of Ziyu's held gaze, she gasped as well.

The squid ink had rearranged itself into piles differentiated into a series of *zhuyinfuhao,* the Chinese alphabet used mostly for spelling and as a pronunciation guide. It looked like a wonky keyboard, one where the *zhuyinfuhao* were not collected into typographically clean letters, but bleared and smeared splotches of the letter forms, all black blurred. It even had five strokes denoting tone at the quadrant of the pizza near Jingfei's knee, though the streaks were a bit wobbly. Even if the markings were all smudged up, it was clear to Ziyu that this was a form of communication.

"Quick," said Ziyu, swallowing the errant jalapeño. "Grab a squid circle."

Jingfei looked hesitant, but Ziyu elbowed her. “It’s spelling,” Jingfei said, as if she finally found her tongue.

They grabbed the rubbery looped band. Ziyu looked back at her Grandma.

Is this your doing? her eyes asked. No response.

“I’ve seen this on TV. In that American movie . . . I can’t think of the name now,” said Jingfei, her voice quavering.

Jingfei’s fingers felt soft and delicate as they brushed against Ziyu’s digits slick with oil. The squid circle budged. They started.

Ziyu breathed out a breath of cheese and fish. She could smell it as she finally remembered to inhale again.

“It’s happening!”

Jingfei nodded, her eyes wide.

The squid circle slid across the pizza, leaving cobweb strings of melted cheese in its wake. Amazingly, the ink that it glided over did not smudge, but stayed the same blurriness in its lettering.

First, the squid circle settled on ㄨ (“w”) and ㄛ (“o”) and shifted towards the third tone ˇ, a V-shaped black blemish, like a bird flying in the sky. It moved to ㄅ (“b”), ㄧ (“i”) and ㄥ (“ng”) and to the tone mark ˋ that whipped downwards. It cut through a flurry of fish pieces and picked up some seaweed confetti as it headed towards ㄅ (“b“) and ㄨ (“u”), using the same tone mark ˋ as a follow-up.

Ziyu used her free hand to dip her fingers in the jasmine tea. Luckily, it wasn’t too hot. She scribbled the formed letters onto the inside flap of the pizza box, creating dark stains of the words that bled into the cardboard fibers.

The room darkened as a downpour began outside, creating a clatter of raindrops against the windows. The panes banged, stopped, then banged again.

When the squid stopped moving in her fingers, Ziyu looked up at Jingfei who shuddered. They both turned to the box, soaked with streaks of jasmine-scented stains:

ㄨㄛˇ ㄅㄧㄥˋ ㄅㄨˋ ㄒㄧˇ ㄏㄨㄢ ㄑㄧˇ ㄙ

They said aloud, "我並不喜歡起司 (Wǒ bìng bù xǐhuān qǐsī)," an incantation that allowed the phonetics to cohere into meaningful words.

Jingfei jumped up. "*I don't like cheese,*" she whispered pointedly. "It's exactly what you said about your grandma."

Ziyu stretched, sticking her finger in her mouth to lick the oil off.

"Ew, don't do that. You don't know what that stuff—" Jingfei said, gesturing towards the smudges of squid ink, "—will do to your body."

"I already ate a whole slice," said Ziyu, but just as she said that aloud, her stomach churned.

The rain was falling in sheets now and a thunderclap filled the air. The room turned bright white, then pitch black as the power went out.

Ziyu could hear Jingfei whimper.

"Hey, it's okay," Ziyu said, as she took her hand, but Jingfei pulled away. Ziyu forgot her fingers still all had traces of the pizza. But, at this point, so did Jingfei's.

Another thunderclap simultaneous to the brilliant light flooding the room caused them to flinch. The storm was very near.

Jingfei seemed to change her mind and reached her hand over to clasp Ziyu's.

Perhaps the cheese was projecting its own greenish light or

perhaps Ziyu was simply imagining it, but now she could see the glossy, smeared letters of the pizza against an incandescent verdant glow of the cheesy canvas.

Jingfei said, "Noooo," drawing out her disbelief. Ziyu shook her head. She wasn't imagining it.

The cheese illuminated upwards, creating a funnel of light that hovered above the pizza. The black smudges broke off the flat X-Y axis of the pizza and infiltrated the Z, the inscriptions lifting up like corpses that gained mobility, like stickers unpeeling themselves from their bound parchment. They combined and swirled in the air, forming a tornado of stretched-out ink before settling into a phrase, releasing itself from that formation and resettling into another phrase.

妳對奶奶這麼不尊敬啊。
妳並知道我不能吃乳製品有乳糖不耐症。

Nǐ duì nǎinai zhème bù zūnjìng a. Nǐ bìng zhīdào wǒ bùnéng chī rǔzhìpǐn, yǒu rǔtáng bùnàizhèng.

"Sorry, Grandma," whispered Ziyu, after she read the shaky letters that scrawled in the air, "How dare you disrespect your grandma like this! You know I can't eat dairy, that I'm lactose intolerant."

Jingfei seemed to lose her sense of fear and nearly giggled. Ziyu shot her a glance.

The storm cackled as if in response to the lack of obeisance.

Grandma lamented on, about her days of suffering in war and famine, and of all the strife she had been through. The least they could do was respect her while she was dead. Words splayed across the air, merging and coming apart.

It was Ziyu's turn to be transfixed. She nodded, a wave of shame filling her that she had cared more about her own dietary wishes than for her grandma's spiritual wellbeing.

Ziyu noted a rustling from where Jingfei was. Jingfei unlaced her fingers and was now moving towards her laptop at the tea table near the sofa. She was typing something. The screen glowed eerie and fluorescent against the green-tinted light coming from the pizza. Ziyu felt a wave of upset and dismay at Jingfei. First the laughter and now she was checking her email!

Grandma, assuming this spirit writing in squid ink was Grandma, wrote about Grandpa and his woes. She wrote about Grandpa's difficult time in the army being one of the smallest men and how he had to fight for respect. She talked about the son they had lost before Ziyu's dad was born and the harrowing escapes they made across the seas to give her and future generations a better tomorrow.

All Ziyu could do was bow and keep silent. The black ink shone and tiraded, becoming even more splotchy. The thunder rumbled in tune with the flow of words. Some of the specks hit Ziyu's face like dark, angry spittle.

After a while, a doorbell sounded and the pizza went dark. Ziyu watched as Jingfei used the light of the laptop to guide her feet towards the door.

Jingfei pulled the door open, the hallway light flooding the room.

"Your pizza," said a spiky-haired girl in a collared delivery uniform. Her nose ring and five cartilage rings that fitted into the lobe of her ear seemed to beg to get out of that rigid, collared outfit.

Ziyu, from her spot in the living room, reached into her pockets, not really understanding. *But, we already got our pizza,* she thought.

But Jingfei beat her to the punch and forked over some crumpled bills.

Once the faint jangling of the door chime above the main door outside announced the delivery girl's departure, the squid ink on the ground rustled again.

"Nu uh, granny," said Jingfei, throwing a few tofu cubes in that direction. They seemed to sink into the cheese like animals caught in a swamp. A clamor of squishy noises came from the pizza and then a burp.

"I did some research," said Jingfei, picking off a few more mushrooms and throwing it over to the other pizza.

"That one's a knock-off. Using the same brand name but the website's all messed up. You can tell with all the spelling errors and plug-ins that don't work. The url also gave it away. Pizza Rara? C'mon. Then I found that it was run by an occultist."

The light emanating from the Seafood Delite knock-off dimmed.

"I don't think it's your grandma. Just someone who hacked into your account and read your grandma's obituary. Programmed the thing to run with this abominable fabulation. There is some phantasmic stuff going on with the whole rendering of words and the light and all that, but it's not your grandma. I exchanged a few rough words once I was able to hack into their site and reach the site owner through chat."

Ziyu listened politely, as Jingfei picked off more toppings from the new pizza to feed the animate one. The animate Seafood Delite devoured them up, aggressive and croaking for more.

Ziyu pointed at the creature. "But, it's right, Grandma or not. I've been thinking a lot about myself, about my part-time job and my break-up, and not really of Grandma's life."

She walked over to the picture frame at the altar, considering Grandma's tender countenance. She put her hands together and head down. She wished Grandma would forgive her for being so selfish.

As Ziyu opened her eyelids, the lights had turned back on and the storm abated. The influx of artificial illumination hurt her eyes. She blinked as she walked over to the sofa, where Jingfei lay sprawled out, alternating taking bites of topping and feeding the knock-off that was still on the ground.

"I'll take this to the temple tomorrow. I think one of the shamans will know what to do with this," said Jingfei.

Ziyu grabbed a mushroom from the new steaming pizza, popping it into her mouth. The juice coated her lips, filled her tongue with a fragrant earthiness.

"No, leave it here. It'll remind me of my Grandma."

"You sure? It's not a problem. You've helped me out before, Ziyu."

"It's my duty. I'm doing this for me. Maybe one day when I'm ready, I'll take it over to the shamans myself. But, right now, I can't stand to leave it there. Besides, it's a good reminder. For all the times Grandma sacrificed and put her life in danger, for her future generations. It'll remind me how to be good like her."

"Suit yourself," said Jingfei, but she sounded unsure. The ravenous gulping of the thing didn't help.

Jingfei pushed a few onions aside and grabbed a submerged pepperoni. She looked as if she'd throw it at Seafood Delite, but she must have changed her mind, popping it into her own mouth instead.

They sat around quiet as the sound of the knock-off pizza devoured pieces of dough, a cannibalistic beast in Ziyu's living room. They picked at the new pizza, sometimes grabbing a few mushrooms, sometimes the peppers with charred edges and sometimes taking bites of the dough with generous helpings of tomato sauce. The pizza was hot and tasty, and the cheese was particularly flavorful with its melty stringiness.

Jingfei intertwined her fingers around Ziyu's, as they used the free hand to feed themselves and Ziyu's newly acquired pet.

"Thanks for being here for me," said Ziyu, shifting in the sofa, nestling her back against the pillow propped up against Jingfei. "It's been a tough week."

Jingfei's fingers squeezed back as a reply, slipping with pizza grease.

D.A. Xiaolin Spires steps into portals and reappears in sites such as Hawai'i, NY, various parts of Asia and elsewhere, with her keyboard appendage attached. Her work appears or is forthcoming in publications such as *Clarkesworld Magazine, Analog Science Fiction and Fact, Strange Horizons, Nature Futures, Vice Terraform, Uncanny Magazine, Fireside Magazine, Andromeda Spaceways Magazine (Year's Best Issue), Diabolical Plots, Factor Four Magazine, Lady Churchill's Rosebud Wristlet, Toasted Cake, Pantheon Magazine, LONTAR, Mithila Review, Reckoning, Issues in Earth Science, Liminality, Star*Line, Polu Texni, Eye to the Telescope, Liquid Imagination, Little Blue Marble, Story Seed Vault,* and anthologies of the strange and beautiful: *Deep Signal, Ride the Star Wind, Sharp and Sugar Tooth, Broad Knowledge, Future Visions,* and *Battling in All Her Finery*. Select stories can be read in German, Vietnamese, Spanish, Estonian, and French translation. She can be found on Twitter: @spireswriter and on her website: daxiaolinspires.wordpress.com.

Memories of a Rose Garden

Beth Goder

"I'm going to write a rose garden," I told Matthew, so I found hills as blank as paper and wrote each individual petal, a softness of grey and yellow and green. I specified thorns curled outward, the rough feel of the stone paths, the beetles who would brush their wings against us feather soft.

The words unglued from the paper, wiggling up industriously one letter at a time, and as they became part of the world, settling down into the earth and finding their shape there, Matthew reached out to touch the pen held lightly between my fingers.

—

It has been so long since I wrote the rose garden. I look back on myself at sixteen, through those layers of years, and it is like peering through muddy water. How can I remember how I truly was?

I learned, at that age, that writing has power, so I am writing down my story to see if I can catch the truth of it.

—

A rose garden can be a wild place if you write it the right way. I wrote brambles, disorder, paths that twisted nowhere and everywhere, the sharp beaks of birds.

The evening roses cradled us. Matthew asked me to write little things into the world—clouds in the shape of frowning mouths, yellow buttons, packets of mint tea, which we boiled in the patch of sunlight written bright by the pond choked with algae, sunlight which glowed even in the dark, even in winter.

Once, he asked me to write his name into the bark of trees, into the grass, into the sky, but I wouldn't. I didn't want to write him into the world more than he already was. It was a wrongness he asked of me, but I didn't have the courage to tell him so.

—

I'd found the pen at the back of Persimmon Books, the used bookstore down Fifth Street where I worked when I was in high school. I was reshelving a textbook on plant biology when the pen fell off the shelf, the cap a little sharper, maybe, than a regular pen, and the blue plastic shiny and scarred, but looking normal aside from that.

When I tried to write a poem about dandelions, white fluff materialized in my hands.

I made up rules for how I would use the pen. The pen had come to me without my asking, at a time when I needed it, and so it seemed like I should use it to put gifts into the world. I wrote daisies into the cracks of concrete. I wrote rain and yellow leaves, and a certain softness that comes when the sun is rising over the mountains and the sky stretches out. I liked to write beetles with iridescent wings, watching them turn from words into something real.

I think what I wanted more than anything was to write a place for myself in the world, a place where I could fit, but I didn't know how to do it, so instead I wrote puddles and snails and once a rose garden that was mine.

—

"Let me try it," said Matthew. We were sitting in the rose garden on chairs woven from dead leaves. His face was never more beautiful than when he wanted something, filled with an intensity that could have shadowed the sun.

"It's mine," I said, the anger in my voice startling me. But the pen wasn't mine. It wasn't anyone's.

Beetles brushed past his face. He swatted at them, nearly hitting one with the back of his hand. He had been so angry when I wouldn't write the beetles out of the garden, as if it was so easy to take something out of the world once it was in. "I would write something no one would ever forget. I would write myself immortality."

"The pen isn't for that." I clutched the pen close to my body, under the sleeve of my ratty red sweater.

When I was sixteen, I loved him. That can be hard to remember. My memories of him are like obsidian lodged under the layers of my past, jagged pieces that won't dissolve. The good memories are the hardest. There was the tender way he blew on my soup when we ate at Chrysanthemums (I couldn't stand hot soup), or the graceful arch of his eyebrows, which was most apparent when he was reading, or the time he placed his hand over my eyes, light as beetle wings, when we hiked up the mountain path and came to a bluff, and I was suddenly, intensely afraid of heights. He didn't mind the things about me other people minded—my aloofness, my old clothes, my tendency to forget that I had said something and say it again.

I didn't know then that it was possible to love someone, and for them to love you, and to still be capable of causing so much harm to each other.

—

I knew something was wrong when no beetles came to greet me at the entrance to the rose garden. I searched for them under petals and in the sky. No soft wings beat in the air.

—

When I was sixteen, I used the pen to put gifts into the world.

In my twenties, I would have used it to try to change the world; sweeping changes, impassioned and rash and thoughtless.

In my thirties, I would have destroyed the pen, for power is a dangerous thing.

In my forties, I would have thought very hard about how to put goodness into the world, and done it. I would have examined the consequences, rejoicing at good outcomes, finding my way through my guilt at bad ones.

Now that I am in my fifties, if I found such a pen again, I think I would use it to put gifts into the world.

—

I found Matthew pacing by the dead leaf chairs. His face held righteousness and shame. When I think back on this memory, I am struck by how young he looked.

"Why couldn't you let me have a place of my own?" I said, my voice loud and hard. "Because you didn't make it? Because it was mine and not yours?"

He lunged for the pen, and in my astonishment I let it slip from my fingers.

He had no paper, so he wrote against his skin, and the words sprang up. He gave himself invincibility, immortality, wealth. The words were too heavy to come into the world. They sank against him, drilling down into his arms.

"Stop," I said. "You can't exist this way."

The words strangled in his throat, coasting over his body. He had asked for too much. He had asked for things that could not be.

I grabbed the pen and coaxed the words back in, one letter at a time. As I pulled the ink from him, he crumpled forward, his breathing harsh, his eyes fluttering closed.

With the unwritten words reabsorbed, I felt the power contained within the pen. I could have written him immortal. I could have written it for myself.

"Where are the beetles?" I said.

"I trapped them by the pond."

I found the beetles in cages made from brittle sticks and thorns.

Freedom, I wrote, striking the pen against the air. It was a hard word to make come alive, for what sort of shape should such a word have in the world? But I wrote it, and the cages dissolved.

In their new life, they were not my soft beetles anymore, but something changed. Wildness came to them, and joy. They pelted Matthew, who cowered behind his hands, and then they flew away.

Ink ran out of the pen in rivers. Ink drenched the garden, filling the gaps in the stone pathways.

Matthew sank with his arms full of new skin, impressions of beetle wings indented in his face. The ink ran around him but would not touch him.

The pen dissolved in my hands. A little bit of ink splashed into my mouth. It tasted like honey and lavender, and the scent of Persimmon Books.

With the beetles gone, I knew the garden wasn't mine anymore.

—

I saw Matthew again when I was in my thirties. He wore grey slacks and an expression like his father's, calm and tired.

"It's been so long," he said. He tried to greet me with a hug, but I shook his hand.

We talked of nothing. I never asked him about the garden. I almost wonder if he would remember. I think with experiences like that, you either remember them intensely or not at all. I gave him a recipe for peach cobbler, and we said we'd go for coffee, but of course we both knew we never would.

—

I hope someone has found the garden, with the dead leaf chairs and the algae pond, with the roses in strange colors that are nothing like the sunset, with the ink-stained stones. I imagine a girl finding her way there and breathing in the scent of leaf mold and petals, knowing she is home.

I think sometimes about the bit of ink I swallowed, and wonder if, like the beetles, I am changed from it.

When I had the pen, I only wrote what I thought should be true in the world. I think that's what allowed my words to pull themselves up from the page and make themselves real.

The words I am writing now stay on the page, and I myself must go out into the world. It is hard, sometimes, to do it, but I remember that the way I shape my own story has power. I remember that I can write myself into the world, one word at a time, the way I once wrote a rose garden, and this gives me a sense of belonging that I never had at sixteen. Sometimes, I catch the truth of things, and watch as my words make their way into the world, taking shape, settling in the places they were meant to be.

Beth Goder (she/her) works as an archivist, processing the papers of economists, scientists, and other interesting folks. In the past, Beth has played percussion in a community band and been a member of a Renaissance Faire dance troupe, but now she spends most of her free time writing. Her fiction has appeared in venues such as *Escape Pod, Fireside Magazine,* and *Flash Fiction Online*. You can find her online at bethgoder.com.

Today, I am a Fountain Pen

Lawrence Miller

Author's Note: Today, Jewish young people (and adults) of all genders can celebrate becoming B'nai Mitzvot, or Children of the Commandments. For most of Jewish history, this rite of passage was sadly reserved for boys and was a simple affair, at which the father of a boy would declare that his son was now legally responsible for his actions, and the boy would "become a man" in the eyes of society (and the law). A few hundred years ago, regional traditions of celebration around this ceremony sprang up, including in Poland, where this story is set. The giving of gifts increased in popularity, and in the late 19th and early 20th centuries, fountain pens were especially popular gifts. A more modern tradition arose for the boy becoming Bar Mitzvah to deliver a speech as part of the ceremony. These speeches so frequently included variations of "yesterday I was a boy; today I am a man" that they became known as "Today I am a Man" speeches. These two factors were humorously combined in a joke told by Jewish comedians about a boy who is so excited to receive gifts at his Bar Mitzvah, that when he steps up to deliver his "Today I am a Man" speech, he says "Today I am a Fountain Pen" instead. With fountain pens no longer as popular gifts, the joke is now dated, but remembered with fondness by the older generations. The title comes from that tradition. I grew up reading and hearing Jewish folktakes, and this is written in that style. The main character's name, "Rivka Pippik" more or less means "Rebecca Belly-Button" in Yiddish. I received a fountain pen as a Bar Mitzvah gift myself, and now as an adult, I carry a fondness for them, which through Rivka's stories, it is my pleasure to share with you.

1.

Once there was, or there wasn't, a girl named Rivka Pippik, who lived in Chelevka, a shtetl about two hours' walk from Lodz. Every morning, as Rivka's older brother went to study Torah with the old men, and Rivka's older sister went to mend clothes with the old ladies, Rivka followed her Zayde Shmuel to his workshop. Together they would turn wood into bowls and vases, bangles and boxes, stools and spoons, and of course, goblets. But her favorite things to make were fountain pens.

When Rivka Pippik was 12 years old, and she was tall enough to reach the treadles on the lathe and strong enough to use them, Rivka's Zayde Shmuel asked Rivka why she liked making pens so much. "I suppose it's because the smallest scrap of wood can be drilled and turned, and find a new life," she said. When Rivka first started coming to her Zayde's shop, her uncle Hershel was still making the pen nibs by hand, and the barrels of the pens were one solid piece. But now there was a factory in far-off England. Rivka's Zayde Shmuel had ordered some fittings of brass, and a shipment had arrived, and they now had hundreds of fine nibs and tiny, delicate feeds just waiting to be used.

Rivka decided to turn a pen for her friend Anzelm as a gift for his upcoming Bar Mitzvah. As she worked, Rivka's thoughts meandered back to her first days in her Zayde's workshop: seeing his chisels and gouges, his wood blanks, waxes, and oils, and of course his lathe—sitting on her Zayde's lap, a chisel in her hands and her hands in her Zayde's hands. She smiled to herself as she guided the gouge along the turning wood, humming a tune she remembered her Zayde humming to her. Rivka's Zayde offered to drill and work the oil into the barrel and cap, and Rivka accepted, and they assembled the finished pen together, Shmuel fitting it into a fine laquered box when it was complete.

When Rivka's Zayde Shmuel passed away a week before Anzelm's Bar Mitzvah, Rivka considered keeping the pen for herself, as it was the last project they had worked on together, but

Rivka decided that her Zayde would have wanted it to go to its intended recipient. Rivka understood then that this pen represented not only the end of her collaboration with her Zayde, but also the start of her career as the sole woodworker of the Pippik family.

Rivka watched Anzelm's face, a study of focus as he read from the Torah, his eyebrows furrowed as he guided the yad across the parchment and occasionally stuttered his way through, and Rivka felt pride in her friend Anzelm and in her work on the pen, and in her Zayde Shmuel, and it was with true pleasure that Rivka handed Anzelm the laquered box that Saturday afternoon.

This pen would be the finest Anzelm would own in his lifetime, and he treasured it always. Anzelm found himself drawn to writing with it in times of joy and in times of sorrow, and especially at times of transition. When Anzelm used the pen he felt confident and bold, and became known by his family and friends as a man who embraced new beginnings in all their forms.

2.

When Rivka Pippik was 19 years old, and she had arranged a favorable marriage for herself to Zocha Krawiec, the 21-year-old son of a successful tailor from Lodz, her father Chaim asked her what she intended to do once she became a wife. "I suppose I'll make more buttons, so Zocha can use them in his father's shop," she said. Rivka's father shrugged, smiled, and asked no more questions after that.

As the 26th wedding anniversary of Zocha's parents Esther and Oskar fell about a month before the wedding, Rivka decided to make fountain pens for Zocha's parents as gifts. Rivka visited the most expensive furniture maker in Lodz and bought from him two blanks of dark Wenge, a wood so hard Rivka had to sharpen her gouge three times while turning the two pens. As she worked, Rivka imagined the life she was building with Zocha Krawiec, how happy they would be, what an attentive father Zocha would be to their children. For Zocha's father, Rivka turned a bold curve, and oiled the wood so it turned nearly black, the striking grain shining through, as though revealing all the vibrant shades of black previously unseen by human eyes. For Zocha's mother, Rivka turned a more delicate curve, ornamented the body with scrollwork, and oiled the pen to the same dark shade as its partner.

Oskar and Esther treasured their pens for the rest of their lives. Zocha observed (but never told Rivka) that while his mother had disapproved of Rivka previously, now she was optimistic about the life Zocha and Rivka could build together. Esther and Oskar found themselves drawn to these pens whenever life was bringing them exciting news; they used the pens to sign Zocha and Rivka's ketubah (Zocha's mother Esther and Rivka's mother Hanna were the first two women to ever sign a ketubah in Chelevka). For the rest of her life, Zocha's mother insisted on being treated as a partner in the tailor shop, and for the rest of his life, Zocha's father agreed.

3.

When Rivka Pippik was 24 years old, and expecting her first child, her mother-in-law Esther asked her what she would do when the baby was born. "I suppose I will turn fewer bowls, since they take so long and babies need to eat so frequently," she said. Rivka's husband Zocha smiled and stroked Rivka's cheek with the backs of his fingers, tenderly. Rivka's father-in-law Oskar told Rivka that his banker, Szymon Abramczyk, had noticed Oskar's pen, the pen Rivka made for him on the occasion of his 26th anniversary, and had asked Oskar where he had purchased it. Oskar had proudly explained that it had been made by his daughter-in-law. Would it be possible, Oskar inquired, for Rivka to turn a pen for Mr. Abramczyk as a favor to Oskar? Rivka of course agreed, and Oskar smiled, all the way to his eyes, first at Rivka and then at his son Zocha. What a wonderful match we made five years ago, Oskar thought.

Rivka Pippik hired a cart to take her to the sawmill in Brzeziny, where she examined a number of slabs before selecting one of cherry burl. Upon her return to her workshop, Rivka began scoring lines on the slab, dividing it into blanks, some the size for knife handles, the others the size for pens. After she had cut the first three blanks, Rivka felt the pangs of labor, and asked her uncle Hershel to call for Zocha. Rivka knew that Zocha and the baby were still hours away; she breathed first deeply, then quickly, through the next contraction, then finished cutting the blanks. As she cut, Rivka daydreamed about someday turning the business over to her own child. An hour later, when the contractions were too close together for Rivka to do much work, she returned home. An hour after that, Rivka's mother Hanna arrived with the midwife. An hour after that, Rivka's uncle Hershel arrived with her husband Zocha. An hour after that, the baby arrived. Rivka looked at the baby, and the baby looked back. Rivka thought the baby was the most beautiful thing she'd ever seen. "I shall call you Shayna," said Rivka Pippik to her daughter.

When Shayna was two days old, Rivka Pippik returned to the workshop, still saturated with the joy and love she felt for

Shaynelah. Rivka finished the pen for Szymon Abramczyk that morning, and gave it to her father-in-law Oskar when he visited that evening. Oskar invited Szymon Abramczyk to Shayna's Simchat Bat (Shayna was the first little girl to ever have a baby naming ceremony in Chelevka), and delivered the pen to him there.

No one would have accused Szymon Abramczyk of cruelty or coldness, but after receiving the gift of the pen turned by Rivka Pippik, he found his heart more open to love of all kinds, sometimes of a kind he'd previously not thought possible. Szymon Abramczyk became more generous in his work at the bank and in his private life, and his fortunes increased as he did so. He found himself reaching for this pen to sign loan contracts, and all of those debtors became successful and repaid their loans in full and on time. His reputation with the bank increased, and Szymon Abramczyk later moved to Vilnius to head the bank's prestigious branch in that storied city. In Vilnius he met and fell in love with a poet named Piotr Wielepolski, and while they could not marry, they became inseparable. Szymon survived the January Uprising with his spirit of generosity intact, taking no position in the fighting and helping to pay for the care of injured conscripts and insurrectionists alike. Szymon Abramczyk died peacefully, with Piotr at his side, at the age of 84.

4.

When Rivka Pippik was 39 years old, and someone had set fire to the Chelevka synagogue and all that remained of the torah was a bundle of scorched parchment and one half of one of the rollers, Rabbi Altschuler asked her if she would be willing to make new rollers for a new torah, as her Zayde Schmuel had once made for the now-ruined torah. "I suppose I cannot do less than my Zayde did. I will turn new *atzei chaim*. Please leave me what remains of the one turned by Schmuel."

And so when Rabbi Altschuler and the congregation of the Chelevka synagogue buried the charred bundle of parchment in a genizah, they did so without the remaining pieces of the oaken roller; two disks and an ornate handle. By the time the new synagogue was dedicated, its ark contained a new torah scroll with *atzei chaim* constructed by Rivka Pippik. After the first shabbat service in the new synagogue, Rivka Pippik approached Rabbi Altschuler and presented him with a pen of fine oak. A slash of burned wood scarred the cap of the pen; Rivka had filled the scar with shellac and finished the pen with beeswax. Holding the pen one could hardly feel the difference, and the weight and balance were perfect. Could this pen be, asked an astonished Rabbi Altschuler, what remains of the original torah handle? Such a gift! Rivka patiently explained that the work of turning the wood had already been done years before by her Zayde Schmuel. Hardly a gift at all. Rabbi Altschuler smiled and patted Rivka Pippik's face. Such a mensch, he thought, from a family of mensches.

Rabbi Altschuler kept the pen Rivka Pippik made from the burnt torah handle at his desk in the new synagogue in a place of honor. When he retired and young Aaron Chelewski became the new rabbi of the Chelevka synagogue, Rabbi Altschuler gifted the pen to him and explained its origins. Rabbi Chelewski kept the pen on his desk until many years later, when he died while composing a sermon. The pen was discovered on his desk, though not in his hand, and he was buried with the pen in his breast pocket. Neither Rabbi Altschuler nor Rabbi Chelewski ever used the pen, however; holding it made them feel haunted. But neither could either man bring himself to be free of it. Some ghosts must be, if not welcomed, at least borne.

5.

When Rivka Pippik was 61 years old, and her daughter Shayna's daughter Adinah was old enough to become Bat Mitzvah but Rabbi Chelewski would not allow girls to become Bat Mitzvah, Rivka visited Rabbi Chelewski and asked him to reconsider. "I suppose I can do no less for the great-granddaughter of Schmuel Pippik, the granddaughter of Rivka Pippik, and the daughter of Shayna Pippik," Rabbi Chelewski answered, glancing at the pen she'd made of the burnt etz chaim still displayed on the desk. If Rivka noticed the glance, or indeed the pen, she made no sign. Rivka thanked Rabbi Chelewski and left.

At her workshop, Rivka Pippik found one last cherry burl blank remaining from the slab she had bought just before Shayna was born. She got immediately to work, using her gouge to reduce the blank to the size of a pen, shaping a bold curve, adding scrollwork, brushing on and wiping off a light coat of stain to accentuate the detail, and finishing with wax before drilling and assembling the pen using one of her Zayde's last English-made nibs and feeds.

Rivka Pippik's granddaughter Adinah read from the torah, standing on a bimah that had survived the fire of the old synagogue (Adinah was the first woman ever to read from the torah in Chelevka), and the entire village agreed she was the most confident B'nai Mitzvah of her generation or the one before. Adinah received five fountain pens that day, including two others that had been purchased from her grandparents' shop, but she treasured the cherry pen given to her by her Bubbe Rivka most of all. All five of the pens wrote beautifully, but only the pen of cherry burl filled her heart with joy when she wrote with it. Later when she was married and her husband Mikhail went off to fight in the Great War, Adinah composed all of her letters to him using the cherry pen. Reading the letters always brought him joy, and after the war, writing with the pen always reminded Adinah of Mikhail's safe return from the front. Adinah used the pen when teaching her own daughter Malka her Hebrew letters. When Malka decided to dedicate her life to the study of torah, Adinah made her a gift of the pen. "May you use it in good health," said Adinah to Malka. After they fled to America to avoid the occupation, Malka became a Rabbi and moved with her husband and children to Ohio (Malka was the first woman from Chelevka to enter Rabbinical school). She kept her mother's fountain pen with her on her desk for the rest of her life, and used it to compose her most joyous sermons.

6.

When Rivka Pippik was 83 years old, and her knees hurt and her eyes were rheumy, Shayna told her Adinah and Mikhail were taking Malka to America, and that Shayna was going with them, and asked if she would please come with them. "I suppose," Rivka answered.

Together with her daughter, her granddaughter, and her great-granddaughter, Rivka Pippik visited her husband Zocha's grave one final time. Rivka placed a pebble on top of the gravestone. "Zie gezunt, my love," Rivka said, and Shayna smiled, a tear in her eye. Rivka Pippik asked if she could make one final stop, and of course Adinah agreed. They walked slowly (Rivka Pippik now did everything slowly) to the workshop where Rivka had spent almost every day since she was a little girl, when it had been Rivka's Zayde Shmuel's workshop. Rivka slowly gathered her chisels and gouges, her wood blanks, waxes, and oils, and placed them carefully next to her lathe. She found a matchbox containing a few old nibs and feeds, and she set to work.

As she worked Rivka's mind wandered, with pride, through memories of raising her family in Chelevka. Of Shayna, from age 7, helping her father Zocha with simple sums in the shop. Of Shayna, from age 9, learning from her cousin Moshe, each night, everything he'd learned at yeshiva that day. Of her husband Zocha asking their daughter Shayna, age 25 and with her own husband and little baby girl, to take over keeping the books in the shop. Of Shayna, age 29, agreeing to teach Hebrew letters to the little boys of Chelevka when Rabbi Altschuler retired, if (and only if) she could also teach the little girls of Chelevka. Of Adinah, age 10, studying torah alongside the boys of Chelevka. Of taking over the shop when Zocha died. She thumbed the notches she'd carved in the leg of her workbench every year on Shayna's birthday to show how tall she had grown, until she was taller than the workbench, and the notches she'd carved in another leg of her workbench on Adinah's birthday, and the notches she'd carved in a third leg, rising only partway up the leg, on Malka's birthdays.

Rivka Pippik paid little mind to choosing the wood; the first blank on which her hand rested was the one she chose. She asked her granddaughter Adinah to work the treadles, and she turned a simple, functional body and cap. Rivka applied a wax that would protect the wood but not add much in the way of beauty, and assembled the pen. "Now we can go."

"Bubbe," asked Rivka's granddaughter Adinah as they walked to the old delivery truck Shayna had borrowed, "who did you make that pen for?"

"For myself," answered Rivka Pippik. "Today, I am a fountain pen." Rivka did not look back as they drove away.

Lawrence Miller (he/him) grew up in Tampa, spending most of his formative years attending Trek, Comic, and Anime conventions, and playing D&D in the living room as there are no basements in Tampa. He currently lives in Pennsylvania with his spouse, two children, and a dog, and spends his weekdays writing software to help physicians become better physicians. His hobbies include folk dancing, knitting, and when time allows, snow skiing and small-boat sailing. Lawrence has personally said hello (and received a response) to Terry Gross on 5 separate occasions. He can be found on Twitter at @ldpm.

A Pencil Golden and Rich

Rai Rocca

Maria looked at her husband, saw his shame, and cried, "Why don't you breathe a little?"

"I'm fine," he said.

"Drink some water."

"I don't want to."

"Alright, what are you missing?"

Carlos Jiménez recalled two thousand dollars. He recalled the house he painted and fixed and polished. The house was not for him but rather for a man he knew as John. The man had greeted Carlos with a smile and had gone on to point at all the things that needed fixing. Three weeks had passed, Carlos had perfected the house, and John refused to pay for the work.

"How could he take advantage of us? It's winter. Doesn't he know winter is the worst time for workers like me?"

For the first time in Maryland, Carlos started to cry. Maria held him, and the tears made them feel young as though they were in Peru again. Carlos did not think that injustice like this would follow them to this country.

"Baby, he threatened me. He told me he would call the police if I kept asking for my money. He'd call ICE!"

Carlos would not have cried if he had known that his seventeen-year-old daughter was not sleeping but rather listening to every detail from her room. His daughter, Isabella, began to shake. Her father's crying transformed her and silently, she began to cry as well.

Her room was light blue—her father had painted it. He was everything on her mind when she began to have a vision. There in that vision, she saw her father conjuring up John's empty house with paint and carpet and light bulbs—the most beautiful blue light. Carlos, floating tall and happy, then invited her in saying, "Come, hija! Come see the house I made," so she walked in to see the beauty made by her father's hands. She looked at his hands and in them were a yellow pen and a black notebook. "Oh, this? This is where I add up the cost of all the work and material to give the man the total price. Here, it's yours."

Isabella, now in her room, stopped weeping and looked at her hands. In them were the pen and notebook. Amazed, she took them to her desk and opened the binding. Contrary to what her father had said, the pages were empty. She took the pen, went to the first page, and wrote, "Two Thousand Dollars".

The pen glowed. Smiling, she continued writing, "The man owes my father, Carlos Jiménez, two thousand dollars."

She looked at the pen and it started growing in size, started changing shape and color until it was unquestionably golden and rich. The weight was golden, and as she continued to write, she began to realize she could write truth to power and power to reality. The pen became timeless, and she wrote as time snapped around her.

She began to see her ancestors' complete lives and realized the images were not imaginations but rather right in front of her. They began to ask her to see them for who they were, the people that again and once again slid, stumbled, wept, and slayed their way into the new world. The Incas, the Catholic kings and queens, the Chinese—the characters were her and she was the character. Isabella, still in her room, was someplace else now. Questioning the origin of the pen, she started to fear the newness of everything. Isabella tried to dismantle the device.

Instead, the pen stuck to her hand and transported her to shopping centers all across Latin America. Centers in Buenos Aires, Quito, Lima, Cochabamba—they were beautiful and the people there spoke her root languages. Holding her pen, Isabella cried again, "Is this really mine? Are you with me, amigo?" The pen replied, "These are your peoples, this is your ground! Look around you. Please, take it all in before I have to go."

She moved through those Latin American cities and saw the houses. She saw the houses and knew this was a place constructed by people like her father. She waved at the construction workers. One of them looked, smiled, and whispered, "recém-chegada". She did not know Portuguese but knew the man had said, "newly arrived".

"Come with me," the pen said. She looked up and was suddenly a baby again. She saw her mother and father, now in their twenties, happy in Peru. It took seconds to realize she was at a birthday party. Her own party—the cake stated she was turning two. She looked around to see her aunts and uncles and grandparents, and she realized the only word coming out of their mouths was "Love". Love in different tones, but it was all love. Isabella looked to her right and saw the pen, now small enough for her baby hands. In that moment, Isabella was the happiest baby. "One last stop," the pen whispered.

The pen transformed her back into a seventeen-year-old and she stood there in the middle of one more Latin American market. She looked up and in the middle of the mall was the man, John.

The man looked at the girl and laughed. "No matter what you do, your father will always suffer. He will never have documents. He will never breathe again until he is dead."

Isabella listened but did not cry. There in Buenos Aires, there in Quito, and there in her room, Isabella looked away from the ugly man and started writing a letter. She did not stop writing until every detail came pouring from her memory. As she finished, the golden pen melted into a regular, yellow pencil. She was in her room again, and she wished she could have taken pictures of all she had seen across America in those fifteen minutes. She wished she could magically create documents for her father, magically make their small house as big as the houses he worked, but for now she breathed.

With the notebook in her hand, Isabella would go on to take her words to every street of the Maryland city until the people would finally listen. Until she found a lawyer she could trust, until she could see her father standing proud in the mornings while preparing himself for another house, she would never stop. For now, she walked to the kitchen where she found her parents calmer. She hugged her father. "Everything's gonna be okay."

"I know, Isabella."

Isabella went to sleep. The next day, she woke up and the pencil remained regular, yellow, and fragile. She went to school and knew that she could not fly anymore, could not teleport anymore, but as she saw the hundreds of faces that surrounded the halls, she saw the blue light of her room, she saw the houses constructed, and she saw love. She held her pencil tight.

Rai Rocca (he/him) is a sophomore at William and Mary studying Government and Hispanic Studies. I immigrated to the US from Lima, Peru when I was two years old and since then have found that writing is one of many ways to reclaim and reconsider the identities given to us. Feel free to contact or follow me on Twitter @Rai_Rocca and lastly, injustices like the man taking advantage of the father in my story are commonplace in America, and not enough magical pens exist. Make it known!

Material*Skin*

Tlotlo Tsamaase

She2 future-stitched her name, a virtual umbilical cord still leaping between now and sometime-then. Future-stitched and still sore, my static thickens the air with tension. The buzzer fuses its noise into my warm studio apartment. I hobble to the door, check the peephole. Sign in: Emelia Tladi, your alias, after all this apartment is in your name; it makes it easier if I'm not here. The voice comes through as code, not Morse. She2 grows past-ward, time slow and languid. They say she's good at finding people. I need her, but I can't trust her yet. I censor my identity. The door unlocks, She2 steps in, logged into my room now. I must run a scan in case she leaves something behind. The air can't differentiate us, seesawing reality.

"Where have you been?" She2, a swirl of perfume energy and virtual dissonance. "What happened? Did you get it?"

"It's in the cloakroom," I whisper, nothing but blurry melanin and brown eyes. Your Material*Skin*. You must have been in a hurry when you left, leaving a smudge of your Material*Skin* behind, like a fingerprint on a mug.

She2 swishes by, click-collects the encrypted skin-coat, a taut alias with a past to run to. "No one must know. We can only change the past if the future wants it altered. I'll be back once I find anything about her." She pauses. "Reneilwe, you don't want her to see you like this. Take care, take a shower. Sleep, joh."

"Just do everything you can to find her."

Where'd you go? Did you leave of your own volition? Did someone take you?

*** She2 has left the room.**

—

I'm left alone with silence, blinding daylight, and a sleeping skin slowly coming to, forming identity in the hazy hours of the morning. I took your Material*Skin* in the mild, midnight mornings, the internet-intoxicated owner passed out, still logged-in, but timed-out. They had some of your stuff in their home. I found your favourite mug with a piece of you still clinging to its handle. When he woke up from his hangover, I shook him, but no answers fell from his lips.

In here, we were like dolls trapped in boxes, our minds floating, staring out from our box at fluorescent-lit faces wearing thick headphones, in crooked bodies, crooked fingers tapping at the keyboard and their gamer sets, twisting us into stories. That's what other people thought. But this was heaven for us. Freedom. But for you to earn money, you must stay a mute doll. These are the things I've come to learn once you've disappeared: your body became taboo, unless it was slovenly spread across their screens, like butter to bread, a toast for their hunger.

But what remained important was that we were together, for years. Sometimes the online current wished to separate us, the sinews of the oceans flowing in and out of us, our love-grimed bones ecstatic in the dark. And now I've lost you, your Material*Skin* non-existent in our future. I have to swim back to the past. Swim back or else lose you forever. But it's hard to ease into the past. The past is a tsunami, fast overwhelming me.

I'm not a smoker, but my lungs cry for a smoke. I sit in the hammock, knee brought up to my chest. I borrow fire from the sun, the smoke wavers in the garden. I stay there quietly, thoughts stewing, thighs freezing, daylight and smoke entangling, red roses blushing in the heat.

"If I change the past, then she can remain in my future. *Or* stay in the past, for that is where she is and will always be," I whisper to nothing, but to something. The air shrinks, notices something in itself; translucence is deception, even it can tell. See-through materials hide things, things it can't decipher.

"I'm bugged," I whisper to herself. "I'm bugged. Is that how they took you?" My head falls forward, thoughts brimming with plans to find you.

*** Reneilwe has left the room.**

—

I'm out of the box. I keep on thinking what I could have done better, but I know I wouldn't have met you without the iBona. Eight months back, my brother Thamiso took me to a department store, said he had something that might interest me, the iBona, a VR sim game with its immersive login set. "You used to love these life simulation games before they became VR," he'd said, tapping the glamorous human-sized box. "It's the rave nowadays."

"Ja, but it's so expensive. I owe medical aid, last month's rent. I haven't paid internet—and this needs internet." I shuffled the shiny box back into its row in the aisle we were in, pushed the trolley as we moved further through the department store.

But later that week, Thamiso dropped by home with the iBona loaded into the back of the department store's truck, the driver and assistant wheeling it into my bachelor pad and connecting it, with the landlord peering through her kitchen window, eyeing it in such a way that would prompt her to raise the rent because "the electricity bill is too high."

He wrapped his arm around my shoulders, smiling. "This is your Christmas, birthday, and New Year's gifts all wrapped up into one gift: the iBona. I'm done for the year."

I jumped and hugged him, always appreciative of any gifts. "You know you could have just given me the money to pay expenses, right?"

"There is more to life than just paying bills and working, sis," he said, hugging me tighter. "Have fun with it, mate." He worked at a bank, something to do with fraud risk management and counterfeit-something, so money flowed in easily, and that's how he took care of our family. He had dreadlocks, with the lower part of his hair shaved. He somehow managed to carry that off professionally.

Thamiso squeezed my shoulder, his expression suddenly solemn. "I hope this cheers you up." I'd started my first dose of anti-depressants and the first two weeks were rough, exhausting, nauseous—they stole my appetite. "Apparently the iBona can be used as a dating site, too" he said, winking.

I was so excited to get the iBona started that night, even though I had a long shift at the newspaper the following day. But it was a life simulation game where you see everything, feel everything, just as in the real world. I used to be addicted to these sim games long ago, being in charge of an avatar's life, being able to start life from scratch to success, and if it didn't work out, start again.

—

The café, slow jazz. My cappuccino is turning cold. Thamiso enters, walks through with a swagger that has the women at the table across from ours staring at him.

He fist-bumps me before sitting down. He's wearing jeans, a jean jacket, and a retro shirt. "What's up, ma? You look . . . terrible."

"I met this girl online," I say, my sadness watering me. "Through the iBona."

He laughs. "Joh, here I thought you lost your job."

"You don't understand," I whisper, eyes wet. "We've been chatting for eight months. She's great. Funny. We lived in this sim city, in this studio apartment that we decorated together. We'd stay up late watching movies, changing night to sun to read novels out in our backyard, swimming in the cold—anything and everything we wanted. We ruled the night, we ruled the day. It was the only thing that's been keeping me alive this year. An escape from this job. My horrible job. Then one day I logged into our home: radio silence. I looked through the cupboards, our filing system for recent logins into our home, recent activities, the history. There was no whisper of her. She was gone."

Thamiso knuckles his forehead, eyebrows furrowed. "You never thought to get her number, joh?"

"It never worked." I stifle a sob.

"I hope you never gave her money," he says, sniffing a scam.

"No, she's not like that. She's never asked for money, or made strange requests. I keep thinking that something bad happened to her. I just don't know what to do."

Thamiso reaches for my hand and takes care of everything as I disappear from the world.

—

*** Reneilwe has entered the room.**

Emelia Tladi, that was her alias. I can't find her anywhere, only other Tladi's. I step into the box, our home, not necessarily with form—with mind, with soul. I built our home when I joined the sim game. Initially when I logged in, it had only a green landscape and hills lulled by the soft blue of sky. It started with the construction, a handful of contractors who I instructed to road-stitch lanes and highways, to densify neighborhoods with residential towers, to build factories, malls, recreational areas. I picked an area for a suite of multi-residential units, one of which I'd live in. Our studio apartment's on the lower ground floor with a spacious garden. If we had a dog, this would be its playground.

As an avatar, now that I had or was building the city, I had other tasks to complete, like getting a degree, opening up a business. That's how I met you. At the university that overlooked a river. I still remember you, before all else went: blue-flamed Afro, eyes lined in night, mouth of drug. You were wearing black shorts, boots, a crop top. In class, with your friends, you'd laugh and knock your head back. My eyes would travel the length of your braids, thinking about wrapping my hand around them and yanking hard.

I did the big chop—shaved off my relaxed hair, years ago. I wore it in bantu knots that weeks later you'd done. I'd invited you home, and we were sitting in the lounge, the TV on, you had me sit between your thighs, as you took a Shea butter mixture and twisted my Afro into bantu knots. In a couple days I could undo them to portray curls for the weekend braai our friends were hosting. That was life for us. I miss those slow nights, the crawl of brown skin, long limbs sleep-entangled with each other. I'm stifled in this sadness, recalling the memories.

A knock. The door, steel-cold, wood-solid. She2's frame in the peephole, looking haggard. Senegalese braids sweep past her knees. Her long dress slept-in, worked in. When I open the door, she drags herself in, drops on the couch.

"Eish," that's all She2 says. That word rolls out with anger, exhaustion and hopelessness. "So that Material*Skin* you gave me, I followed its history, its trail." She2 ruffles for something in her duffel bag. "This is all that I managed to get, joh. Her . . . "

"Material*Skin*." Like a torn piece of garment. It's pixelated, unreadable in our game. I bring it to my nose. "It smells like Emelia," I whisper. "Where did you trail this?"

Your scent has left codes in places in people—their mouths. They can't wash it off. I can smell the fury in your scent. We're in different places, different times, probably. The Material*Skin* is the only thing that identifies us, it's the only elixir that can allow avatars to be born into the real world—*only* if provided by a real-world human.

She2 sighs. "In another game. Not just any game, but some shooter game. She was in some trance, fam. Said I was the enemy. She shot me! Can you believe that? I almost got wiped out when I made contact."

She2 readjusts her thin-framed glasses, looking rather uncomfortable. "But I've terrible news. She . . . um . . . she's not real." I give her a strange look, then she adds, "Not real like you and I." She switches from one butt cheek to another butt cheek, not sure what to do with herself. "She's just an avatar, ja."

The skin you wore is not your own. Not your own as in not like mine, not where I come from: outside the box. You wouldn't just leave me, with all the plans and dreams we had. The internet is intact to your eye structure, so why didn't you make contact?

Send an email? A DM? As I stared at you, in the dream-feed shot that hung across the wall in our lounge, my iBona feed displays last recent posts, snapshots of your skin emitting smileys, LOLs, TGIF and hashtag #Blessed in a spectrum of emotions.

I stumble, fall to my knees. She2 hurries into the kitchen, fetches me a glass of water to gulp down. She guides me to the lounge.

"You know what you have to do next," She2 says.

"I know, but if I can't find her, then I can't help her," I whisper.

"The only way she can continue to live, to be here, or try to get out into *our* world is if you share your *skin* with her," She2 says.

"Why didn't she just tell me? Ask me?"

"It's a big thing to ask, and sometimes quite a selfish thing," She2 says. "Your skin will birth her but it will mutate you, it'd be painful for you. Do you really love her that much, joh? I mean, you're gonna have to take care of her for quite some time. Will your salary even support you both out of the box?"

"I love her. I have to save her. I can't let her die. As long as we're together, we'll do alright." Out of the box, I'd need to keep the iBona connected to my plasma TV. With my skin, she'll be able to crawl out from it, flop onto my living room floor, real as flesh and bone. It'd be a searing pain for me, but we'll be together. And she'd have something that no one ever gave her. Life. Opportunity. I love her, I truly do.

*** She2 and Reneilwe have left the room.**

—

*** Reneilwe has entered the room.**

Weeks later, I log in into our studio apartment. I switch on the dream-feed, filled with many questions. Many questions I want to ask the past you. Skins are boundaries we never wished for. On the shelf above our bed, I reach for a disk full of memorabilia that can be slipped into the skull-port to fuel once again the things I was forgetting. Who am I? Where am I? What is my purpose? All these questions are my yoga. Slowly, the memories eddy, stream into my mind. The room revolves, changes into months ago, on our bed: you undoing your braids, me reading a manhwa.

I hurl the manhwa aside. "Where are you? Please tell me where you are?

You giggle. "I'm right here, silly."

Of course, you'd say that. The past you. Today, you'd know what that question means.

"What do you speak? Kalanga, Zulu, Xhosa?" I ask, afraid to aim for the truth. "How does it feel living in here all day? In this box. Trapped. What do you do?"

You stare through the skylight at the stars. "This is my normal just the same as that world is your normal."

"But what do you do all day?"

You laugh, kicking up your feet. "I do avatar things. Shop when I'm told to shop. Act broke when I'm broke. Run around running errands, winning, but failing sometimes. Then I come home just like you come home." Sometimes you'd pixelate, get zapped out of bed—explaining it away as part of your job—but I realize now it must have been when your owner had logged in, wanting to play. So you whisper, "It's a weird job, isn't it? It's my job to be logged-in all the time. But"—you looked around the room—"this is my quiet place, where I get to choose what I want." If I didn't know the truth, I wouldn't be able to tell how sly you were being. You were never going to tell me the truth.

I grab your hands, stare into your eyes, hoping for a miracle. “Don’t you want to get out?” I ask, regretting it almost.

“What? Like, you?” The light leans into your eyes, the irises flickering. And I see it, the truth lighting itself up in you. “What’s the point of that question? You know I don’t have a body out there. Not like you. I wasn’t born like you.”

*** Reneilwe has left the room.**

—

*** Emelia has entered the room.**

I rush back home as soon as I see the notification. I leave work without notice. I stumble into my bachelor pad, and the iBona, sensing me, injects itself into my body.

*** Reneilwe has entered the room.**

You are home, but outside the open front door where our neighbors see you, the sun golden, your brown skin flawless and clear. Hurt in your eyes. You are slowly feathering away, the tinges of dusk dissolving you. “Renee, I’m so sorry,” you whisper. My heart leaps to meet yours, hugging you, kissing you.

“They’re deleting me. Wiping me out,” you cry. “I have deformed my bones for them. How can they do this to me?” You stare at me, yours eyes still a hazel beauty. “I didn’t know how to tell you. I thought it’d be easier if I just disappeared from your life before I really disappeared. But you’ve been looking for me everywhere. I’ve been so hungry for you. I just had to see you.” And I see it’s been a hurdle for you to migrate between games to see me because the current is forcing us apart, together we keep.

I kiss your tears dry. "Shh, don't cry, babe."

You fall to your knees, face soul-battered, arm outstretched as if telling death to stay at bay. Lips are loose with prayers. No one moves, waiting for your death to sail the air. I do only what I should. I unfurl my Material*Skin,* wrap it out around you to shield you from the burning cold of death. You remain in my arms, in my life—together, as the last light seeps from the virtual sky, we escape the box, we escape my real-world plasma TV, onto my bachelor pad's floor. With my Material*Skin* you are a real human girl, true to form, with real flesh and bone. Home. Welcome home, lover.

Tlotlo Tsamaase (she/her) is a Motswana writer of fiction, poetry, and architectural articles. Her work has appeared in *Clarkesworld, Terraform, Apex Magazine, Strange Horizons, The Dark,* and other publications. Her poem "I Will Be Your Grave" was a 2017 Rhysling Award nominee. Her short story, "Virtual Snapshots" was longlisted for the 2017 Nommo Awards. Her novella *The Silence of the Wilting Skin* is forthcoming from Pink Narcissus Press in May 2020. You can find more of her works on tlotlotsamaase.com; Twitter at @tlotlotsamaase and on Patreon at patreon.com/tlotlotsamaase.

The Last of Your Kind

Vijay Varman

I wonder if the Dodo knew,
That its species was so few.
Or how the Tasmanian Tiger dealt,
With the solitude it must have felt.
What is it like to be the last of your kind?
To outlive your brothers and one's intended design.

For decades I was used to write,
Novels, poems, and letters alike.
Some were beautiful, others were graceless,
And quite a few were a little bit racist.

The letters were the first to go,
Replaced by a system with a strange bright glow.
Digital messages so easy to send,
Were merely the beginning of my uneventful end.

As the years leisurely went by,
The dust often brought a tear to my eye.
Post-its, drawings, and the simplest notes,
No longer feasible as a final lifeboat.

Too many eras blur on by,
And humankind has conquered the skies.
Silent I sit in a museum of history,
Appearing to some as a confounding mystery.
200 years since I last was used,
So I spend most of my day choosing to snooze.

But soon the funds for me have dried,
My future no longer for others to decide.
All I can do now is wait for the end,
Humanity's last ever ball-point pen.

A resident of London in the United Kingdom, **Vijay Varman** (he/him) is a scribe who enjoys writing for both the page and the screen. Though he dabbles in a variety of genres, his first love is for science-fiction. To pass the time between writing gigs, Vijay also spends his time working in the Genealogy industry and behind-the-scenes in London's West End theatres. "The Last of Your Kind" is Vijay's first publication. You can find out more about his worldly thoughts at vijayvarman.com or on Twitter as @CircleofCine.

Memory Malfunction

Minerva Cerridwen

With a hiss, the door slid open, revealing a human in dark grey trousers and a short-sleeved suit jacket that showed off a pair of well-defined biceps. Pinned on the jacket was a small badge with the words: 'Deabun, she/her'.

"Mx S1812L," she said. "Please, come in."

The android who'd been waiting in the corridor got up from his metal chair. "Call me Sibill. I prefer not to use an honorific."

"Then we've already found a commonality." Deabun smiled and stepped aside.

The android's black robes, interwoven with an intricate silver pattern, flapped around his ankles as he walked into Raddert & Deabun's main office.

The room's interior could not have looked more different from the undecorated corridor with its metal walls and soulless chairs. Cream carpet padded the office floor, deep green cushions lined the chairs and walls, and a tan, velvet tablecloth covered the oval desk. Behind it, three large wooden cabinets displayed all kinds of vases and trinkets. It wasn't the kind of room Sibill expected on a spaceship, but then again it did fit Raddert & Deabun's business—and certainly seemed cosy enough to spend a lot of time in while managing an intergalactic company.

A second human was seated at the desk: tall and brown-skinned, wearing eir grey hair in a small bun and a comfortable striped jumper over eir soft form. As Deabun closed the door and took a seat next to em, Sibill sat down across from them and quickly checked the other company owner's badge.

"I'm honoured to meet you, Mx Raddert, Deabun," he said.

"Wonderful to meet you too," Mx Raddert replied. "We've read your application with great interest. You achieved an almost perfect track record at your previous firm. And I imagine the dragons of planet Firepit are not the easiest of customers."

"I've never had any trouble," Sibill said loyally, unwilling to confirm any stereotypes about his former clientele at HEH—*'we'll Help Expand your Hoard'*.

"Why did you leave HEH?" Deabun asked.

"The work was all on just one planet. I'm ready to see more of the universe," Sibill answered.

Raddert nodded. "We've experienced first-hand how learning about other cultures enriches a society. Both directly through art objects *and* by communicating with people all over the universe in order to do business."

"Not *only* to do business," Deabun said, smiling. "I met my wife on Haunt two standard years after we started the company and we definitely didn't just talk about the chandelier she was seeking to sell."

"As you like to remind everyone," Mx Raddert teased, before returning eir full attention to Sibill. "There is, of course, a small issue that complicates the matter of your recruitment." E lifted the thin tablet in eir left hand, on which e had Sibill's file open.

"Yes. My memory is defective."

Deabun frowned. "Your job would be to buy and sell antiques on planets in many different galaxies. We were delighted to see an android apply, as the long journeys are more straining on a human or foochsian body, but without the ability to remember a lot of cultural details and the range of values a particular object may hold in the eyes of different people, we're not sure how this is going to work."

"I developed this malfunction three years ago," Sibill pointed out, "and you've seen my sales at HEH. I may no longer be able to retrieve anything from my long-term storage, but the skillbases hosting my behavioural protocols and language files are still available, as well as my short-term memory, where I can save information for up to twenty hours, depending on how much new data there is to process within that time span."

"Perhaps that was enough to remember everything you needed on Firepit, but our company sends out ships to trade with millions of cultures," Deabun said. "You'd need to be able to negotiate with sellers to obtain the best possible price for us, yet without hurting them. And to determine a reasonable price adapted to the local market for the objects *we* sell. You would have to learn about all of these people and can't afford to forget what you learned."

"I won't," Sibill said. "I'm good at filing details."

"But what good is that if you can't recall those files?" Mx Raddert asked. "We have a proposition. Since we would be very excited to take you on, we could arrange your restoration, at no cost to yourself. Providing you with a new storage drive would offer us some security, as our insurance might not cover mistakes caused by your defect, considering we knew about it before hiring you."

Sibill had to blink his round, black eyes a few times in shocked indignation before finding himself able to reply. "Replacing my memory drives would change my very identity. If that's what it takes, I'm withdrawing my application. Good day." He stood up.

"No, wait!" Deabun called.

Mx Raddert pressed a hand to eir heart. "I'm so sorry. Had I known that would be the consequence of such a procedure, I swear I would never have suggested it. My deepest apologies, Sibill."

Sibill studied the startled expressions on the two humans' faces for a moment before sitting down again. "Apology accepted. Look, it's clear that employing me would be advantageous to both of us. I promise I know what I'm doing. But it would require your trust, and I understand if you can't give me that. I know there's much at stake and that wasting a light-years-long journey on me would be a blow to your finances. All I can tell you is that I'm driven to explore new environments and to put my extensive language skills to good use."

Mx Raddert and Deabun looked at each other for a long moment, apparently communicating without words. Sibill knew that telepathy was not a skill humans possessed, but decades of close collaboration could induce a surprisingly similar phenomenon.

"Okay," Deabun said finally, turning back to Sibill. "We want to give you a chance. Your first mission will be on Mysta. Does that sound good to you?"

Somewhere just behind Sibill's left hip, a whirr sounded as nervous tension uncoiled. He was getting an assignment in a different galaxy right away! Delighted, he held out his right hand for the human custom of shaking. "That sounds marvellous."

The android had personalised his office. It wasn't as luxurious as that of Raddert and Deabun, but behind the standard oval desk was a shelf with gorgeous old books, a colourful abstract landscape painting, and a small showcase with a dozen short, rounded sticks. In the corner farthest from the door, a low table displayed the statue B sought to buy. B could barely contain their excitement at finally seeing the artwork in person, but still managed to focus on the new Raddert & Deabun representative instead.

"You are exactly on time," the android remarked with a pleased smile.

"My species may not be known for their punctuality, but I know yours is." B flopped one of their long ears down over an orange eye in the equivalent of a wink and pressed one of their three pairs of limbs to their heart in greeting. "Sibill."

"B. Shall we?" Sibill gestured at the desk and started walking around it. Although the limbs supporting B's plump body were much shorter than Sibill's legs, they quickly fell into step. Side by side, they walked two full circles around the table as Mystan etiquette prescribed, before sitting down across from each other.

B rustled their shiny, deep brown feathers appreciatively and nodded towards the statue. "I couldn't help but sneak a glance already. It's in fine shape, isn't it?"

"It was well looked after," Sibill agreed. "The only damage is a small crack in one of those pieces of glass."

"Not bad for its age." B stood up again to take a closer look. The statue, carved out of grey stone, represented two characters: the first was a fat, woolly creature with several sets of wings; the other a tall, very flexible figure coiled lovingly around the first one's chest. Both of them had oodles of eyes all over their bodies, those of the coiled figure all partly hidden behind dark, round eyeglasses.

"It's beautiful." B turned back towards Sibill. "Do you know its history?"

"The piece was created two centuries ago on planet Haunt," Sibill replied. "It was based on a visual entertainment show that, at the time, never reached the popularity the makers had hoped for. Still, someone clearly cared enough about *Excellent Premonitions* to depict its two main characters in their art. Only a few standard years ago, the show was picked up again and became successful throughout the entire galaxy."

"You bet it did." B grinned. "I became obsessed with it. When I saw this statue in the Raddert & Deabun catalogue, I wanted it immediately."

"And here we are," Sibill said. "The price you mentioned in your communications before I arrived on Mysta sounded more than acceptable. Is there anything else you would like to know before we move on to the paperwork?"

"I think I'm ready to sign the credits over to you," B answered.

"Then please excuse me for a moment while I go and alert the transportation bots, so you won't have to wait too long once we're done."

"Of course." B sat quietly while Sibill left the office, the door sliding shut behind him.

Then they jumped off their chair. Sibill was amazing! His summary of the artwork's history had been perfectly correct. He was polite to Mystan standards, knowledgeable about the merchandise; nothing had indicated his lack of long-term memory. Raddert and Deabun could be assured that hiring Sibill had been a good choice. B would make sure of that in their report.

But the question remained *how* Sibill had accomplished it. Somehow, Raddert and Deabun didn't seem curious; as long as the results were good, they didn't really care whether the work had been done with or without a functional storage drive. But after having seen Sibill in action, B needed to know.

They quickly rounded the desk and smoothed a hand over its surface. There was no hidden tablet that could have aided Sibill. The desk drawer didn't offer any explanations either; it only held a bag of Narbuvian marbles, probably meant for sale or trade.

B scanned the office thoughtfully, their gaze passing by the bookshelf thrice before they realised that some species used thick objects like that to hide secrets. Secrets like a device that could transmit information directly into Sibill's short-term memory!

They grabbed the nearest book, opened it carefully . . . But there was no room to hide anything inside. Page upon page was filled with ink. B couldn't read most of the text, as it hadn't been written in their language, but they recognised just enough species names to realise that the neat, square handwriting was listing traits, customs, and economic backgrounds.

"I'm afraid those aren't for sale," Sibill said from the doorway.

B had been so amazed by the book that they hadn't even heard him enter. "I . . . I'm sorry for snooping. I just wanted to understand how you're working your magic."

Sibill pointed at the decorated sticks in the showcase. "Analogue pens. Most androids don't hold them in high esteem, but they truly are wonderful filing tools."

"I see. So all of these books are . . . your long-term storage?"

"I haven't written in all of them yet, but yes, that is their function," Sibill said. "I use an intricate system so I can quickly find every necessary piece of information and read up on what I need before meeting a client."

"Well, you passed with flying colours!" B reverently put the book back on the shelf. "I better come clean with you now. You see, I befriended Raddert and Deabun quite a while ago. They're also *Excellent Premonitions* fans and we got talking online. When you signed your contract, they sent you to me first so they would be able to get some feedback on how you were doing. From their *Mysta-ry* shopper, as they called me."

Sibill let out an amused snort. "I understand there wouldn't have been much mystery if they'd checked whether I was okay with them telling you about my memory, but I better remind them they owe me that particular conversation."

"It wasn't *just* a test, though," B hastened to say. "I really do want to buy the statue."

"I see," Sibill said, smiling. "Would you do me a favour, B?"

"It's the least I can do after sort of tricking you."

"Don't worry about that. But would you please not tell anyone else how I remember everything? I rather enjoy the speculations that I may be the only android who performs through witchcraft rather than technology."

B grinned. "Let's make you into a legend."

Minerva Cerridwen (she/her) is a queer writer and pharmacist from Belgium. Without her to-do lists, she would forget half of the things she's supposed to do. Pens feature heavily in some of her hobbies, like handlettering and drawing, and less so in others, like yoga and baking (except when writing recipes). She co-wrote a story in *Five Minutes at Hotel Stormcove*, and the revised version of her novella *The Dragon of Ynys* will appear in 2020. For news, keep an eye on her website: minervacerridwen.wordpress.com.

Shared Space

A. P. Howell

Tracey spent a third of her day in the cubicle, so she thought of it as hers.

Decorating her apartment was overwhelming. But a cubicle? That was a manageable amount of space. A chunk of wall was dedicated to a coat hanger, and much of the rest was covered with printed out procedures and codes, regularly consulted and frequently annotated. The free space on the walls and the doors on the built-in shelves housed cat pictures and art cards, Impressionist landscapes and Escher architecture and nature photos. Her wall calendar depicted European castles, heavy gray stone fortresses to mountaintop Schlösser.

Tracey put some poetry magnets on one of the drawers. At first, she'd tried to come up with a poem every day; then she aimed for Haiku Friday, which only lasted two weeks. Every once in a while, she came up with something new, but though they were terribly neglected she refused to take the magnets down.

She could have gotten a plant, but she tended to kill house-plants. At least, she had when she was younger; as a responsible adult, she might have better luck. But it would be humiliating to have an audience for her incompetence, and depressing to watch a plant die in her space.

Baseball was boring, basketball too squeaky, football a blood-sport, and women's professional soccer a faded dream, so Tracey had a Buffalo Beauts team pennant hanging up. If the goal was fitting in, the effort was only a qualified success. Rooting interest in a sport generally went over well, but the Beauts weren't a popular hometown team or players of a nationally televised sport. At least she'd educated people about the existence of women's hockey, and that counted for something.

Tracey wasn't especially neat by nature, certainly not in the privacy of her own home. But for all the personalized touches, the cubicle was not private. People who warranted offices might be able to joke about stratified piles of paperwork, but Tracey knew there was a short, direct line from "messy" to "disorganized" to "unprofessional" to "unreliable" for a woman who only warranted a cubicle. And it was nice to have clear space to spread out when necessary, without having to do the work of making space before doing the work that had to be done.

The cubicle looked pretty much exactly like the last cubicle she'd had in this office, except this one was closer to the water cooler and farther from the bathroom. More importantly, from the perspective of office geography, she and a few of her colleagues were now a few steps closer to their respective managers' offices.

Since the move, neatness had become a matter of courtesy. Her new cubicle was one that the call center team used when making evening and weekend calls. Tracey found the shared space irksome, like a secret demotion, even though it had no real impact upon her. She worked nine-to-five, only overlapping with a few of the call center staffers who started early. Listening to them reciting their scripts made her feel a little better about days spent manipulating spreadsheets and reporting queries. At least she didn't have to talk to random people on the phone. Tracey had no idea how they maintained a pleasant phone voice throughout their shift; she could barely avoid embarrassing herself ordering a pizza.

So her response to the secret demotion was secret solidarity with her unseen counterpart. She made sure the desk was clean, her hand cream and other personal items unobtrusively stashed, pens and sharpened pencils and Post-It notes plentiful. She wasn't sure exactly what, if anything, the call center folks used aside from the phone and the computer, but Tracey wanted to be a good hostess and helpful colleague.

Her efforts were silently appreciated, or perhaps unperceived, for some time. But one morning, she was greeted by a single Post-It note stuck below her keyboard. She expected a routine note—"Come see me when you get in" or the like—but there were no words.

The Post-It had become a canvas. One of her landscape images—an impressive rock formation—had been rendered in blue ballpoint. Tracey was impressed. The cross-hatched lines were preternaturally parallel. Had the artist used a straight-edge? She moved the blue-on-yellow image to a safe part of her desk; it was too charming to risk crumpling.

New sketches appeared each morning: soulful kitten eyes, impossible geometries. Soon her red and black pens entered the fray. Tracey was particularly impressed by a sunset of red sky, blue sea, and black shore. She didn't even mind that the pens weren't making their way back into the desk organizer, but were instead scattered around the desk.

The following Monday, Tracey found her soft green editing pencil near the keyboard. The number 2 graphite pencils—one pinprick-sharp, thanks to the electric sharpener by the copier, and one thin-leaded mechanical pencil—flanked her open notebook.

Her notebook. She'd bought it at the drug store so she'd have something other than the legal pads from the office supply closet.

It was always tucked away in a corner because she wanted to be polite to her unseen deskmate—who apparently poked around and flipped through her informal meeting minutes and semi-legible task reminders and didn't value even an illusion of privacy. Tracey should have felt offended.

And yet . . . the picture was beautiful. It was a rendering of Caernarvon, this month's castle, beautifully detailed and textured. Most of the work was in graphite, with just hints of green incorporated for depth and the illusion of life. Tracey wished the artist hadn't used notebook paper. The blue lines made the image less frame-worthy (though Tracey pinned it up on the cubicle wall). Before she left for the day, she grabbed a few letter sized sheets of paper from a printer tray and left them next to her keyboard.

Throughout the week, Tracey's deskmate made good use of the paper. Hands drew a fluffy kitten, a buffalo roamed the coast of Northern Ireland, and carefully smudged pencil rendered water lilies in monochrome. A single Post-It note was covered with interlocking swans, but the letter-sized sheets were the clear favorite.

Tracey refreshed the paper every night as a courtesy. She assumed the call center staff could find the printer—maybe they even used the printer—but maybe they sat down and stayed chained to their desks by their headsets. She wanted to make life easier for the unseen artist. The world, and her little corner of it, needed more art.

It brightened her day as the company ramped up for crunch time, the point in the business cycle when everything hit at once and tasks seemed to take forever to deal with or manifested in unexpected ways. Leaving at 5:30 became a challenge; 5:00 was right out. From experience, Tracey knew the days would continue to stretch for a few weeks, but she didn't have kids or dogs or any other obligations that made it difficult to stay until 6:00 or 7:00 or later. No need for workload conversations with her manager or anyone else, which was good, because Tracey disliked confrontation and liked having a job.

On Friday, a woman Tracey didn't recognize approached her cubicle. "I'm Ellie." She had a nice smile: even white teeth and cheeks that reminded her of a chipmunk. "I'll just be in the kitchen until you're done."

The words took a second to register. "Oh, right. Nice to meet you. Tracey," she added, even though her own name was on the cubicle. "I'll try to wrap up quickly."

She supposed she ought to resent having to rush, that her company didn't give her the time and space to complete the work they told her to do. She ought to feel resentful on her own behalf, and Ellie's: regardless of how much time she was forced to spend twiddling her thumbs, Ellie's nightly call quota would doubtless remain unchanged. She could, if she were particularly uncharitable and illogical, feel resentful of Ellie herself.

But instead, she felt a rush of gratitude for their clashing schedules. Her unseen deskmate now had a name and a face.

"I was curious," Ellie nodded at the Beauts pennant, "so I went down the NWHL rabbit hole."

"Oh?" Most people stopped at the revelation that women played professional hockey.

"I think I could parrot back most of the stats, which isn't really saying much since the league hasn't been around that long," Ellie said. "But I was even more interested in the ownership drama. Plus the trademark stuff. And the strike! I really hope the player's union gets what they want, but I'm nervous. Women's leagues come and go so fast, I'm afraid it's just about to go the way of the Canadian league . . . "

"They're so undercapitalized."

"I wouldn't mind, if that was like a cultural decision to treat sports as games, but men's sports are so ridiculously overcapitalized. And the public expenditures—" Ellie paused and grinned sheepishly. "I talk a lot. I talk as my job. But my calls aren't nearly as interesting."

"Glad I can help."

"I love your cube, too."

"It's our cube, really. You spend as much time here as I do."

"But you've done a great job decorating it."

"Thanks for your help." Tracey gestured at the sketches. "They're beautiful."

Ellie cocked her head. "I didn't make those. I haven't been scheduled for a week—I took a few days off before crunch time. I assumed you drew them. They really are lovely. Whoever made them is quite the artist."

"Yes," Tracey agreed. She had the sense that this was a mystery to be solved, but she couldn't muster much interest. She'd wondered about her deskmate, and she was learning about her deskmate, and that was enough for now. "Maybe I'll join you in the kitchen before I head out, hit up the vending machine. One candy bar for the road."

"Just not E5," Ellie warned. "Things always get stuck in E5. But I've learned the trick for feeding the machine dimes. I could just use dollars, but I wanted to keep trying. There's always something new to figure out."

Maybe Ellie would figure out the answer to the artwork; but for someone who conquered a vending machine's quirks, she didn't seem too worked up about it. Tracey saved her spreadsheet, logged off, and stood up. The work could wait until tomorrow, when her desk might be graced by a new piece of artwork not created by Ellie. It was a reason to look forward to another day in their shared space.

A. P. Howell (she/her) was raised in upstate New York, moved to Pennsylvania to attend Bryn Mawr College, met a boy Scottish Country Dancing, and lives happily with him and their two children. Her handwriting is atrocious, somehow reminiscent of both Palmer Method and the Richter Scale, so she is more likely to type than write longhand. She fondly remembers doodling ballpoint pen marginalia in college and the India ink stain on her finger in high school. She currently works in a cubicle, which she does not share with anyone else, and can be found online at aphowell.com and tweeting @APHowell.

Mystical Woo

Victoria Hollis

Seeing the pen in Annemarie's hand the week before he went to Chicago shocked him.

"Peanut, where did you find that?" He took it from her hands; the "Michael" stenciled into the cap was rough against his fingers.

"In a briefcase. I can't get it to draw."

Fountain pens were always finicky, and this one might still have a will of its own. "Where did you find it?"

Annemarie led the way to the briefcase and a black leather journal. Mike sat on the floor, journal on his lap while Annemarie peered over his shoulder. "This is a magic pen, and anything I write with it comes true in a day. Watch." He wrote in his distinctive script on the first blank page. *I love Annemarie more than anything.* He felt it—the sparkling in his stomach—*yes, Annemarie is the best thing in my world.*

She frowned. "We can't see that, Daddy, and I know that anyway. Do something real."

"Okay, smarty-pants, what should I write?"

She fidgeted. "I got a math test tomorrow . . . Can I have my leopard coat if I get an A?"

She'd been eyeing that jacket for weeks. "I did math in college. Maybe you've got some of my talent," he said with a little poke. "And we can open a department store with your clothes—"

"Please?"

Mike laughed. “Okay, fine.” He put pen to paper again. *Annemarie will do well on her math test and get her leopard coat.*

“Now we wait.” He closed the cap before sticking it into his shirt pocket. Annemarie’s dubious look made him pause—does it still work?—but he poked her again. “After we eat, we’ll study for your test. We can help the magic, right?” He pulled her across his lap for a ferocious tickle fight. Her giggles were their own form of magic—

“Playing around?”

Aleja stood in the doorframe, just a hint of warmth in her eyes.

“We do that sometimes, you know,” he said with his voice perfectly neutral.

Her lips pursed. “Gavin and I are going to MOMA. Put Annemarie to bed at a reasonable hour.”

She left in a whirlwind of perfume and diamonds. Annemarie whispered, “Do you think Mommy likes her new boyfriend? Can you write about it in your magic book?”

—

Where had it gone wrong?

The quiet of the Brooklyn loft and thoughts of his college reunion brought the uncomfortable question forward, drawing it out as painfully as his differential equation proofs.

In the alumni magazine, he had nothing to fear: a married father, a risk manager with a growing New York hedge fund.

In the depths of his heart, the lies were thick and tangled, an ad populum fallacy.

He glanced at the journal on his desk; his fingers caressed the pen.

Could I have made it better if I had just figured her magic out?

—

Michelle, the bringer of dimples and magic.

You couldn't miss her—bangles, large earrings, a patterned scarf tied around her riotous curls. Convincing anyone walking through campus to sign this petition, to attend that rally, to fight for the rights of the disenfranchised.

He'd arrived for the first debate team practice and found her on the other side of the room. She'd winked at him and said, "Did you think I was just another pretty face?" And she soundly trounced him that first round.

Michelle had a wide range of knowledge, and that drew him to her flame. And she was eccentric, with her fashion sense and her flaming-heart liberalism, and then she'd get started on what she called "mystical woo": crystals, tarot, all strange to his logic-driven brain. Against his thoughts, he kept her at arm's length, friendly but not friends, attractive but not his style.

Senior year she thrust a black journal and a polished wooden pen at him.

"Okay," she began, "the journal I bought, the pen I had made, and it's entirely tuned to you. It's mystical woo, but it's good. Write your desires down in this journal, and they'll come true within a day."

He blinked.

"It's *true*." She sighed, frustrated. "Now you can create your own destiny. I can because I have nothing to lose. But you've got the weight of yourself on you. This gives you a fighting chance."

Had she really been able to see that within him?

Mike thanked her, took the pen and journal, and packed them

in a box. Graduation morning he felt her hug, saw the last flash of her dimples, and heard, "Don't forget to create your destiny, and don't forget me."

He forgot.

Until the pen and the journal reappeared in his first apartment. Hungry, weary, and ready to escape his Bronx closet and his dead-end internship, he wrote: *I will get a job in day trading.*

Two days later, TradingScreen had found his resume.

The journal rested in his hands daily, the pen wore grooves into his hands. *I will live in Brooklyn, I will close this deal with Enron, I will get the promotion to Risk Management.*

Yes, yes, yes, the journal agreed. Mystical woo—and the thought of Michelle's dimples—was beautiful. He considered emailing her to thank her, but there was never enough time.

One of the Enron execs had been treating his team horribly for over a month. Running on alcohol, adrenalin, and two hours of sleep, his anger curled into the page: *I want them brought to justice.*

He watched as the news leaked out and the stock plummeted. Then, as everyone tried to cope with the upheaval and loss of September 11th, their gold-plated corruption was brought to light. The Enron loss was devastating to his firm, even as he felt the exhilaration of justice. Jobless and tired, he shoved the journal and pen into a box at the back of his closet.

New York healed, and so did he. Richer, but overworked and lonely, he made a few desperate scrawls using the journal and pen. *I will find someone to create a financially strong and independent family with.*

He met Aleja at a work conference the next week. She was a gorgeous, smart, driven junior coder for a startup firm. The conference fell during a summer lull, and he didn't see the "hope you're doing well" email from Michelle until a month later—just a month before he sent the news to the alumni magazine. Married: Michael S. Caviness '97 to Alejandra Davila, July 27, 2004.

Within five months Aleja was pregnant. Mike wrote: *I want our child to be the light of my life.* Born to: Michael S. Caviness '97 and spouse Alejandra: Annemarie Catalina, May 18, 2005. Annemarie's hazel eyes held a mischievous twinkle from the moment she was born.

There was no need for magic anymore. Life was good. Mystical woo was what you made it. He tucked the pen and the journal into an old briefcase, thought that he should reach out to Michelle to tell her that he finally understood and to wish her well.

Then it started.

Aleja, with a colicky baby, grew exhausted and irritated. Spending too many nights at the office, too many post-work drinks. A world on edge, with growing uncertainties in the market and fears of a never-ending war.

Annemarie turned three. They celebrated with a trip to FAO Schwartz, a screaming match over his need to escape to the office (secretly the bar), and a shocking announcement: Aleja had been cheating on him for the past two months and had no intention of stopping. The Great Recession hit their investments the next week, leaving them as little more than roommates who couldn't divorce.

—

The investments had stabilized. Annemarie had adjusted to their new lifestyle. At least Aleja was still present. He'd just broken things off with Sarah and wasn't interested in diving back into the dating pool . . .

The journal fell open in front of him, its pages still carrying the faintest smell of 9/11 ash and dust.

Create your destiny.

What *did* he want?

He wrote: *I want to be happy.*

The sparkling in his stomach rose, made his hand shake just a bit. On impulse, he added: *I hope to see Michelle at the 15th in Chicago.*

—

"How'd your math test go, Peanut?" Mike swooped Annemarie up for a hug.

"You were right, Daddy! I'm pretty good at math once I think about it!" He could already imagine it: the test with a bright red A on the top. "Can we get my leopard coat?"

"Let's wait. Nana sent you a package."

"Me?"

"Yeah. I thought you might want to open it first."

It did not surprise him to see the coat, with a note from his mother: *Alright, I caved! Is this the one? But won't Annemarie look just darling in this? I wish you'd come to Washington for Christmas this year.*

"Daddy, your magical book did it! Can I write something in there, too?"

Mike had said not yet, but he opened it on the plane and saw her block print. *I WANT MY DADDY TO BE HAPPY TOO. LOVE, ANNEMARIE.*

—

He heard panels on UChicago's role in changing the world,

networked and schmoozed at the luncheons, and felt a flutter of attraction at the handsome woman giving the fundraising pitch. Michelle's riotous curls were nowhere in sight. He'd heard the names of deceased classmates during the memorial service that night, felt his breath catch as they began the Cs. They passed her name.

Emboldened, he wrote again. *I hope to see—really see—Michelle Collins at the gala dinner on October 12.*

—

The banquet room glowed with dimmed lights and brilliant candelabras, crystal flutes sparkling with champagne, a rainbow of shimmering evening gowns offset by black tuxedos. Mike adjusted his cufflinks and looked for curls in vain.

"You don't recognize me, do you?"

The fundraiser from yesterday stood before him.

"No." He gave her a brilliant day-trader smile. "But I did donate stock toward the class gift already."

"All those years debating, and you forgot zany Michelle?" She smiled, dimples on display.

The throb of the journal struck him.

"Don't feel bad." She pulled out an empty chair. "No one knows me anymore. You have to play the part if you want to beat the system from within. How have you been? I heard you got married and had a baby. Are they here?"

A trap at every conversational turn. "I thought I'd make my first time back personal. How are you? I was . . . hoping I'd see you."

She let his nervousness pass.

After a few years of "finding herself," she had stumbled into fundraising at UChicago before leading an individual giving program at one of the Smithsonian museums. She was always happy to know someone who knew people with money, so she pulled a business card from her purse along with a wooden pen. "I'll add my cell number."

The pen resembled his, down to the "Michelle" stenciled in the cap.

"Hey, that looks kind of familiar," he teased.

She frowned. "So embarrassing. You don't still have yours, do you?"

"Of course," he said, surprised. "You told me to create my destiny. Sometimes I do."

Her expression held a mixture of surprise and sadness.

"You mean yours worked?"

He threw his hands up. "You're sitting here, aren't you?"

After a moment of visible shock, Michelle dimpled again.

"I bought those things as a set. The shaman from the botanica on the North Side told me they were guaranteed to work. Mystical woo, right?"

Her voice shook. He reached for her hand and the pen across the table. "Yeah. Mystical woo."

"I wrote pages about how I could get this, buy that, find that job. And about how you'd finally see me as more than zany, flaming-heart liberal, debate partner Michelle. But you never did."

She'd liked him the whole time?

Michelle shrugged. "I got everything else. Maybe I wrote the parts about you badly. But that was a really wild time. So I let that go and focused on work. Becoming my best me. And I feel good."

She gently removed her hand, handed him her card.

"Glad it worked for you, Mikey. Look me up if you come to Washington." She rose to leave.

He reached for her hand but caught air instead. "Wait."

He felt the sparkling deep in his core, just as the swing band tuned up.

"Dance with me," he begged.

She laughed as her eyes sparkled. "Why not? It's a reunion, after all."

The fierce desire rising up in him as she moved, strong and confident and lithe, in his arms while dancing. The clink of their glasses, and the champagne bubbles that tickled their noses over the third. The sly smile she gave him, and his painful need to touch her, to place his hand at the small of her back.

They tipsily leaned upon each other while she babbled. "I have a room here. And I know what I wrote but you're married. This all must be a dream, but—"

"My marriage isn't real. You can say 'yes' with no issue," he whispered, and waited.

"Yes," she finally answered, and lifted her lips for his kiss.

—

He snapped awake at 3:33.

Michelle slept the sleep of the loved next to him, her tawny body curled into the sheets and into his arms.

Should he have? Not that it mattered to his marriage, but was this disrespectful to Michelle?

The answering throb coursing throughout his body said he was following the path of destiny he'd plotted, despite whatever the pen had done.

A feeling itched. He shifted to see the bed's side table. A black leather journal, similar to his, lay there, quietly radiating power and love and truth.

He managed to leave the warmth of her embrace. It felt personal to pick up the book and read the words she'd only meant for herself, but she'd left it here, facing him. He felt sure she wanted him to see it. He snapped on the lamp.

June 1, 1997. Commencement Day. *I'm so excited to start speaking truth to power! . . . But I will miss Mike and I hope he understands just what his pen can do. I want to see him today and hug him just once.*

August 27, 1998. *Rick said Mike's about to move to New York. I hope he does well.*

April 10, 1999. *Rick laughs when I ask how Mike's doing. He hates his job. I hope he finds whatever he needs in that finance stuff . . .*

September 11, 2001. *I don't know how to start the peace and healing from all of this . . . Is it selfish of me to hope that Michael's okay? It doesn't matter. I want him to be safe and sound and alive.*

June 15, 2002. *I should reach out to Mike but I'm afraid.*

He flipped ahead a few pages, keeping up with his own chronology.

May 12, 2004. *Legal aid is okay, but I've been thinking that my volunteer fundraising for UC is making a bigger difference for students. I should apply there.*

Someone who could help create a financially strong and independent family . . . He kept reading.

June 2, 2004: *I finally emailed him! I know he's busy. May he respond to me when he can.*

September 1, 2004: *Mike got married. He didn't contact me and I guess I know why. I hope he and his wife are happy.*

December 25, 2004: *I know I should make him write to me, but I won't! I can't!*

July 1, 2005: *He has a daughter now. Guess he doesn't need my good wishes anymore.*

May 15, 2008, a few days before Annemarie's 3rd birthday: *Okay, self, listen up! It's been over 10 years now. It's not going to happen. Stop carrying a torch for Michael Caviness and start carrying one for yourself.*

November 2, 2009: *Barack Obama will be the next president of the United States, and I will be in Washington by the time of his inauguration! If we all use the woo, it will happen!*

A few days ago: *I saw Mike's name on the reunion attendee list: now that's someone I haven't thought of in a while. Wouldn't it be nice if I saw him?*

Two nights ago: *In vino veritas! I will see Michael Caviness during the reunion, and he will really see me, and find the new me attractive, and ask himself, what if!*

He retrieved his own pen from his tuxedo pocket.

I like both Michelles, the free spirit from school and the elegant woman who feels so good against me tonight. Sorry it took me so long to understand.

Criterion: Michael Caviness wants to see where this mystical woo with Michelle Collins is going. He will do everything he can to keep it alive.

He left the journal on the table before climbing back into bed with her.

—

Layers of implications, he thought, as she blew him a kiss on the way to her departure terminal. He controlled his own destiny, sure—but would his happiness always depend on her since she had the other pen? Or was their power their own? Could they really change the world?

He pushed the risk management questions away. Mystical

woo is what you make it, as he'd told her. "I like that," Michelle had said, dimples on display. "Let's start by using it for good, one day at a time."

She had written in his journal—*I want you to be happy too! Return to me soon, and don't forget me this time.*

Staring at the pen, he laughed. He scribbled during the flight home. How Aleja deserved to have Gavin's love, and how Annemarie loved her too. How Annemarie would grow up happy, healthy, strong, and loved. How he would work smarter instead of harder, and love more. How Michelle would enjoy seeing them later this year.

Feeling the sparkling in his stomach as he took a cab into the city, he knew that his mother would love having Annemarie, Michelle, and him in Washington during the holiday.

Victoria E. Hollis (she/her) was born and currently resides in North Carolina. While she has finally figured out how to put her English degree to good use for marketing and fundraising in the performing arts, this is her first published work of fiction—thirty-six years after she first caught the writing bug in kindergarten. She hopes to publish more fantasy, romance, and New Adult works in the future. Victoria also loves classical music, college basketball, and conversation, all things she'd love to share with you on Twitter @vikehollisrites.

Charcoals from an Unidentified Chicago Artist

Dawn Vogel

1871.

The city was aflame.

The sky glowed red and eerie, even at a distance. Sometimes roiling smoke blotted out the glow, but it lurked within the clouds, baleful and destructive.

She sketched the view from her rooftop. But more than that, she imagined the buildings downtown and drew them as they might look gutted by fire.

When the fires burned out and the city cooled enough for people to return, she went to see the destruction, like so many others. Her imagination had served her well. The newspaper men gladly paid for even the sketches.

After the fire, after the city began to rebuild, her drawings took on a certain style. She had worked so long in charcoals, all her work had cross-hatched lines and smudges. But the brand-new cerulean blue oil paint turning to ash on the canvas sealed her decision.

She stopped making art.

1893.

The World Columbian Exposition was magnificent. The buildings were architectural marvels, decorated and lit in the most inventive ways. But it was also underlain with a pervasive frenetic sadness, the last desperate attempt of a city reborn from the ashes to prove itself to the world.

It was what the world wanted of her—the triumphant return of a lost artist, when she wanted to move beyond that life. But the beauty seeped into her soul.

She drew.

No one knew what to make of the wisps of smoke that found their way into her drawings. Some decided they must be artistic clouds, added to give the otherwise featureless background some depth.

But when the cold storage building burned two months later, they wondered, as did she. Was she prescient? Had she been touched by the Great Fire?

After she completed her sketches from the cold storage building fire, she returned home and put her drawing supplies away, tucking the box beneath her bed, into the farthest corner, and filling the space around it with boxes of books and drawings. She'd shut away that part of her life once. Perhaps she should do so again.

1894.

Half a year passed before she began the arduous task of retrieving her tools. Another artist might have gone out and purchased new supplies, on credit if need be, to begin work faster. She could not. Teaching everything except art paid her bills, but little else.

The famed White City was burning, a direct parallel to the Great Fire. That which had risen from those ashes now returned to ash.

Now those people who had wondered about her prescience had more reason to suspect. She was invited to show her artwork from the Expo, along with her newest pieces of the burned-out ruins, at the police precinct. They asked her whereabouts at the time the fire started, even as they marveled over the emotion infused into her drawings, smoke clinging to the lines and making their eyes water as though they bore witness to the flames. The police reviewed her portfolio and knew she was not to blame, only exceptionally talented.

Or, in her mind, exceptionally cursed.

1903.

She had become the artist the papers called when something burned.

This time it was the newly opened Iroquois Theatre. The fire was out before she arrived, but the building still smoldered in the frigid winter air. So too did the bodies stacked around the building—too many to transport away on icy roads with limited vehicles.

She stood away from the building, telling herself it was perspective, as she tried to sketch its original lines. But her gaze returned time and again to the bodies.

She was tired. Fifty-six years old, no family, still teaching for a pittance. In another life, she could have been among the dead—seated in an expensive orchestra level seat, just in front of the stage where the conflagration had started.

She wiped away a tear, smudging charcoal across her face, and looked at what she had drawn. It was the scene inside the theatre, as she had imagined it. Worse than she had imagined, even.

She tucked the sheet into her sketchbook and began a new drawing.

1910.

The city was burning again.

That was how it always felt, when the calls came in.

This time, she could not bring herself to get out of bed. The years of smoke had taken their toll, and she breathed with a rasp even on good days.

Her days as the fire artist were at an end.

1958.

She'd been dead more than forty years, but the city had called her back. Though she was insubstantial, she had her tools.

A school fire this time. And being a ghost, she witnessed it from the beginning.

There was nothing for her to do except draw.

When she finished, she drifted until she found her old art box, filled with stacks of her drawings, tucked beneath her great-nephew's bed. His father had carried it from her apartment when she died, and her great-nephew had kept it with him since. Though her sisters may not have known what to make of her art, at least her extended family saw some value in keeping it.

She lifted the lid and placed her newest sketches atop the others, dating back almost a century.

1971.

"Package, sir," the clerk said.

The smudged and tattered wrapping paper covering the package was spattered with chunks of melted snow and salt. But the box beneath was solid wood, untouched by the elements.

The curator coughed as smoke tickled at his sinuses and throat—not like cigarettes, but something thicker and older, like the world afire.

The handwriting sprawled across the top sheet. "These belonged to my father, though he was not the artist. We hope you can find a home for them at the Art Institute." No signature followed.

The curator shuffled through the pages beneath. Charcoals of a burning building. As he examined them, he identified the name of the building worked into the stone façade—Our Lady of the Angels School. He recalled that fire—it had been all over the news as a great tragedy.

He dug deeper into the pile. Most of the drawings depicted fire or its aftereffects. An old theatre. The White City. The Great Fire, even. The drawings spanned an incredible amount of time. He rubbed his eyes, the smoke permeating the paper making his eyes water.

He lingered over one drawing, blinking to clear his eyes. The World Congress Auxiliary, the building in which he now sat, rendered in precise detail, though evoking loss and destruction.

He peered at the drawing's lower corner, bearing a smudged "T. L.", as though it had been rubbed many times over the years.

He called out to the mail clerk. "Do we know where this came from?"

"Couldn't quite read the return address, sir, though I know it came from within the city."

The curator's mind was already awhirl with thoughts of the exhibit this trove would unlock. He'd have to check all the dates and try to identify "T. L." But the title in his mind would be better than finding the name associated with the artist. *Charcoals from an Unidentified Chicago Artist.*

Dawn Vogel's academic background is in history, so it's not surprising that much of her fiction is set in earlier times. By day, she edits reports for historians and archaeologists. In her alleged spare time, she runs a craft business, co-runs a small press, and tries to find time for writing. Her steampunk adventure series, *Brass and Glass,* is available from DefCon One Publishing. She is a member of Broad Universe, SFWA, and Codex Writers. She lives in Seattle with her husband, author Jeremy Zimmerman, and their herd of cats. Visit her at historythatneverwas.com.

Pointy Chances

Robert Kingett

Just before the bell rang, I dropped my pen. Immediately panicking, I dove under my desk to hunt for the rainbow-colored treasure I had found last year. I was hoping that it would whimper or cry out or something to let me know where it had landed, but the pen seemed to have a mind of its own when expressing any sentient behavior. Even though my blurry vision couldn't distinguish the object near me, I grabbed it and held it up to my face to see if it was, in fact, the special pen. It was. It swirled with the rainbow of colors I loved so much. Sighing with relief, I went to stand up and banged my head on the underside of the desk, causing it to tip over along with my chair. A few other students in the class winced, stopping their clinking braille writers to turn towards my monumental accident.

"Whoa," Jesse said. "Are you always that hard-headed, there, Nick?"

"You are such a riot," I playfully fired back, rubbing my throbbing head. Jesse unfolded his cane and came over to help me up. I could see the deep black of his skin in front of the bright fluorescent lights as his blurry form came into focus. I took his outstretched hand as he pulled me to my feet. Still holding his hand, I caught a glimpse of a flashy grin before he patted me and went back to his seat.

In my shirt pocket, I suddenly heard my special pen groan amidst the whispers of other students.

Oh yeah, I thought, *now you have something to express. How funny.* Shaking my head, still rubbing it, I looked for the familiar blurry outline of my best friend Amanda, who was still sitting in the front of the room, furiously typing on her electronic braille notetaker next to other students unzipping their backpacks. As I walked towards her, and her form became clearer, I noticed that she had changed her hair color yet again. This time, it matched her icy blue eyes.

"How strange," I said, dodging a few tapping canes as some classmates left early.

"What's that, your face?" The pen chuckled in my pocket after her reply. Upon hearing the high-pitched chortle, Amanda giggled, leaned towards my shirt pocket, and started talking to the pen as if it, instead of I, were her best friend.

"It's good to see you didn't lose your sense of humor, Pointy."

"You know I don't like that nickname," I snapped. "And, no, I was referring to your extremely bright blue hair."

"I was very tired of having green hair. Anyway, why didn't you ask Jesse to sit with us at lunch today? You had the perfect opportunity, you know?"

"He wouldn't want to be asked out on a date while in the midst of saving me from a disaster."

"I didn't say 'date.' I said, 'lunch.'" The pen sighed in my pocket. Amanda suddenly sat bolt upright, turned towards me, and stared towards my voice.

"Oh my gosh. You're still afraid of telling him how you feel, aren't you?"

"Quiet!" I hissed as the bell rang and various students around me snapped their canes open, put their large-print or braille books away, and began shuffling out of the classroom, creating a rhythm with their canes.

"Why should I be quiet?" Amanda said, to the backdrop of cell phone screen readers around us. "No one's gonna pay attention to me, anyway. They think I'm weird." I glanced at the black T-shirt she had on. Enlarged white letters spelled out, in print and braille, *I totally see you.*

"Gotcha," I said, nodding absently.

At that moment, a cane briefly thwacked me on the leg. I turned and saw Jesse making his way out of the room. He looked very strong and confident, and extremely cute, with his buzzed hair and eye-catching smile and his huge, warm hands, holding onto his cane with very firm muscles on his arms.

"Oh, goodness, I'm so sorry," he said, smiling.

"Your cane looks nice," I blurted. I could immediately feel my heart beginning to pound and my face growing so hot that the Earth's temperature rose a few degrees.

After giggling, Jesse said, "Well, I'm sure yours looks really nice too, Nick." He smiled again and started to head out but stopped and turned back to us.

"Oh, hey, Amanda. Sorry about that. I'm just in a rush because the school library has some new audiobooks by black authors I want to check out. I didn't want you to think I was ignoring you." The pen sighed in my pocket. Jesse laughed, probably thinking the pen was Amanda.

"Oh, no worries, dear. I was admiring my non-perfect cane."

As Jesse laughed, turning towards the doorway leading to

the hallway, I took a deep breath and cleared my throat. "Bye," I called. Despite my throat clearing, my voice cracked.

As soon as he was gone and we were left alone in the classroom, Amanda walloped me, hard, with her cane pouch after I sat the pen on the table before us.

"You seriously are afraid of him, like he's a mad scientist or something. Why?"

"I'm not afraid of him. I'm afraid of my own feelings . . . like, what if he's not gay?"

"That's why," she said with an emphasized thump of her cane pouch against my arm, "you use Pointy to express how you feel. Let them do the writing."

I sighed and put the pen back in my pocket, where it cooed happily. I distinctly heard canes thwacking against walls and lockers slamming shut.

"You could charm Jesse with your personality," Amanda said. "You really could. I mean, it's not like he can see your brown hair and green eyes, after all."

"Yeah, yeah," I replied, leaning on an empty chair. The trouble was, I didn't feel great, or smart, or inspirational, or witty. I felt ordinary. I didn't understand what the pen saw in me that made me worthy of Jesse. The pen had told me before that we both were very caring people. That time Jesse had signed his name in my yearbook last year, our junior year, the pen had been able to glimpse his true character. But what if it was wrong about me? I was sure the pen wasn't wrong about Jesse, because in my eyes, Jesse had a heart of gold. He'd often give hungry kids lunch money because the school district didn't believe in free lunches. Jesse, like me, believed that was a huge issue in the system, but still, he wanted to ease their pain. He never asked for anything back.

"Look," Amanda said, "Pointy said before, they would be willing to help. And, they are a pretty good pen, it seems, I mean, morally speaking, so, why not use Pointy? Pointy wants to help, so let Pointy help."

"But Jesse doesn't want me," I said. The pen began to whimper in my pocket, but I plowed on.

"I'm serious."

"I don't think so. I think you're wrong." Amanda said. "Catch him at the library before you go to the dorm today. Talk to him. Ask him to eat lunch with you on Mystery Meat Friday, during lunch period," she giggled. The pen giggled too. I sighed and stood up. I walked over to my now-upright desk, retrieved my cane, and popped it open. Feeling dread, I made my way to our school library.

My heart continued to pound as I entered the library and began making my way to the braille books. Jesse was a bit old-school in the sense that, even though he loved downloading braille books online and reading them on his refreshable braille display, he said it was still epic to hold a book in his hands.

The longer I searched for his blurry familiar form, the louder my heart seemed to pound. I mean, what would I do if I actually ran into him, what would I say if I actually— Suddenly, I yelped and leaped back. I realized that I had just crashed into Jesse.

Whipping around, he caught me as I tripped on a chair while backing away from him. Holding onto his vice-like grip, I gasped for air as he looked at me worriedly. Seeing the concerned look on his face made my stomach do a somersault. Oh, wow was he handsome . . . and caring, and he was holding me . . .

"Nick?"

"I was thinking about you and wasn't looking where I was going," I babbled. The pen chuckled in my pocket. Jesse was still close enough for me to see a grin dance across his lips and light up his eyes.

"What a coincidence; I never look where I'm going," he said with that broad grin still touching his eyes. "But, um, you said you were thinking about me?"

"Well," I murmured. "I mean, I was thinking about recommending you a book. You know, because, well, you read books . . . and I read books, too, but anyway, there's a black book—I mean a black writer you should definitely check out because he writes LGBT literature featuring . . . " I trailed off, staring at his face. I began to hear my breathing increase in volume. My heart was pounding even harder, and my breathing soon became very rapid.

"LGBT?" he asked, curiously.

"Yeah," I choked. His forehead furrowed, but then he gave me a small smile before hugging me.

"Whoa Nick, your heart is beating so fast. Are you okay? Here, let's sit." He took my now-sweaty palm and sat down at a back table still near the braille section. He still held onto my hand as we sat down. He then took my hand in his huge, warm hands and gripped it tightly.

"Let's take a minute and breathe. Okay? Let's calm down." He calmly inhaled then exhaled a few times before I realized I was supposed to copy him.

When I calmed down, he went back to the shelf and retrieved the braille book he was looking at before.

"This book is an LGBT fantasy by a black writer. I think you'd like it. Mind if I read to you? Actually, wait, I have an idea." He took out his braille display and went to go get some print paper for me. When he returned, he smiled after setting the paper down before me.

"Let's have some fun," he said, eagerness in his voice. "Let's make a TBR list for each other. We both like to read, so wouldn't it be great if we could get to know one another through our book lists?" He paused before continuing, "Oh, and don't worry about the print. I'll have someone read it to me." The pen squeaked excitedly in my pocket. Jesse smiled and then suddenly chuckled.

"I always knew you were cute."

"Cute?" I repeated, like I didn't understand words. He smiled and began typing on his braille notetaker. His looked to be a newer model than Amanda's, so I wondered if he wasn't secretly looking me up online or something. I took the pen out of my pocket and set it on the print paper. I first made my book list, which transformed into braille. Beneath the book list, I placed the pen on a free spot. Before writing, though, I bent down and whispered to it, "Help me."

The pen gave an excited sigh and began composing. I watched my arm move across the page with a flourish. I, unfortunately, couldn't tell what the pen was creating because the words were turning into braille faster than I could read.

After a few minutes, Jesse got up and went to a wireless printer nearby. He handed me a large-print typed sheet.

"I hope the font size is good enough," he said. "I just coded a conversion program into this thing, so I hope my coding skills are good."

"I'm amazed," I gasped, feeling extremely impressed and touched. I set his book list aside and looked at my book list I was giving to Jesse, filled with perfectly spaced tactile dots. I cleared my throat, adjusted myself in my chair, and picked up the paper, handing it to Jesse.

Upon taking the paper and feeling the braille dots, Jesse's eyes bulged. "Wow! This is a really pleasant . . . " he trailed off, his fingers carefully going over every contraction, every letter. He didn't move. He sat there, still as a statue, but with a look of pure shock on his face. When he was done, I looked over to see a tear rolling down his cheek.

He read the paper again, this time letting the tears flow more freely. When he was all done, he gaped at me.

"You . . . you . . . are so sweet. I love your book list, and I love your note. I really do."

I took the paper back from him. The dots were transforming into bold, print, block letters again. Before I read it, though, I turned to Jesse.

"Look. I have something I want to confess. I've had a crush on you for a while now. I've liked you ever since we did that English project together back in freshman year. The one where we had to argue for banning problematic classic literature in schools? You were so poised and so ready. I felt like you were better than me in every way. I thought, also, that you were extremely nice and someone that was worth getting to know. I guess what I'm trying to say is, you make me want to be who I know I am. You're an inspiration to me, but that's because I feel so average and ordinary, that I just looked up to you a lot. But I've realized that I do have a lot to offer someone. I've got a few quirks about me, but I'm a pretty okay person. And, I feel extremely comfortable being myself around you. You're the first person I ever wanted to improve alongside. You know?"

He didn't say anything for a while. He just sat there, staring at where my voice was coming from. Finally, he said, "I've always thought you were really smart. I also always thought you were really cute. And, again, I love your book list. I'm glad you opened up to me. I really am. It would definitely be an honor to be your friend . . . " He gave a small laugh as he added, "and possibly more. We can share book lists together, even if we break up."

I laughed along with him. My heart ballooned into extreme admiration and peace. I let out a huge sigh then turned to Jesse.

"Can I eat lunch with you tomorrow? I'll start checking these books out today and let you know which ones I cried over because the endings were so sweet."

"Of course. I'm going to go check out these books, but I'm really honored you opened up to me. Thank you, Nick. You're very strong." As he stood up to leave and unfolded his cane, he gave me a small hug before departing. I picked up the paper, the one Pointy had written on, and read the note below my book list.

Hi, Jesse. As you know, I'm Nick. After you read my book list, I have something I want to tell you. But I don't want to tell you through writing. I want to tell you with my own words. But just know that, even though what I want to say is very scary, just know that it's all good things about you. I've always been too afraid to approach you, until now. I really, really, like you. I even love you as a friend, and possibly more. But I've always been afraid to speak up for myself, until today. I know this is nerve-racking for you, but I swear, you won't be disappointed in what I have to say. The reason I'm telling you this in person now is because you've given me hope and courage. Here I go, but whatever happens, I just want you to know that I will always love you. Even if we detest each other's books.

Robert Kingett (he/him) really loves fiction podcasts. His favorite fiction podcast series to date is *20 Sided Stories*' Pokémon season. When he was in the third grade, he tried to start an advocacy campaign to give all senior citizens stuffed Wishbone dogs to try to better their lives. As an adult, he enjoys trying fun desserts, such as fried ice cream. He has absolutely no idea how to talk to charming bookish boys on the bus. He loves introducing friends to live lit events when they're not working. His website is blindjournalist.wordpress.com

Old News

Gustavo Bondoni

"It just isn't fair," Sofía said.

"What isn't?" her grandmother replied absently from the kitchen. She took care of her every other Saturday, while her parents worked.

"The people on the news, they want their land back."

The sounds of cooking stopped and footsteps approached. Her grandmother glanced at the television. A noontime news program was on, transmitting live from Patagonia. "Many things in life aren't fair. If they get their land back, what will happen to the people who live there now? A lot of people live on that land today. Rich people, poor people, some of them have nowhere else to go."

Sofía thought about that. Grandma was always right, but something still felt wrong. "I just wish there was some way I could help."

"There are many people who could use some help, Sofi."

"I would help them all, if I could, Abu."

Her grandmother looked down at her, eyes bright, but she said nothing.

—

On Sofía's 12th birthday, her grandmother pulled her aside, out of sight of her parents.

"What's up, Abu?" Sofía asked. She was pert and pretty in her brand-new yellow dress, and her mother had allowed her to dye the ends of her hair green.

Her grandmother looked at her sternly.

"If you had the power to change the world magically, what would you do?"

Sofía hesitated. There were so many things. But something she'd seen that morning on an Instagram post jumped out at her. "I would feed those little kids. You know, the ones in the camp in Italy. They can't go back home because of the war."

Her grandmother nodded curtly, once, and then her habitual smile returned.

—

The following Saturday, Abu sat her down and placed a piece of paper in front of her.

"Read it."

Abu's writing was nearly impossible for Sofi to decipher but she made the effort: "I, Sofía Viviani, will only use my magic to help those who truly need it." It was puzzling. "What is this? What magic?"

"It's a promise. You have to sign it." Abu held out an old fountain pen, old and made of metal, not the cheap plastic used by school children. "You have to sign it with this."

"Why?"

"Because if you sign it with this, it will become real. The pen is magical. What you write with it happens in real life."

Sofía studied the older woman's face, but there was no trace of humor in her expression, so she thought about it long and hard. "Give me the pen."

Abu watched her put down her name and then shook her head when Sofi tried to hand the pen back. "No. It's yours now. Be wise."

—

Sofía didn't help children in Italy. Not at first, anyway. She got distracted by the protestors on the news again. Tehuelche people were out on the streets of Bariloche, Argentina's most important mountain resort town.

It was, the news reported, the largest concentration of Tehuelche people in the century and a half. She was shocked to see how few of them there were, perhaps two hundred, all told.

"It's not right," she said.

—

It took her nearly two weeks to decide to take the pen to school, and when she did, she felt ridiculous for having brought it along. She suspected it was gold, and if she lost it she would be in real trouble. And, now that she thought of it, the mere idea of a magic pen felt incredibly silly.

So the day wore on and the pen remained in her bag. At 4:03 PM, just two minutes before the bell dismissed them for the day, she pulled it out and rushed a quick sentence: *Palermo Day School's seventh graders will be on a field trip to the Museo Sarmiento tomorrow (Friday).* Then she hid the sheet beneath her desk, hoping no one had seen her. When the bell rang, she forgot all about it.

—

Until the next day. The teachers formed them up and led them into buses. Their destination? The Museo Sarmiento, where the Tratado Chegüelcho, the first treaty between the Patagonian tribes and European settlers, was on permanent display.

Too shocked to believe it wasn't all a coincidence, Sofía still hedged her bets. She wrote: *The treaty will not be under glass, and I'll be able to write on it without anyone seeing me.*

To her shock, this, too, worked.

It wasn't easy. Bringing herself to deface a document of priceless historic significance was nearly impossible.

But she needed the wording. She needed the names. She couldn't build something like this herself: her attempts to do good would wreak havoc. She knew enough to know that.

The problem was that was pretty much all she knew. What would happen to the people there now? What were the native people even claiming? She was woefully uninformed.

Sofía stood before the document, smelling the ancient paper and trying to read the script. One line jumped out at her: it spoke of land to the south of a river.

Not knowing what else to do, feeling the clock ticking, scared of being discovered, nearly crying in frustration, she reached out a trembling hand and scratched out the line after that one, replacing it with: *everyone involved will use the land as much as they truly need, and not more than that.*

Then she ran away.

—

Sofía brooded on the bus ride back from the museum, ignoring her friends. Had she changed anything, or would the museum discover the vandalism and come after her?

The afternoon passed in abject terror, fear of being called to the principal's office, expelled. Could they send a twelve-year-old to jail?

What had she been thinking?

The final recess of the afternoon found her hiding in the library, the one place where they would never look for her.

As the fifteen eternal minutes dragged, her eyes fell on the large map of South America on the wall. Strangeness penetrated the fog of her terror and she focused on it.

The familiar triangle that was Argentina was absent, replaced by three different-colored polygons. The northernmost was labelled Argentina and directly to the south was a green area, simply named the Eternal Peace Nature Reserve.

She was trying to make out the name of the southernmost portion when the bell rang.

—

"Abu," she said the next day. "I have a question."

"What is it?"

"Why give the pen to me? Why don't you help people yourself?"

"Ah, so you believe in it, now?"

"I think so."

Abu thought before speaking. "Each person has to use the pen in the way that suits them most. I was young, but unlike you, I could only see what was right in front of me. Well, maybe that's normal: it was a time of suffering I could see first-hand, and I didn't have the same sources of information you do. I helped our family. Not economically, but I made sure we led long, fulfilling lives … even if we're poor. When I realized that the world had bigger problems, it was too late for me to channel the magic differently. Believe me, I tried."

"I think I did something, but I'm not sure what."

"It works that way, sometimes. What happened?"

"The Nature Reserve. Eternal Peace. I think I had something to do with that."

"Sofi, the Reserve has been there for a century and a half. It's one of the greatest things ever done during the colonial era, a sudden attack of humanity in a brutal time. It's still used as an example of how things might be done when wise heads prevail." She shook her head. "I don't think you could have done much there."

"And the country to the south of that?"

"Jerun? What about it?"

"Is that where the Tehuelche live now?"

Her grandmother looked confused. "Many people live there; our best friends, our greatest allies. Since the treaty, we've worked together to maintain the Reserve. Everyone has benefitted. You'll learn all about it in high school. It must have been a great man who decided to add those critical words. Too bad historians can't agree on who it was."

"Oh." Sofía suddenly understood how it worked, the price she would pay. Loneliness would be her lot. "I hope I can do good things like that. Using the pen, I mean."

"Yes. That's a good guide." Her grandmother stroked her hair. "I knew you'd understand. That's why I chose you."

Sofía shivered. She understood more than her grandmother—or anyone else—would ever know.

Gustavo Bondoni (he/him) is an Argentine writer with over two hundred stories published in fourteen countries, in seven languages. His latest book is *Ice Station: Death* (2019). He has also published three science fiction novels: *Incursion* (2017), *Outside* (2017), and *Siege* (2016) and an ebook novella entitled *Branch*. His short fiction is collected in *Off the Beaten Path* (2019), *Tenth Orbit and Other Faraway Places* (2010), and *Virtuoso and Other Stories* (2011). His website is at gustavobondoni.com

Illumination

Joy Givens

Strasbourg, 1440

Summer wind, rippling across the moonlit grass, teased the two veils. Armored only with the prayerful girdle books at their waists and the penknives in their pockets, Sister Aurelia and Sister Ennelin crept away from the abbey.

The wind seemed to breathe on them, an affectionate inquiry: *Daughters, what adventure draws you from your cells tonight?*

Aurelia, a postulant with eyes as bright as fresh pots of ink, led the way. "Keeping this secret from you has been pure torment," she whispered. "My heart overflows to share it." She brandished her penknife at the darkness. "When you see what this man has wrought, your eyes shall think themselves bewitched."

"I should hope not." Ennelin gripped her silver crucifix as she followed. Only a few years older than Aurelia, but nearly ready to profess her vows, she was weary from the day's work and wary of trouble. And stealing away from the abbey was *more* than trouble. Only her dearest companion could draw her out like this. "Child, you said this was of greatest importance—such importance that it merits secrecy even from the abbess."

"Oh, yes." Aurelia pressed her ink-stained fingertips together. "Please forgive my cryptic words, sister."

Ennelin nodded, but her own forgiveness was of little consequence. If they were caught roaming Strasbourg after dark . . . even their exceptional talents with quills would not save them from disgrace.

She followed Aurelia's gaze toward the still river. The moon upon the glassy water would afford them enough light to walk safely. "How did you happen upon this discovery?"

"Well . . . I had heard a rumor of a new invention, and after witnessing an administration of last rites at the south end of the city . . . I allowed my feet to wander on the return to the abbey."

Ennelin smote one hand against her forehead. "Good heavens."

"*But* in my wandering," Aurelia rushed to add, "I caught a glimpse through the window of his workshop. And I saw—"

"Whose workshop?"

Aurelia trod along the riverbank, avoiding the mud. "Johannes of Mainz."

Ennelin gasped. "The *goldsmith*?" she whispered fiercely. "Not he who fashioned those pilgrimage mirrors and claimed they could capture holy light? That charlatan?"

Aurelia nodded. "The same. Though—forgive my dissent, sister—I believe he was merely the metalworker, not the merchant of that scheme."

Ennelin glared into the darkness. "And what has he to show for his labors this night—reliquaries that make gold mysteriously vanish?" Shaking her head, she turned back. "This is a fool's errand."

"No, it isn't!" Aurelia laid a hand on Ennelin's arm. "It is not foolishness, I promise. I nearly ruined two pages of calligraphy in my distraction, and I could hardly hold still through vespers tonight. If I cannot share with you the excitement that burns in my heart, I fear—oh, I fear I shall burst into flames!"

Ennelin sighed, but a faint smile softened her mouth. "Flames, child?"

Together, they moved as softly and silently as clouds along the banks of the River Ill. The workshop of the goldsmith lay not far from the abbey. Ennelin clasped Aurelia's ink-stained hand in hers, aching from hours spent illuminating letters and illustrations in the leaves of a new Bible. Still, they walked with the bold energy of believers embarking upon a pilgrimage.

The smoke of extinguished fires, the detritus of work animals, and the blooms of oleanders all added their scents to the night wind. Even in the warmth, Ennelin took a deep breath and shivered.

Their destination, a small shop of sturdy frame and thatched roof, lay on the eastern outskirts of the city. Despite the late hour, lantern light spilled through the glass window of the goldsmith's workshop onto the dry ground. Every other building in the borough was as dark and silent as a gravestone.

"Look inside," Aurelia whispered, drawing Ennelin alongside her beneath the window.

Ennelin made the sign of the cross upon herself. "Mercy . . . " She rose up on her toes and peered over the sill.

In the flickering light, Johannes of Mainz laid a small piece of paper across a frame on his workbench. He pushed a rod back and forth over it. By his side lay several mysterious metal tools. His brow furrowed as he set down the rod and stroked his long beard. Then, slowly, deliberately, he peeled back the paper from the base beneath it.

Johannes crowed with the pride of a rooster at sunrise. A

small cry slipped from Ennelin's mouth, and her hands flew to her heart.

Black lettering, sharp and clear, now shouted against the cream of the paper. That multitude of skillful, even characters would take precious time with a quill. This man had produced it in moments.

What sorcery is this?

With another victorious shout, Johannes kissed the paper, dappling his beard with black ink. Ennelin touched her own lips, still specked with lapis lazuli from licking the tip of her paintbrush to a point. "How can this be possible?"

"It is just as before," Aurelia whispered. "He has laid all the lettering in reverse. When he coats the frame in ink and presses the paper across it . . . "

"A facsimile." Ennelin began to shake. She gripped Aurelia's hand as if it kept her tethered to the earth.

On the other side of the glass, Johannes laid the paper on the oilcloth-covered floor and placed another piece upon the frame. After repeating the miracle before their unblinking eyes, he set the paper to dry beside the first.

Ennelin dropped back onto her heels and sagged against the wall. What had this man done? What great, fearsome power had he unlocked? And from whence had it come?

"Merely think," Aurelia murmured, her eyes glowing. "Think of how quickly words may be printed this way. Does it not burst your heart with joy? Pages multiplying upon pages, like Jesus multiplying fishes and loaves for the five thousand! Mills shall hardly be able to supply quires of paper fast enough."

Ennelin pressed her hand to her stomach. Nausea rocked through her. The thought of this goldsmith and his compatriots reproducing pages with unnatural speed, selling indecent materials, pamphlets, perhaps even entire books . . .

"Hearken," Aurelia gasped. "He is coming out!"

The sisters staggered around the far side of the workshop and held their breaths. Had they been sighted?

The door banged open, then shut. "Not even a drop left in the shop to celebrate," Johannes of Mainz muttered. "Preposterous."

Coins jingling in his purse, he strode away without a second glance. He cut between the other buildings like a cat in a churchyard, and his footsteps soon faded.

Ennelin exhaled slowly. Her stomach churned.

Aurelia leaned against her with a faint groan. "Forgive me. I should have prepared you more fully. The awe is nearly unbearable even now. Oh, just *one* glance more before we return."

She pulled Ennelin back to the window and gazed into the shop. The fire crackled low in the hearth, and a lantern still burned upon the workbench. "To think of what this invention will mean! How it will change . . . everything."

The night wind puffed up their habits like the sails of ships on a rough sea. A sudden gust blew around the corner of the workshop with a *bang* that snatched at Ennelin's heart.

Aurelia yelped. "The door! Oh, *no* . . . "

The wind rushed through the flung-open doorway, into the shop, and rustled the papers on the workbench. One whirled into the air and landed atop the lantern. A curl of smoke.

"Quickly!" Aurelia tore around the corner and into the workshop.

Ennelin's spinning mind stopped on the open door. Providence had lit a path for them. She hurried after Aurelia into the shop without a word.

Aurelia snatched the singeing paper off the lantern just before it could catch flame. Aside from harsh scorching, the paper was unmarked.

"To think how easily it could have been . . ." She dropped to her knees and made the sign of the cross upon herself. "*Laus Deo.*"

How easily. Ennelin looked around the shop. Lampblack, sweat, and burning wood perfumed the air. Each inked paper on the floor chorused the same phrase:

AVENTUR UND KUNST

Enterprise and art.

Aurelia took several deep breaths and clambered to her feet. Her fingers hovered over the glistening frame. "He has shaped each character out of metal, then laid them out in reverse order to form his words. 'Enterprise and art.' It is . . . oh, it is brilliant."

"It is *dark* magic." Ennelin's lip curled. "Child, do you not see that this is a vehicle for sin? It must be stopped."

Aurelia flinched as if Ennelin had struck her. "Stopped? What do you mean?"

"Think of what this machinery will produce—what it will propagate. The Holy Word, like the texts we faithfully copy and illustrate?" Ennelin shook her head. "This goldsmith will produce whatever will reward him most handsomely. Words of the fallen world. *Enterprise* and art. Prideful, aberrant missives that will breed and spread like plague."

"But, sister—"

"Do you not see it?" Ennelin's voice sharpened. "This invention is the most deceptive work of the devil. Who will devote their hours to the Word when every tawdry comedy and bit of gossip can be recreated in this way? These devices will deaden the Church." She pointed to the door. "Providence has brought us here this night and opened this door to us. If we act swiftly, you and I can yet save Christendom from this unholy contraption."

"What?" Aurelia's voice shook. "Sister . . . "

Ennelin picked up the singed paper. "He departed so carelessly that he left his hearth and a lit lantern unattended, with the door hardly latched. If we had not been here, this paper would have surely caught his workbench on fire."

The paper trembled in her hand as she held it beside the lantern. If the workbench caught flame, the oilcloth upon the floor would also. The walls and framing would catch, and the thatched roof would burn faster than tow. Such an inferno would surely melt the lettering. The goldsmith's work would be gone.

"But we *were* here," Aurelia quavered.

Ennelin set her jaw. "Perhaps to bear witness, nothing more."

"*Ennelin*. You propose destroying this man's work. His invention. His space."

"The God of Israel destroyed Korah and his rebellion with fire."

"But He spared the three thrown into Babylon's furnace," Aurelia countered. Her spine stiffened. "What if we were led here not to bear witness to destruction but to intervene and stop it? And who are you or I to judge the virtue of this creation?"

"The light of admiration blinds you!" Ennelin exploded. "This man's invention will steal the power of the scripted word. We are scribes because we respect this art as sacred, a duty to transmit the divine to the world." She stamped her foot upon the oilcloth. "Johannes zum Gutenberg does not respect our art, nor our heavenly commission. If we allow his invention to propagate, words will be bought and sold. *Truth* will be bought and sold."

In the dim light, the sisters glared at each other, Aurelia's hands hovering in guard above the frame, Ennelin's hesitating beside the lantern.

The embers upon the hearth crackled.

"Sister," Aurelia finally spoke, her voice quiet and slow. "What if this invention is itself a heavenly commission?"

Ennelin's face twisted. "Oh—"

"No, truly. What if it is not magic, but the hand of God? What if 'enterprise' means not worldly fortune but boldness of faith? What if this device has a capacity beyond what we can envision, an ability to disseminate the Scriptures more widely than we could ever hope to do with our quills and brushes?"

Ennelin's fingers tightened against the paper. Tears spilled from her eyes. "Then what if it blights the holy texts we create with our own hands? What if our lives' devotions are of no consequence? What if—" She gulped. "What if the holiness I seek to illustrate, with every fiber of skill and love I possess, is discarded upon a rubbish heap and burned to ashes? What, then?"

Aurelia sank to her knees beside the bench and laid her hand upon Ennelin's. Her voice was low. "Is not the pain you fear precisely what you would inflict upon this man?"

"I do not know," Ennelin choked out. "And I do not wish to cause anguish. But when I look upon that frame, the fear—it . . ."

Releasing the paper, Ennelin sagged to the floor. Shame blazed on her cheeks. "I suppose it matters not if these devices are destroyed," she muttered. "The idea will remain. We cannot put out the flame that he has lit . . . but think how it will spread." A sob burst from her. "What if it consumes us?"

Aurelia embraced her. They sat quietly together, shoulders shaking as the hearth's coals hissed lower.

The night wind whistled against the window.

Aurelia let out a long sigh. "Ennelin," she whispered, "we cannot prevent destruction by destroying. We cannot walk by fear, only through it."

Ennelin nodded against Aurelia's shoulder. "I know you speak true. I know we are called to walk by faith." With a shuddering breath, she sat up straighter. "Faith that our work matters. That this invention is not borne of—of sheer arrogance." She grimaced. "That whatever it ignites will not engulf us."

A small smile lit Aurelia's face. "Faith that we can walk through fire?"

Ennelin wiped the tears from her cheeks. "Bless you, sister."

She looked down at the papers laid on the oilcloth. She traced the air above the printed words as if each were a labyrinth. Finally, she found her crucifix with one hand, grasped Aurelia's shoulder with the other, and closed her eyes.

"Agnus Dei, Qui tollis peccata mundi, miserere nobis." The prayer, as familiar as breathing, tumbled off her tongue. *Lamb of God, You who take away the sin of the world, have mercy on us.*

"And," she added, "let us continue to serve Thee, in . . . in boldness of faith and art. Amen."

"Amen," echoed Aurelia.

The sisters rose from the floor. Ennelin retrieved the singed paper and carefully burned it on the hearth. They slipped out of the workshop, leaving not so much as another leaf of paper disturbed. With the door securely latched, they interlaced their arms and walked through the darkened borough.

The night wind breathed upon their veils, a gentle commandment: *Walk boldly, daughters.* The patient light of the moon illuminated their pathway home.

Author's Note: I am immensely grateful to Sara Ross of Kent State University for her support and invaluable guidance on the historical aspects of "Illumination," as well as her decades of friendship. Sara, you're a princess and a scholar.

Joy Givens (she/her) is an educating, caffeinating writer of stories and the lucky mother of two tiny superheroes. By day, she runs a tutoring company, volunteers with her church and several other organizations, dreams up new recipes for her hungry loved ones, and occasionally conquers Laundry Mountain. By night, she pens "fresh, fierce, fantastic" fairy tales and other fiction for children and young adults . . . and occasionally stays up too late laughing with her dear husband. By morning, she's usually quite tired but excited to do it all again. joygivens.com

A Blank Canvas

Ethan Hedman

"Okay, Hap, it's showtime." Ameivia cracked her knuckles and took a deep breath, retrieving her lucky stylus from its usual place in her jacket pocket. She clicked its activation switch and it sprang to life with a bright blue glow and a gentle hum. "We came all this way. Let's see what we're working with."

The lights in the holobay dimmed as a rough representation of the surface far below loaded into the center of the room. Ameivia walked around it, peering at the pockmarked landscape. She gazed at the tiny newfound moon as a whole before sending it into a slow spin with a gentle flick of her wrist. "There's potential," she muttered, tapping her stylus here and there, each small poke marking another tiny dot on the transparent globe. "Do we have a resource scan yet?"

"*Affirmative,*" came a quiet response from between her fingers. A handful of pings danced across the lifeless moon as the holographic array program, the onboard AI tied into the stylus which Ameivia had affectionately rechristened as 'Hap,' began interpreting the scan data. There were some common ore deposits found beneath the surface of the natural satellite, but nothing that would be particularly useful.

Most formers hoped to unearth rare materials from simple mining worlds to attract more funding towards their future projects. She'd done exactly the same on all of her previous expeditions, cajoling the Terraforming Institute's interest with detailed cost-benefit analyses of resource-rich terrain, but had grown tired of the corporatization of her work and longed for something different. She didn't want her latest world to be built around optimized extraction, to be nothing more than a pleasant-enough work colony. She wanted to make something beautiful on a truly blank canvas, a canvas which wouldn't be judged for its usefulness or production, and her canvas was finally in sight.

"Here we go," she said, closing her eyes as she swept her stylus across the map with a sweeping flourish. Ameivia imagined the intersection of earth and water in her mind and let them fuel each movement, her every stroke planning a future cut in the landscape to create shorelines and basins. She only opened her eyes after the first burst of adrenaline was finally out of her system. Eventually she began carving gentle, rolling hills from the edges of the moon's jagged craters, layering thick swaths of color over the top of each one to plan the types of grass which would soon grow below.

Ameivia spent her days almost entirely in the holobay, stylus in hand, humming and swishing with each and every movement as she poured her energy into forming what she hoped could soon be her home. Even when she wasn't poking and prodding at the map itself, she used her trusty stylus to scroll through thousands of palettes, noting comfortable color combinations in the sorts of dirt, soil, and foliage which would complement the soft lavender tone she'd chosen for the sky and sea.

Finally, after poring over every detail of the little world-to-be, from its rivers and valleys to its peaks and caverns, Ameivia made her way back to the cockpit. It was the one part of her vessel which had been largely ignored during the long process of creation. She nestled into her timeworn chair with a warm cup of hot chocolate in hand, taking a sip as she stared out at the nearby moon in its natural state for the last time.

"Okay," she whispered as she set her mug aside. "I've done everything I can." She retrieved her stylus from her pocket and slid it into its holster on the ship's control console. "It's your turn, Hap."

Dozens of tiny dashboard indicators began to flicker as the ship received the plans from the stylus, launching its small fleet of terraforming drones to begin the long process of creating a livable world. Ameivia watched as they soared out towards the moon, barely able to see the beams of bright energy from the first bursts of laserwork on the surface.

She took another sip of hot chocolate and closed her eyes, picturing the world she had poured so much love and attention into, feeling it starting to form just outside the confines of her ship. "We did good," she said, reaching out to touch the stylus. "And now, we wait."

Ethan Hedman (he/him) is a speculative fiction writer from South Florida, the land of heat, humidity, and hurricanes. His work has been included in a variety of publications, including *Gunsmoke & Dragonfire, Unrealpolitik,* and *The Hamthology*. Ethan's full bibliography can be found on EthanHedman.com, his little corner of the internet.

One Story, Two People

Nicole J. LeBoeuf

Rachel is ten years old when the fountain pen wakes her up in the middle of the night. It's always had an irritatingly scratchy stroke. By the glow of her old Winnie-the-Pooh nightlight (which no one but Erin is allowed to know she still has), she watches the pen scrawl its noisy way across the big sheet of butcher paper covering her desk for precisely these occasions. She does not, N-O-T *not,* go over to read what it's writing. If she's told Erin once, she's told her a thousand times: No late-night scripts when they've got an important test the next day.

Next morning, Rachel cuts the message out and brings it to school. Five minutes before first bell, she shoves it in Erin's face. "What does this even *mean*?"

"Hello to you too," Erin replies coolly. She reads the message: 'What time is it when you are now?' Huh. Dunno. Wasn't me."

"Well, who in the world *else* could it be? You loaned your pen to someone without telling me? Or you think there's a third one out there?"

"I don't know, not on your life, and maybe?" Erin thinks a moment, then brightens. "Maybe it *was* me. Future Me! Trying to figure out which Past You she's got ahold of. You should answer her. I mean me."

"Get real."

"The realest! It's like I keep telling you: the pens work via some kind of quantum entanglement nonsense. Ergo time travel.

Cue ee dee." Erin studies the paper more closely. "Future Me has nice handwriting, though. Can I borrow this? I want to practice."

Rachel had become fascinated with fountain pens the summer before fifth grade. She was delighted when, as the final stop on their annual back-to-school shopping expedition, Mom took her to the fancy stationery store on the west end of downtown. Rachel could choose any pen she liked, Mom said, so long as it was reasonably priced. Thankfully, the one Rachel fell in love with cost just this side of what Mom considered reasonable. It was big and chunky, what Fountain Pens Online called "cigar-shaped," in a deep midnight blue spangled with stars. Rachel wanted to fill it with indigo ink and write poems about space with it.

The elderly lady running the register that day pulled out a bottle of ink (black, oh well) and a scratch pad so Rachel could try the pen out. Then she reached into a drawer and pulled out another pen, identical in design but bearing obvious signs of wear and tear. "Special offer," she said. "Buy one, get one free."

Rachel blinked. "Really?" The lady nodded, smiling. "Oh, wow, that would be *awesome*!"

"Then you'd have a spare," Mom said, "just in case you lost one."

"Mom! There is *no way* I'm going to lose something this cool."

"Of course not, honey. Maybe you can give one to your little friend at school."

"Her *name* is Erin." Rachel rolled her eyes, then grinned. "And I bet she'll love it. Thanks, Mom."

The lady behind the counter had been observing this

mother-daughter interaction benignly. "And thank you for giving it a good home," she said. "I couldn't sell it on its own, given its, shall we say, less than pristine condition. But I know for a fact that its previous owner treated it very well."

Home again, Rachel wasted no time filling both pens' converters from the bottle of "Bleu des Profondeurs" ink Mom had let her pick out. "Deep blue," the lady behind the counter had translated. "Like the night sky between the stars." Rachel took out a spiral notebook and began to write down that very sentence.

She'd only got three words in when the second pen stood itself upright and also began to write, echoing every line and scribble she'd just scrawled. Rachel stared as it worked its way from the capital L through the final T in "night" then lay gently back down next to the three words it had written on the desk's polished maple finish.

"Oh, crap," muttered Rachel. She rushed to the bathroom for something to clean up with.

She'd intended the pens to be a surprise for Erin when they saw each other on the first day of school. Erin could have the brand-new one, and Rachel would keep its second-hand twin. But after this development, the news couldn't wait. She gave Erin a call.

"So you're saying these are, like, cell phones, except they're pens? Huh. How does it work?"

"How else? Magic."

Erin made a game show buzzer noise: *Ennh!* "Wrong answer! Try again—with science!"

"Oh, you want science? When school starts on Tuesday, we are going to do *all* the science with these pens."

And they did. Just as Rachel had hoped, Erin was scientist enough not only to believe what was happening in front of her eyes, but also to devise multiple experiments. "Like, how far away from each other can they be for it to work? What if you're holding the pen too tight when it receives a message, or it's got its cap on? Does there have to be ink in them for it to work?" Rachel, quickly growing bored with Erin's methodical testing at recess, suggested that they just start using the pens and see.

In the weeks that followed, they passed notes to each other in class and between classrooms. They gossiped late at night across the distance between their houses. Sometimes they even did their homework together. When Erin's family went to Florida for the holiday break, Rachel didn't have to wait for Erin's post-card to arrive—she already knew what it said. Erin was the one who started calling it *scripting,* "like texting, only in handwriting instead of on a phone." They never found a distance too great for the pens to cross, and if one was unable to write the message at the moment it was sent, it wrote it as soon as its keeper took it out to write with.

But Rachel never got Erin to admit it was magic. "It's got to do with quantum entanglement," Erin said. "They've done experiments with subatomic particles. This is like that, only bigger." She sent Rachel links to articles full of phrases like *relative simultaneity* and *spatiotemporal nonlocality,* which Rachel ignored. As far as she was concerned, magic was magic, and you don't look a gift unicorn in the mouth.

The mystery message arrives in early March of their fifth-grade year. Rachel can't get it off her mind. One night soon after, she pulls out that scrap of butcher paper and writes down the current time and date. She leaves the cap off the pen for the rest of the night, even though she knows it'll mean fully flushing the nib the next day.

During some gray predawn hour, she wakes from vague nightmares to see—still no further words added to the scrap of paper. On impulse, she opens a spiral notebook and writes, "Hey, Erin, what time is it when YOU are?" Within minutes, her pen transmits an answer: "Five thirty, what are you even doing up? Go back to bed."

One night when Rachel is sixteen, she parks her mother's car in the half-deserted lot of a dive bar on a highway known for beautiful views and not much else. Inside, two men are playing darts; the dart boards occupy the brightest spot in the whole dim place. The bartender stares absently at a football game on the TV. The only other person Rachel can see is a college-aged guy sitting alone at one of the tables placed haphazardly across the much-abused wood floor. He looks over at her briefly as she comes in, then goes back to glaring in the direction of the restrooms.

The moment Rachel enters the ladies', she can hear Erin sobbing. "Erin? I'm here. I'm sorry it took so long—I left the house as soon as I got your script." Erin doesn't immediately come out of the stall, but Rachel hears her unlock it, so she goes in. She finds Erin perched like a bird on the toilet seat, hugging her knees to her chest and shaking.

Rachel hugs her. "You OK, hon?"

"Asshole stole my cell phone," Erin whispers. "No, don't try to get it back. Just take me home."

As Erin gets to her feet, Rachel sees the message Erin wrote on the unfinished wood wall above the toilet paper dispenser: HE'S SCARING ME PLEASE COME—ROLLING ROCK BAR HWY 93. Rachel reaches out a finger to touch the big block letters. The ink smudges. She looks down at the stain and then up at Erin in shock. Rachel's pen received the message fully forty minutes ago.

The hint of a smile crosses Erin's tear-streaked face. "Yeah," she says. "It worked." She does not explain further.

When she gets home, Rachel pulls out the old scrap of butcher paper with the two messages on it. Now there are three. The third says, "How about now?" It's in the same handwriting as the first, both of which resemble Erin's. Rachel remembers Erin admiring the handwriting; she also remembers she never gave Erin the message to take home and practice from.

"It's the night I rescued you from that creep," Rachel writes. "And your first experiment with temporal nonlocal whatsis, I guess."

She puts down the pen and nearly screams when it leaps right back up again. "Not first experiment," it scripts. "First success."

"Well, thank goodness for THAT," Rachel writes back with a shaking hand. She underlines THAT several times.

She leaves the cap off and keeps half an eye on the pen for the rest of the night, but nothing else appears to be forthcoming.

—

Rachel stays in town for college. She takes classes in journalism and creative writing. She self-publishes chapbooks of poetry. She falls in and out of love with a series of what her mother calls "nice enough boys." The fourth one she winds up marrying. He's got a stable job in residential real estate and a fondness for board games which Rachel almost comes to share.

Erin attends one prestigious STEM university after another, collecting degrees like some people collect stamps. She studies particle physics and quantum mechanics. "And it's all thanks to you and your quantum-entangled pens," she scripts Rachel, who's congratulating her on winning yet another award. "One day the world will know the truth behind the singularity, and your name and mine will be legend."

"That and five bucks will buy me a latte," Rachel scripts back.

They don't script so much. Texting is more convenient. Rachel's smartphone is content to beep once when a message arrives and then shut the heck up. It doesn't go on buzzing in her purse like a trapped housefly. It never needs its nib cleaned or its converter refilled. But sometimes Rachel scripts anyway, just to remind herself that the magic still works.

Of course it works. Erin's making a name for herself from trying to figure out *how* it works. Not that she says as much to the national papers and scientific journals. Rachel reads each article faithfully; they're full of terms like *relative simultaneity* and *spatiotemporal nonlocality* which she understands little better than when she was ten. But she knows that Erin's drive to unlock the secrets of the universe is fueled by a miracle they share and can repeat any time they want.

Sometimes Rachel pulls out that aging scrap of butcher paper and adds to its contents. "You're forty-three and you just won yet another award named after some dead scientist," she writes.

This time, she gets a reply. "I know exactly when you mean. Keep in touch."

Rachel is sixty-three. The funeral is over. It was too soon, far too soon, and she's sick of hearing everyone say it. She's locked herself in her study, having escaped her husband's mostly abstract concern, and now she's paging through the scrapbook. Articles in national newspapers and scientific journals. Relative simultaneity and spatiotemporal nonlocality. Scraps of paper covered in fountain pen ink, the words written in two distinct hands. A poem or two. Rachel can't bear reading them now.

Finally she reaches the pocket in the back cover of the scrapbook and pulls out a ragged piece of butcher paper nearly covered in short sentences. She lays it carefully on the desk with her fountain pen across it, uncapped. Minutes pass. The pen doesn't move. Why should it? There's no more Future Erin to script her. Maybe there never was.

In a sudden rage Rachel snatches up the pen and writes, "You died last week. Your funeral was today. What the fuck time is it for YOU now?" Then she throws down the pen, heedless of the nib's point or of the ink spattering everything in a five-foot radius. It's orange today. The bottle says "Paleolithic Amber." That is one of many details that just don't matter anymore. Rachel puts her head down on her arms on the desk.

After a minute, the pen slowly rolls back toward the paper. Two inches in front of Rachel's nose, it rises upright, then hesitates as if deliberating over a choice of words. "I'm not sure that's a question that makes sense anymore."

" . . . Go on," Rachel says, as though the pen could hear her.

"Time is a place. Each moment is a room. It's like when we passed notes in school; we don't have to be in the same moment-room to script each other." The pen runs right off the edge of the paper and onto the desk. Rachel reaches for more paper to slide under the nib. "There are other rooms I can visit. There is a room where I have a stroke and die. There is a room where I beg you to come save me from an attempted kidnapping, or worse. And there is a room where I give you a special offer on a second-hand pen: two for the price of one." The pen pauses again while Rachel tries to tell herself she doesn't believe what it just wrote. "I took very good care of it, Rache. Thank you for taking such good care of me."

Rachel snatches up the pen again and writes, half on the new page and half on the desk itself, "That was you? In the store with the second pen?" She can't remember the lady's face anymore. Grown-up strangers were all anonymous when she was ten.

"Just one pen. Just one story, and two people writing it."

The words blur as Rachel's tears fall anew. She won't be able to bear to look at the paper again for hours. Just glancing in its direction will blind her with fresh sobs. But eventually she will remember that fountain pens don't care who died recently, they want to be capped and set upright in their pen holders when not in use, and just as an artist doesn't let grief get in the way of cleaning her brushes, a poet takes care of her pens. And she will come back to the page, and she will see one more sentence in her friend's hand, waiting for her—

"What makes you think we're done writing, Rache?"

—and suddenly all the details will matter again.

Nicole J. LeBoeuf (she/her) is from New Orleans, Louisiana. Accordingly, she's a die-hard Saints fan, and she feels most at home when humidity levels are above eighty percent. Her first professional publication was the short story "First Breath" in the vampirism anthology *Blood and Other Cravings*. Since then, her fiction has appeared or is forthcoming in venues including *Daily Science Fiction*, *Cast of Wonders*, and *Tales to Terrify*, and her poetry in *Sycorax Journal*, *Eternal Haunted Summer*, and *The Macabre Museum*. She and her husband currently live in Colorado, where she skates roller derby with the Boulder County Bombers under the name "Fleur de Beast," and persists in her possibly futile attempts to grow mirlitons and okra. Her favorite fountain pen is the sadly discontinued Sheaffer Agio. She blogs at NicoleJLeBoeuf.com.

The Oneiric Archive

Lorraine Schein

Each morning, I transcribe my dreams
with a silver stylus
to a memory stick
for my dream database.

The Webmaster of Sleep
takes it from my pillow
and copies my digitized entries
for her web archive

then translates the images
from my sleeping brain
by optical character recognition
onto her server

to make them downloadable
and searchable online
dragged into folders
by their repeating themes:
dreams of flying, falling, public nudity,
and recurring nightmares.

Lorraine Schein is a New York writer whose work has appeared in *VICE Terraform, New Letters, Witches & Pagans, Little Blue Marble, Strange Horizons* and in the anthologies *Tragedy Queens: Stories Inspired by Lana del Rey & Sylvia Plath,* and forthcoming in *Eighteen* (Underland Press). *The Futurist's Mistress,* her poetry book, is available from mayapplepress.com. She likes writing with purple pens and believes in precognitive dreams.

Writ Large

Holly Schofield

What happened that day in the Ottawa boardroom, well, it's never been public knowledge. I think the story needs to be told today. For context. For truth. And because of what I'm about to do before I leave the podium tonight.

On that world-altering day ten years ago, I'd stood up and walked to the end of the boardroom table. The Sollid Neurotech Research Ltd. board members stared at me every step I took. I really hate demonstrating stuff. What I can accomplish perfectly when I'm alone, I always screw up in front of an audience. But I had no choice back then, not if I wanted to keep the project going and keep my job.

I started off really badly. Hey, I was young back then. Young and naïve. I thought an apology would help. I said, "I'm sorry about the incomplete report. I was working on something else last night. But I've licked the problem of the tinnitus and the headaches. Well, mostly. Can I just tell you about the MindScribe instead? Um, I can write out different sizes of smileys? And I can—"

"Smileys? *That's* the complexity you've achieved? After four months of effort? Our clients need a serious communication neuroprosthesis, not some gimmick. If we can't patent it and supply it to them, how do you think we make any profit here?" Don Anderson, CEO of Sollid, flicked a fingernail at his tablet like it was my nose. "I hereby make a motion to cancel the whole project. Who'll second it? Jonathan?" He turned to the copycat dude-in-a-suit at his elbow, one of the ten board members he knew he could count on.

"Seconded." No hesitation, no inflection, no actual thinking needed. I swear, Jonathan would lick Anderson's boots. Even *after* he'd walked through cow manure.

Sollid had been a good company until Anderson got appointed. He was such a snake, ruling the company by cronyism, backstabbing, rumour-mongering—if a management technique was manipulative, he was doing it. Now, he was glaring at me from beneath his rusty gray curls. "Our twenty-four-year-old hotshot may come through with something viable at some point, but this is not the outcome nor the timeline we've been hoping for. Tennan is good, but not that good."

"Tennan is very good," Olive said flatly. "When you give them a chance." She was a lowly admin assistant but she never hesitated to speak her mind.

I remember thinking: neither should I. And that's what decided me. I was going to do it! I'd take the risk of presenting the prototype even though it didn't work right yet. I jammed the MindScribe headset on and squeezed my brain cells hard. At least, that's how I think of it, even now. Like trying to force out a burp, only in your head.

Symbol-based communication has existed for years: pointing at boards by whatever means the person is capable of—a finger, a stick held in the mouth, an eye movement. Concepts—*yes, no, want, don't want, good, finished*—can be conveyed really easily. Well, really easily *if* the person can move some part of their body. But if you can't, you live without self-expression of any kind. Our clients, MedFelicity, were a medical conglomerate out of British

Columbia, interested in thought-to-text solely because of their paraplegic patients.

I got excited just thinking about it. Consider people with locked-in-syndrome. A pen for your brain, a pencil for your mind: a real neural translator would be a life-changer. Not just for simply telling a caregiver, "I'm thirsty," but for the sheer human connection that a person desperately needs. Like my Aunt Fran and her four-year coma-that-wasn't. Because of her, I got into disability tech. I was hanging around all the new machines at her bedside and learning about EEGs, fMRIs, and electrocorticography even back then in high school.

I started into my presentation slowly, just a gentle squeeze in the ol' prefontal cortex. A yellow smiley appeared on the big screen that ran the length of the boardroom wall and also on everyone's tablet. I overlaid it with the toothier version of the emoji so it seemed like an animation breaking into a huge grin. Anderson jumped and I grinned.

"Thought-to-symbol has been possible for years." Anderson blew out his lips.

I tried not to sound as ticked off as I felt. Had Anderson even read the summary of the project's targeted goal? "Yes, Don, but only with a lot of terminals implanted under the skull, usually using ones already put there for treatment of epilepsy." Did he have any idea how lives could be improved if I could get this to work right? I drew in a long slow breath and recentred myself by recalling Aunt Fran's multi-nuanced "!!!" when she could finally communicate in symbols after years of silence.

Next, I concentrated on that frothy feeling in my forehead and squeezed harder. Making words was much slipperier than symbols, but I'd "canned" some of them into the software, as if they were PowerPoint slides. With just a little effort, words appeared on all the screens.

NOT JUST EMOJIS

It came up purple Comic Sans, because I was a twenty-four-year-old snot.

"Text? I assume it's stored in the software. Still, drawing on it is impressive." Hugh glanced at Anderson uneasily. Unlike the Chair, Hugh had a degree or two in some non-neuroscience or other. He wasn't all bad. He even brought donuts to the employee lounge once in a while. But it was a shame he rarely strayed outside of his role of corporate stooge.

"Displaying stored text is a mediocre outcome with limited functionality. Let's redirect the budget to something that will increase our bottom line." Anderson frowned. I swear, the man's posterior superior temporal lobes have dollars where his neurons should be.

My head began to ache. Any minute now, he'd call for a vote. And I'd be out the door, on the cold Ottawa streets, jobless, and homeless too. Most of my stuff was in a storage locker back in Kitchener. I still hadn't gotten around to renting an apartment here, working all hours and unrolling a sleeping bag whenever I needed a nap.

Hugh caught my eye. "Can you do something *un*scripted?"

"Um . . . " I probably could. More likely, though, it would fail spectacularly. And that would only support Anderson's argument for cancellation.

Anderson crossed his arms. "Gentlemen, it's time to vote. Let's repurpose these funds."

I suppressed the fuzzy tickles I could feel between my ears, like a quill pen scratching on my brain. Maybe if I just tried talking to Don? I mean, talking had worked for thousands of years, right?

I tugged down my Sarek T-shirt, wishing I'd gone full blazer. "Folks, I know it's nowhere near launch-ready. The decoding-to-text needs a lot of work. And we need hardware that isn't so uncomfortable." I scratched where the electrodes had rubbed bald spots on my temples. "But the product is viable. I just need more time."

Olive spoke up. "It's true, Mr. Anderson. Tennan can do it. I believe in them. Our mission is to be responsible to the shareholders, right? The MindScribe would benefit so many people, it's sure to make a profit! And you don't want Tennan going to the competition, do you?" She gave one of her patented fake smiles.

"I'll remind everyone that we've all signed an NDA. And that the intellectual property belongs to SNR, Ms. Ng." He didn't even bother to look at Olive but caught the eyes of the board members instead. "Does anyone have anything of *real* value to add?"

Olive had put up with so much. From Anderson, and from ambivalent Hugh and wimpy Jonathan and silent Stan and all the rest of the board members who just watched from the sidelines as he gaslighted her over and over.

I couldn't take it anymore. A thought formed in my head, a giant bubble that grew and grew. There was no stopping it. It burped its way out and lit up all the screens.

ENOUGH WITH THE DISRESPECT, ANDERSON.
IT'S TIRESOME

"I take it that's unscripted?" Anderson's mouth tightened. Another bubble immediately formed and popped.

OF COURSE IT IS, YOU JACKASS

I blushed, Anderson glared, Hugh snickered, and a couple of board members laughed out loud.

I sat down and took off the headset. "Sorry. That's why I didn't want to mention the breakthrough I had. So far, I don't have a way to filter the unscripted stuff. It just slips out. So it's clumsy for the sort of targeted communication MedFelicity wants. And think of the privacy issues. It's a major flaw. I'm sorry."

"Slips out, eh?" Anderson suddenly perked up. "So, if I were to ask you something you wanted to keep secret, you'd just blurt it out?"

"Well, with this model, probably. But I'm trying to make a neural gate that will sift through—"

"Put it back on."

I hesitated.

"Do you want to keep your job here? Put it on."

I slid it over my head, one ragged fingernail scratching my ear, disgusted at myself.

"Tell me the truth, Tennan, are you sleeping in the employee lounge?"

I bore down. I swallowed. I bit my lip. Every trick in the book, but still it leaked out.

NO, YOUR OFFICE SOFA IS MORE COMFORTABLE
EVEN THOUGH I SPILLED CHAI ON THE FANCY EMBROIDERED PILLOWS

That was it. It was over. I'd be tossed out on my butt. And forced to pay for the pillows.

But Anderson was smiling. I stared at him, completely thrown.

He strode over and patted my arm. “Don’t you see, dear? That’s not a negative outcome. The military will be begging at our doorstep for technology like this. Interrogating a prisoner is so much easier when you can literally pick their brain.”

I stared at him, horrified. I’d only thought of it as a bug in the software, a nasty flaw reducing the purity of communication. I’d never imagined the sort of evil purpose that Anderson had leaped on. My mind flared and the screens all burst into furious red and orange swirls, dancing like flames.

The board members broke into loud discussion. Hugh pounded on the table, a vein in his forehead pulsating along with the pixels on the screen. Ten voices, all clambering at once, no one listening. Really, what it comes down to is they were all struggling to translate neural impulses into tongue-and-mouth manipulations to produce audio sounds that we’d all agreed had specific meaning. No wonder it was chaos.

I closed my eyes and hummed, trying to recentre. And that’s when I realized what positive outcomes could happen. This was bigger than just helping people like Aunt Fran. This was huge.

This time, I didn’t even try to suppress my thought. It came out in black letters a foot high.

> *WHAT IF WE ALL WERE WEARING MINDSCRIBES RIGHT NOW? WOULDN’T THIS DEBATE BE EASIER?*

“And more honest,” said Olive into the sudden silence. “Maybe we’ve been going about this all wrong. What if we don’t need to develop a gate? What if we *all* receive unfiltered thoughts? If everyone does, then there’s no way not to trust someone. That would change everything—from marriage counselling to commercial transactions to international negotiations.”

She was right. We all lived solo, alone and untrusting. If we could truly know another person's thoughts, it wouldn't just make for clearer discussions; no, we could actually make that connection, the one we all wanted, fill that mental hole we all felt.

OLIVE, YOU'RE A GENIUS.

Anderson was the first to speak. "No, no, no. The invasion of privacy alone—"

Hugh interrupted Anderson. "You know, Don, once I went to a nudist colony. It only took me three days to adapt. That feeling of exposure, of nakedness—well, if everyone is naked, then no one is. This could be the same. I think Tennan is truly onto something."

Stan tilted his bald head. A couple of other board members raised their eyebrows. Someone rubbed their hands together over and over. I thought they all might be agreeing with Hugh although, of course, I couldn't know for sure.

The screens lit up with my thoughts.

WE ARE ALL STUCK IN OUR BONE BOXES IN SOME WAY

My head was bursting.

BUT THE MINDSCRIBE CAN SET US ALL FREE

I raced from the boardroom, heading for the lab, mind roaring, tears warm on my cheeks. Waiting for the elevator, dancing from foot to foot, I could suddenly hear Anderson's shouts being drowned out by Hugh's voice, then cheers and applause.

Of course, y'all know the rest or you wouldn't be sitting in this hotel ballroom tonight in your fancy clothes. How the MindScribe became the hottest new personal device, if you can afford the six-digit price tag. How twenty percent of North America was Scribing by the following Thanksgiving, even if they had to mortgage their homes or get a huge loan. How SNR became the decade's most profitable company and, after Hugh ousted Anderson and raised my stock options, I became a zillionaire. I now have a sweet little condo in the Glebe, a real bed, and about a hundred Star Trek T-shirts. And MindScribe 1.0—duct tape, bulky wires, and all—is displayed in the Smithsonian.

Ironic, isn't it, after a hundred years of personal tech, we all trust what people Scribe more than what they verbally say. Sure, truth hurts, but it also cleanses. Olive had been right.

With the current tech, people who can Scribe are proven to have increased their empathy up to fourfold. That still amazes me. It saddens me no end, though, that there's still about ten percent of folks for whom the tech doesn't work—the list of medical and psychological reasons for that is still growing.

And, sure, some folks are still weasels—are you out there, Don Anderson?—but enough aren't. Most people just needed a little trust in others to break that awful 2010s downward cycle—and Scribing filled that niche.

Lots of you in the audience have helped with climate change challenges, disease prevention, and all kinds of other humanitarian needs. You are all awesome. Give yourselves a round of applause, please.

You've changed the world!

Well, somewhat.

Kind of.

More needs to be done, you know it does.

And I've tried to help, really I have, using my skillset. The filtering gate is pretty good now, right?

Anyway, I thank you all for coming out tonight to this ceremony, especially after the snow that came down today. It's a real honor to be standing at the microphone in front of you all, ten years later, a thirty-four-year-old who's still a snot in jeans and T-shirt, about to be handed this cleverly sculpted golden medallion. The Neuro Award is prestigious even to oblivious nerds like me. And Aunt Fran sure is proud. She told me so.

But I can't accept it.

That's right. I'm turning it down.

I may have improved the tech, but I've failed in another way. I can't get the MindScribe price low enough so that everyone can have it, world-wide. I've tried and tried. The design is so complex, so quantum-neuro-cognitive based, that it's beyond me.

If we don't reach that tipping point—what the marketing people call a breakpoint of saturation—it'll remain an elitist gadget. Everyone who wants to should be able to access a MindScribe, scribbling out their thoughts, sharing their true hopes and dreams. If we all have mental pen and paper, we can write the most amazing plans and stories and love letters. All of us, every stratum of every race, religion, and country. We can really, truly read each other. Isn't that the most awesome thing you can ever imagine?

And there's no time to waste. You've seen the news articles: I spend most of my humungous salary getting injunction after injunction to stop the government from making the MindScribe a controlled resource, a Big Brother monitor worse than anything ever conceived. Men in black suits follow me around and make threats.

It's only a matter of time before they get their hands on it. So, here's what I've come to tell you all tonight: I've given up my job at SNR and put Olive in charge of my legal team. I'm going to spend the rest of my life Scribing my heart out, searching for the next neuro-genius, the person who can carry on where I've left off. The person who can make this truly global.

And y'all can help.

All of you, bend down in your fancy tuxes and dresses. Look under your seats and you'll find a package taped there, Oprah-style.

Go on. I'll wait.

That's right. It's a flash drive containing the open-source plans for the MindScribe hardware and software. I've also just posted those plans on about a thousand websites.

So go home now. Take off your itchy bowties and boob-lifting tape. Scribe these plans to everyone you know.

Let's get the world on the same page.

Holly Schofield (she/her) travels through time at the rate of one second per second, oscillating between the alternate realities of city and country life. Her speculative fiction has appeared in many publications including *Lightspeed*, *Analog*, and *Escape Pod*, is used in university curricula, and has been translated into several languages. She hopes to save the world through science fiction and homegrown heritage tomatoes. Find her at hollyschofield.wordpress.com.

Rhapsody in D Minor

Jannae' Sifontes

As her hoverchair slowed to a quiet hum, finally still in the warm, nurturing light of the stage, Lavoneisha Carson-Harris pulled out the stack of manuscript paper from her bag where it rested on its hook at her side. At first, she'd considered just managing on foot today since she'd woken up feeling rather well. Yvette had lovingly convinced her otherwise, reminding her of occasions when Von had been overeager and underprepared. Happy spouse, peaceful house, right? She huffed a little, her deep brown eyes darting to the side and peering through the curtain of her braids to make sure that the young stagehand who had accompanied her to this point had left. Only then did she pull out the tarnished steel case from her bag. The metal was cold, the texture biting at a few of her fingers as she ran them along the worn surface before finally releasing the latch and removing the pen from within. It was a welcome weight in her hand, even as a slight tremor took over her fingers, the muscles in them starting to give out. This one passed quickly enough, and she hoped it wasn't going to be one of those days after such a pleasant start.

The pen was just shy of being unwieldy—its thickness due to the mystic and mechanical parts residing inside. Otherwise, it was innocuous; it was but another pen of the many in her collection unless you noticed the glyphs on the side. No one would've guessed it played a role in some of the most celebrated symphonies of the past decade. The primary factor being the woman holding it, obviously.

Lavoneisha moved to where the string section would be seated before removing a small audio recording device. She had a process she followed, and it had yet to fail her. Once home, she'd start mixing this recording with the rest, making sure it all flowed as smoothly as she'd imagined. She spared a glance at where the trumpet section would sit onstage, the part she had finished only yesterday. While necessary to this piece, she hadn't wanted to assault her ears with the horns by working on them in the acoustics of the music hall. The violin section, on the other hand . . .

Her hand darted to the page secured on the clipboard in her lap, the paper void of all but the title of her newest work and her pseudonym: LaVonc. She had settled on using the first letter of her married name, not her maiden. Yvette had approved, for both selfish and auditory reasons. LaVonh didn't quite have the right punch. Her pen quickly peppered the page with notes, and the music in her mind started singing throughout the hall, brought to life by pen. She sighed as she composed, a sound of happiness and longing. Critics had noted the favor she showed to the string section, and she gladly admitted it in the rare interviews she gave. Violin was the first instrument she'd ever learned to play, after all.

The truth was, Von mostly wrote her violin pieces onstage like she did now. For a brief moment, she could pretend she was younger and still capable of holding the bow just right, with her fingers flying across the fret. She could feel the strings digging into her fingers, and she missed the sting that stayed after hours of practice. That was before the diagnosis, and it was before she found her grip fading. It was before the loud, heartbreaking clang of her violin on the stage as it fell from her shaking hand which would no longer listen to her brain or her heart. It was before . . .

A clang rang out from the audience, silencing the melodic vibrations of strings as Von came to a full stop and stood up, trying to catch the source of the interruption. That was before realizing how much of her energy she had poured out onto the page through the workings of her pen. Her knees buckled, and she barely managed to fall back into her chair, it dipping down as it adjusted again to her weight.

"Who is there?" she called out, her alto voice carrying easily in the silence.

Slowly, a tuft of brilliant, bluebird-colored hair rose up from the audience, from near one of the exits to the right of the stage. Lavoneisha wondered how she had missed the door opening, but she looked down at the now-filled pages that had spilled in her shock. She'd been lost in one of her frenzies, and she'd been known to overlook much more obvious interruptions.

"I'm sorry," came the soft apology in a deep baritone, and Von bit her lip at the tone of the words. She hoped it was just guilt she'd heard, but it always sounded way too similar to pity in her ears.

"I believe I rented the hall out for the next two hours for a private affair, so give me one reason I shouldn't report you to the authorities for trespassing?"

The hair only grew brighter as the head that sported it came closer to the stage. Von recalled the scattered papers and leaned over to gather them in case it was someone trying to steal her work. Heavens knew, it wouldn't be the first time.

"My cousin . . . she works here, and she told me that LaVonc would be here, so I snuck in to see if I could just hear what you were working on, and I never thought I'd actually get a chance to see you in person, and now I'm rambling . . . "

The words drifted off as Lavoneisha bothered to look up and see the dark brown eyes that might've been her own on skin so many shades darker. At least he'd dressed the part, a black shirt sporting some sort of graphic design and black jeans making it hard to spot him with the stage light in her eyes. Only then did she find the source of the earlier disturbance in the form of the violin he carried awkwardly in one hand. A softness tugged at her heart, and she let out a resigned sigh as she realized that she wouldn't report the kid if she could avoid it.

"You should just go on outta here while you still . . . "

"Wait! Ohmygosh, you're . . . you're!"

His words were awe-filled, and the tone caught her by surprise while the kid whipped out his phone, frantically tapping away with one hand before turning up the volume. While he was still some distance away, Von felt her heart constrict as the sound hit her. She knew what he'd pulled up well enough without seeing it anyway. It was her uploaded cover of "Stereotypes" by Black Violin, the video as old as her dreams of touring the world and playing her own songs.

"That's you, isn't it?"

It was a very loaded question, and Lavoneisha heard the background noise well enough. How did the lively woman dancing on the screen in the video get to this point?

"I'd appreciate it if you kept what you've discovered to yourself," she warned. "I'm not quite ready to reveal this part of myself to the world."

"I mean, I could understand that when you were just getting started." He really wasn't so much a kid, she supposed. Maybe in his late teens, early twenties. "But you're about to kick off your, what, fourth world tour? Ain't nobody gonna be saying you're a good composer for someone disabled. You're just one of the best. Period."

The final note rang out from the video as it faded, her cheesy editing still enough to garner the video almost a million views. And that was the last time she'd checked, maybe a month or so ago. People still commented, wondering what had happened to her. Maybe it was time they all found out, and she celebrated both past and present. She took a deep breath before counting down from four, soothing her nerves the way she always did before a performance.

"So, you wanna hear what I'm working on, or what?" she asked, somehow more excited than when she'd first entered the building, melodies and harmonies now a crescendo in her head.

When he smiled at her, Lavoneisha realized what the theme of her next piece was going to be. But first, she had to finish what she'd started. One note at a time.

Jannae' Sifontes (she/her) is many things to many people, but is currently found being a sister, wife, and mother in the city of oaks known as Raleigh, North Carolina. While her interests range from anime to gaming to jewelry making, writing has been one calling she is always pursuing. Her love of worldbuilding is seconded only by the desire to empower those that feel unheard and inspire a kinder, better world. She has a novel, *Ex Umbra*, and was most recently featured in *Five Minutes at Hotel Stormcove*, also published by Atthis Arts. Feel free to find her on Facebook or Twitter (@ArgentArtisan) and follow her antics there.

Written with Love

Stella B. James

"Emma, can you please explain why there are five boys attempting to beat down my front door?"

Emma winced at her grandfather's question and tugged the edge of her sleeve further down, hoping to hide the evidence a little longer. She knew she should have stayed out of his office. His one explicit rule for staying with him over the weekend was to keep out of the office, and she broke that very rule within hour three of her stay.

"Maybe they have the wrong house?" she asked, her voice squeaking out the last word as her muffled name could be heard through the wood. The other boys, catching on to this, started chanting her name as well.

"Are you in some kind of trouble?" her grandfather asked, pinching the bridge of his nose. Emma bit her bottom lip, unsure how to answer.

Was she in some kind of trouble? She had gone into her grandfather's office, used his things, and now had a mob of boys at her front door. She wasn't sure if she should fear the mob or her grandfather more.

"Define trouble."

Her grandfather sighed, his shoulders sagging in defeat as he turned for the door.

"Wait! You're letting them in?"

"I'm a little curious, aren't you?"

She shook her head, not at all curious. Anxious, terrified, guilty—those were the broad spectrum of her feelings. Okay, and maybe a teensy bit curious.

"Before you open the door, there's something I should show you."

Her grandfather leaned against the door and crossed his arms. It was almost as if he knew she would cave. Emma scratched at her wrist, as if it would buy her some precious time, before lifting her sleeve all the way up to her elbow.

Scrawled on her skin in her loopy handwriting were the names of five boys: Travis Demma, Miles Parsons, Ethan Wright, Scott Lopez, and Chase Adams. She noticed her grandfather's eye twitch, a sign that his blood pressure was on the rise and a blow-up would surely ensue. She braced herself, her fingers clutching the hem of her sleeve.

"Let me take a wild guess," he drawled out, pointing to her arm. "The five guys outside match those five names." Emma nodded and let the sleeve drop. "You used the pen in my office to write that." Emma nodded again and took a step backward.

Instead of an exasperated declaration of 'Just what did you think you were doing?', Emma was met with laughter—loud, bent at the waist, literal knee-slapping laughter. Her brows furrowed as her face set fire, and she decided that this was almost worse. It was one thing to be reprimanded when you already knew you did wrong. It was another to be made fun of and humiliated.

"You have no idea what you just did, do you?" he asked, wiping under his eyes once he'd contained himself. Emma shook her head, watching him with wary eyes. "Emma, who am I?"

"My mean grandfather." There, point for Emma. He sighed

and asked the question again with more emphasis. "You're Cupid," she muttered under her breath.

Emma had always known the truth about her grandfather, but it wasn't special if you couldn't tell anyone. And it especially didn't mean anything if Cupid wouldn't help you in your own love life. He claimed that it wouldn't be fair to abuse his power, and with her at the 'hormone-driven age of sixteen', she apparently didn't know what real love was.

"That I am." Cupid snapped his fingers, and the pen from his office poofed into his hand. He rolled it between his fingers, studying it with mild amusement, before holding it in the space between them, as if putting it on display. "And do you know what this pen you used does?"

"Obviously not." She flushed in embarrassment, not meaning to snap at him, but sometimes it was so hard to 'respect your elders' when your own grandfather looked to be about twenty-five.

"This pen is what I once used to help people fall in love with their soulmates," Cupid explained in an even tone, his eyes steady on hers as if to gauge her reaction. Emma snorted and rolled her eyes.

"Nice try, but I did take Mythology last year. You use arrows. Everyone knows that."

Cupid shook his head, wincing as the boys started in on an attempted serenade that sounded more like squawking seagulls. "Arrows are so medieval and completely inefficient with the growth in population. I went to pens decades ago, writing names on people in their sleep. But then that got troublesome, especially when tattoos came about."

"You don't use the pen anymore?" Emma asked, her curiosity once again piqued.

"Nope." The pen vanished suddenly, and Cupid reached into his back pocket, fishing out his phone. "Technology is great. I barely have to travel with this bad boy."

"What, you like text them or something?"

"No," Cupid scoffed, leaning back against the door. "I have an app, of course."

Gee, they really did have an app for everything.

Cupid's body vibrated with each pound of the door, and Emma worried if the boys would be at this all night. Or all week. For eternity . . . Was this her fate for the rest of her life? Surely they would overwhelm her in their haste to get to her and claim her as theirs the second she opened the door. She could feel the sweat gather at her hairline, but Cupid looked calm and collected.

"So what does this mean? I wrote five names on me with your secret magic pen!"

"You have five soulmates, my dear. Zeus would envy you." Emma did not appreciate his amused smirk, but she needed his help, and fast. Puppy eyes it was.

"Please, grandfather, I am so, so sorry I disobeyed you!" She clasped her hands in front of her for good measure and pouted in an overly obnoxious way to get her point across. "I'll never touch anything of yours again. Now, please help me!"

"Of course I'm going to help you," Cupid said as he shut off his phone and slid it back in his pocket.

Reaching out, he took her hand and gently rolled up her sleeve to study the names scrawled on her arm. Emma's eyes ping-ponged between Cupid's face and her arm, every passing second causing her heart to thrum harder. The boys outside grew restless, her name sounding louder, each plea more desperate than the last.

"So?" Emma prompted, breaking the silence. "What do we do?"

"We're going to have tattoo your arm, I guess," Cupid said, his tone low and laced with sorrow. "How do you feel about full sleeve?" Emma's eyes practically bulged out of her head, and she wrenched her arm away.

Once again, Cupid was laughing. Emma grumbled obscenities under her breath as she pulled her sleeve back down. Cupid breezed past her, stopping just shy of entering the hall bathroom. He jerked his head towards the door, and Emma hesitated just a moment before following.

Cupid hummed to himself, half his body swallowed up by the closet. He reappeared holding a golden bottle that shimmered in the light. Emma would not admit that it was the most beautiful thing she had ever seen.

"You have no sense of humor." Cupid tsked at her in mock disappointment while unscrewing the bottle cap.

"If that's what you call it," she shot back.

"We're going to wash the names off with this," Cupid explained, shaking the bottle a little. "The boys will forget all about today, and you will never use that pen again. Are we in agreement?"

Emma nodded enthusiastically, her smile so wide, she could feel it stretch from ear to ear. Oh, what a relief it was that all this would soon be a bad memory. The entire ordeal had been more than embarrassing for everyone involved.

"It's lucky for me that you have this soap," Emma said, starting the water in the sink. Cupid poured the golden gel over her arm, and Emma took to scrubbing away the five names that were surely giving the entire neighborhood a headache.

Slowly, one by one, the voices died off. The door became silent after a few minutes, and Emma could swear she heard their retreating footsteps. She sagged against the sink, letting the water wash over her arm, and tried her best to ignore the tingling sensation of the magic erasing the ink.

"Meh, I've been known to make mistakes. Aphrodite had this concocted for me after a few blunders." Cupid capped the bottle and placed it back in the closet.

Emma turned off the water and closed her eyes, basking in the silence. She could hardly believe a pen could cause so much trouble. She vowed to herself to not be such a nuisance to her grandfather for the rest of her stay. But one thing still nagged at the back of her mind.

"Were any of those boys my real soulmate?"

A knock at the door interrupted Cupid's answer, and his eyes twinkled as he smiled down at her. "Why don't you go to the door and see for yourself?"

Stella B James (she/her) is a Southern girl who appreciates strong coffee and losing herself in fantastical daydreams. When she isn't writing about the complications of life and love, she can be found reading romance novels of any genre, drinking prosecco while watching whatever she has left over on her DVR, or talking herself out of buying yet another black dress. She has published several short stories with various publications, and is currently writing her first romance novel. You can find her short stories on her website, stellabjames.com. Check out her Instagram @stellabjames, where she shares her writing and inner musings.

The Healer

M. Kaur

"Kakaji! Sultan is ill again. Can you help him?"

Partap Chand glanced up from his newspaper. His neighbor's daughter, Nusrat, was peering over the brick wall separating his courtyard from hers. Putting his teacup back on the saucer, he got up from the bamboo chair and hurried over.

"Get down from there, child. If you fall again, your mother will blame me."

Undeterred, the eight-year-old clambered over the wall and jumped onto his newly planted flowers. Touching her ears in silent apology, Nusrat looked up at him expecting to be told off. Laughing, Partap helped her up and led her to the breakfast table. He always had morning tea outside in the summer months, at least on the days it didn't rain. And this August, in 1947, it had been particularly pleasant. The sweet smell of freedom pervaded the air in Sindh province, in the new country of Pakistan, created just a week ago when the British finally left the Indian subcontinent.

"Tell me about Sultan, what's wrong with him?"

"Colic, the vet says." Nusrat picked up a ripe mango from the fruit bowl on the table and squeezed it before putting it to her lips to suck out the juice. "He says it's time to put him down because he's in pain. But you can help him, can't you?"

Partap looked at the girl, staring at him with hope in her big hazel eyes, and winced. Ever since he had written on her hand

and cured her of a fever, she believed that he could cure anything and anyone.

"I don't think my grandfather's pen works on horses, child! If the vet says it is time for him to go, maybe you should listen."

And there it was, the thing he was afraid of—big, fat, tear-drops in her big, round eyes—threatening to wash away any hope of reasoning with her. Knowing when he was beaten, Partap got up from the table and went inside to get the pen.

"Never use it on your own family," his grandfather had said. "It is only for the benefit of others. Never take money in exchange for the words; they will not work if you don't give them freely as a gift. And never, ever tell anyone what you write, except your son."

Partap had knelt beside his grandfather's deathbed. He could still feel Dada's gnarled fingers on his head as the old man had blessed him before handing over the qalam. The calligraphy pen should have gone to Partap's father by right, but he had passed away ten years ago of typhoid. Everyone in town had shaken their head at the irony of the healer's son, dying of a disease his father had cured in others countless times.

But the gift was not for the benefit of his family, Dada had said, as he watched his firstborn fade away.

"I'm sorry, Partap," Karim Sumrah said. "Nusrat should not have bothered you."

Karim and Partap had grown up together. Living in

neighboring houses, the two men had been best friends since the first day their mothers walked them to the neighborhood school. Their wives were from the same village; they studied the same subjects in college and marched in the same protests during Gandhi's Quit India Movement. The only difference between them, if you were determined to find one, was that they belonged to different faiths. Karim was Muslim, Partap was Hindu.

"Don't worry about it," Partap assured his friend. "I don't mind doing this for Nusrat. I'm just afraid she'll be disappointed when it doesn't work. Dada never said it would work on horses," he laughed as the two men strode to the stables behind Karim's house.

Nusrat ran over with a sheet of paper. As Partap sat down to write on it, she carefully averted her eyes, knowing the rules. No one could read the words the healer wrote; else, they wouldn't work. When Partap had written on her hand, her mother had tied a cloth over it. But Sultan was being led around the stable. The vet said he would be in more pain if he stopped. So, the plan was that Partap would write the word, Nusrat would stuff the paper in a cloth purse, and Karim would tie it around Sultan's neck.

"Have you heard about the riots in Punjab?" Karim asked as the two men walked back to the house later. Nusrat remained at the stable, keeping an eye on Sultan. The vet had gone home, washing his hands of the case, muttering something about "superstitious nonsense."

"It will die down," Partap said, sounding more confident than he felt. "People need some time to adjust, and then life will go back to normal."

"I don't know, my friend." Karim paused at the gate and placed his hand on Partap's shoulder. "I think maybe you should go to Karachi for a while. You have relatives there, and if the violence spreads, you can take a boat to Bombay." He hesitated before continuing. "I've started to hear rumblings around town. Refugees have brought reports of Muslims being killed in India. Some believe that Hindus in Pakistan should pay the price."

Partap stood in silence, gazing at the spire of a mosque, visible next to the saffron flag flying above a Hindu temple in the same street.

"So, did the horse get better?" Partap's granddaughter asked.

It was August in Bombay in 1974, and the monsoon season was in full swing. Partap put down his cup on the table set up in the balcony of their highrise apartment. He liked to have his evening tea while looking down at the bustling street below. His eight-year-old granddaughter, Vijaya, sat beside him, eating piping hot pakoras.

"Yes, he did. And then, Sultan saved our lives in return."

Nusrat had climbed over the wall in the dark of the night to warn them of the attack. Partap and his wife had gathered their children and followed Nusrat to the stables where Karim was hitching Sultan to a tanga. They escaped through the orchard behind the two houses in the horse-drawn carriage while the mob tried to beat down their front door.

"So, the magic does work on animals too. I knew it would!" Vijaya reached for a mango to sweeten her mouth after having devoured the fiery pakoras.

Partap looked at her and smiled. His sons had shown no interest in the gift of healing passed down in their family for generations. They were both doctors and didn't believe a calligraphy pen could have any magic at all. Instead, they put their faith in the pills and powders they dispensed in their clinics. He hadn't written on anyone's hand for a long time. His qalam remained wrapped in cotton and packed away in a small wooden box he hadn't opened in years. Perhaps the time had come to pass it on.

"Never use it on your own family. Never take payment in exchange. And never tell anyone what you write, except the one you pass on your gift to."

And then Partap leaned over and whispered the word in Vijaya's ear.

M. Kaur (she/her) @manjitsekhon is a learning strategist turned creative writer. She is writing a collection of short stories based on her family's experience during the partition of India and Pakistan in 1947. "The Healer" is inspired by her grandfather who was said to have the ability to heal fevers by writing a word on the patient's hand. Her flash "The Red Scarf" was recently published in *Apparition Lit*.

Magical Markers

Lena Ng

Author's Note: This story was inspired by my sister's family friends whose young son passed away at age seven from childhood cancer.

At the end of the eighth ward, in a small room with a grey tiled floor and awash by dim fluorescent lights, there lived a little girl named Rose. She smiled, when she could, though those closest to her noticed the lengthening distance between them, as the fluid dripped from a large bag into a drip chamber and then into her pale, thin arm. She knew, but didn't really understand, that she was dying. Her parents had cried when the doctor, a Taiwanese pediatric oncologist, had said with a sorrowful expression that Rose's neuroblastoma, a cancer which can successfully be treated in many patients, had spread extensively despite the abundance of treatments they had tried.

Rose's days were mainly spent sleeping but she was sometimes blessed with visitors: other children with varying degrees of hair loss, somber relatives from near and far, clowns and other costumed entertainers sent to bring a breath of cheer to the ward. During the day, her constant companion was her grandfather, who liked to read aloud fairy tales about dancing princesses and sweetly singing nightingales. He could transform his voice into that of a talking frog or a questing prince or a noble king. He kept watch over her, watching cartoon adventures or helping Rose to put together puzzles, until one of her parents arrived after work.

One afternoon, as the sun started to kiss the horizon, a small rap sounded on Rose's door. In walked a young woman, her complexion as fresh as a new lily, dressed in a blue dress with blue wings made from pipe cleaners, felt, and chiffon. She carried a small woven basket. "Hello," the young woman said, her voice like a breeze skimming a field. "I'm the Blue Fairy. I'm here to make your dearest wish come true."

Rose's brown eyes, the colour of polished teak, widened on her round face. "Any wish?"

The Blue Fairy brought out her wand, which was made from a wooden tongue depressor and construction paper. "Only the one you long for most."

Rose thought of the other small beds and the other small bodies and tubes and IV poles carrying bags of liquid medication. How wonderful it was when her friends were happy. She scrunched up her face and held her hands over her heart. "I wish . . . I wish I could make other children well." Her grandfather leaned forward in his metal chair and the light of hope brightened his tired face. If Rose was not getting well, perhaps she could help others.

The Blue Fairy gave a sad smile. "I'm sure you will make them feel better." She reached into her basket and gave Rose a velvet-covered book, holding leaves of drawing paper, and a set of felt pens, each a different colour of the rainbow. She waved her wand and there was a small sprinkling of silver glitter. "Have fun drawing with these magical markers. They will make your wish come true." She ended her visit by giving Rose a small kiss on her peach-fuzz forehead and two cherry-flavoured candy canes.

That night, Rose dreamt of laughing children, her little hospital friends overjoyed to go home. The next day and over many days, Rose drew pictures of her visiting friends. For Aidan, a five-year-old boy who loved his stuffed purple hippo, she drew a trip to the zoo with lazy lions and nibbling giraffes. For Tina, a chatty girl too small for her age, a red hot-air balloon floated at the top of the page, her family soaring through the air in a wicker basket. Ryan, his face rounded from steroids, always wished for a dog so Rose drew a puppy in the picture. The sun had a yellow, smiling face and dazzling butterflies flew in the paper sky. The colours of the magical markers blazed across the page.

Many children came and went from the hospital ward. A joyous clanging of a bronze bell would announce their departure, echoing down the long, white hallways. The parents may have believed it was the chemotherapy or radiation that had helped their children, but Rose knew it was her drawings.

One Sunday morning, Rose awoke but the metal chair beside her bed stood empty. Hours passed and then the day, but the chair remained empty. Her parents tried to explain her grandfather's absence; his heart gave out in the night. Rose didn't understand—how could a heart as large as her grandfather's stop working?

By some sad coincidence, that same day, the magical markers ran dry of ink. The pages in her notebook looked as empty as the metal chair. No children left the hospital ward that day; no happy clang of a ringing bell sounded down the hospital halls. Exhausted from grief, Rose fell asleep, her magical markers scattered uncapped by her side.

That night Rose dreamt of her grandfather. It was the Christmas before she became ill. She sat at a long table at her grandparents' house, when Nana was still alive. There was laughter at that table—carefree laughter, not the type that served as a brief respite to grief. A wreath decorated with candles was the centrepiece. The roasted turkey, a beautiful burnished gold, gave the room a delicious smell with its stuffing of mushrooms and marjoram. Her grandparents had a matching glow on their faces, and after dinner, her grandfather, with crinkles at the corners of his eyes, held her hand as they skated over the small pond nestled in the eastern corner of the lot, the ice illuminated by the porch lights and the moon and the stars.

In her sleep, Rose shed many tears. When she roused in the darkness of just before dawn, Rose noticed the faint stain of ink from marker to the paper. Her tears had replenished the ink. Quickly, she drew the last image from her dream: she was holding her grandfather's warm hand.

A few hours later, when Rose's parents awoke, the first thing they noticed was the serene expression on Rose's face. She lay so quietly, so peacefully, she looked as though she were sleeping.

Lena Ng (she/her) lives in Toronto, Ontario. She has short stories in three dozen publications including *Amazing Stories*, from Australia, Canada, the US, and the UK. *Under an Autumn Moon* is her short story collection. She is currently seeking a publisher for her novel, *Darkness Beckons*, a Gothic romance.

Rekindled

Mikko Rauhala

Nera knew something was amiss as soon as she noticed the crow cooing on her porch a mere three weeks after the fall equinox. Mother's next letter, no doubt wishing Nera well in all her endeavors, wasn't due until the winter solstice.

The crow cawed and pushed a small container tied to his leg toward Nera.

"Just a moment, Wisp. I'll get you your treat," she said to the crow. Intelligent as the familiar was, he was still a crow. Headstrong, willful, proud—just as Mother liked it. He would run errands for her, to be sure, but he expected to be properly compensated for his time and effort.

Wisp bobbed his head up and down in acknowledgment. Nera entered her single-room hut, suitable for an independent medicine woman in her late twenties. A simple stone fireplace in the corner to keep her warm, a bed to let her rest her bones, and a stool and a table to write on. A shelf to the left of the fireplace held jars of herbs and tinctures of various kinds, and the shelf to the right was reserved for more mundane foodstuffs. She reached into a jar on the latter shelf, pulled out a handful of nuts, and returned outside.

She crouched next to Wisp, placed the nuts on the porch, and said: "Here you go. Could I have Mother's letter now, please?"

The crow tilted his head, a gesture that Nera had learned to take for a smile, and proceeded to tinker with the string on his leg. As soon as he'd gotten the container free, he picked it up and placed it on Nera's hand. Then he turned to regard the pile of nuts.

"Could you wait a while so I can see if an immediate reply is called for?"

Wisp picked up a nut in his beak, bobbed his head up and down, and proceeded to bite into the treat.

"Thanks," Nera said with a smile. "I'll try to make it quick." Then she went inside and opened the window next to the table. The sun was still high, and the southwestern view was good for evening reading.

Nera popped the container's cap, dug out a small scroll, and spread it onto the table. Despite her age, Mother's hand was as steady as ever. Nera had to squint to make out the tiny letters:

Dear Nera,

I hope this letter finds you well. It occurs to me that we've barely spoken anything of import for the better part of the decade. I'd like for us to get to know each other again, and give Wisp some proper exercise. What say you?

Regards,
Raziela

Nera chuckled. This was a change from the formal pleasantries they usually exchanged four times a year. Not an unwelcome one, though. They'd just sort of drifted apart since Mayview had lost its previous medicine woman and Nera had answered the call. But maybe it was time to reconnect.

Dipping her pen in the inkwell, Nera wrote her agreement on the blank side of the scroll, then rolled the message back into the cylinder. Wisp jumped up on the table, having eaten his fill, and Nera tied the message to his leg. "Thanks, Wisp. Give Mother my best," she said.

Wisp cawed and took off through the open window, disappearing into the sun.

Two days later the crow returned, and twice a week hence. The pace was such that it was all Nera could do to think of something to write back before Wisp would be knocking on her door again.

Mother shared her memories of the early years, how she'd juggled raising a baby and serving her community, not always to her own satisfaction. She wrote about how she'd kept Nera busy with learning about healing herbs and tinctures as soon as she was out of the crib. She recounted how distraught she'd been when the whooping cough had spread throughout the village, Nera falling ill among the rest, but how her medicinal arts had managed to triumph over it in the end.

And she wrote of the bittersweet sensation of Nera coming into her own and leaving for Mayview, of her regret over letting their contact largely lapse while busying herself in her own responsibilities. Nera sent a reply reminding her that they'd both had their hand in that.

As the year marched on and the winter solstice approached, Mother suggested that Nera join her for a quiet celebration. Nera happily agreed and prepared for the journey.

Nera's old home was as it had ever been. The stone house was twice the size of Nera's own, and had twice the rooms—gratitude of a village well served. A diverse herb garden dominated the front yard, its lushness only slightly reined in by the mild winter air. The rest of the surroundings were as nature wished.

A caw from above welcomed her as she approached the front door by way of the narrow garden path. Nera looked up and saw Wisp circling in the sky. She gave him a little wave, and the crow dove down and in through a cracked window at the front.

"Ah, she's here?" asked a familiar voice from her childhood. There was an affirmative caw. "Come on in!" Mother hollered. "It's not as if I've put a bolt on the door!"

Nera chuckled. "Didn't expect you had!" The hinges creaked with age as she opened the door to the main room. It hadn't changed a bit since Nera last laid eyes on it, except for the large piles of paper in every corner of the room. The walls were otherwise lined with shelves full of one odd thing or another. To the left of the door stood a table with some dishes and cutlery on it. A tattered couch lay near the fireplace.

The door to her mother's room was open, not that there was any chance of closing it without clearing some of the clutter first. Nera peeked in, barely catching sight of Wisp's tail at the window as he took off into the air again. Mother sat at her desk with a pile of empty papers on her left and full ones on her right, her quill furiously working on the half-filled sheet in front of her.

Mother raised her smiling face toward Nera, but her hand continued scribbling as she spoke: "Welcome, welcome, my child. It's good to see you after so long."

"Too long, Mother. It's good to see you, and that you're as vital as ever. It's not just my correspondence keeping your hand busy, then?" Nera asked, trying to insert some levity into the obvious question.

Mother's smile widened. "No, it's not. But it is one of my more pleasant pastimes."

"What're you working on now?" Nera asked.

"Come and have a look, why don't you?"

Nera came closer and tilted her head to get a better view of her mother's writing:

"Nera came closer and tilted her head to get a better view of my writing," said the latest line of text as soon as her mother had finished with it. Nera raised her eyebrow. "Nera raised her eyebrow," Mother added.

Nera sat on the spare stool next to the desk. "Well, at least from what I can tell, you're writing what I'm doing *after* the fact," she said matter-of-factly.

Her mother chuckled. "Right you are, my girl. You always were quick to notice such things." Her hand continued to write. A quick glance told Nera that yes, her mother was writing her own words down as well.

"For what purpose are you narrating everything we do, if you don't mind me asking?"

"Why, what does one usually make notes for? I want to be able to remember my dear daughter's visit. Ah. 'Nera pursed her lips, perhaps thinking my memory isn't what it used to be.' My recollection is fine, dear. It's just, you know, sometimes writing things down helps in forming memories. Ones that last."

"I see." What with the piles of text in the house, Nera wondered if her mother's scribal habits had gotten a bit out of control. Then again, Mother seemed very present even as her hand wrote down the minutiae of their encounter. Perhaps she should reserve judgment. "Well, if you think my visit is worth jotting down, who am I to argue?" She gave her mother a smile.

"Worth it indeed. Now, if you wouldn't mind lending a hand, we should probably be getting ready for supper, and I've had my hands full in writing my memoirs. I do have some sweets stashed for the solstice, so fear not, it'll be more than potatoes."

Nera laughed, and they proceeded to the main room to prepare supper, Mother taking her quill and some sheets along.

As they dug into their vegetable casserole at the table, Mother noted that she'd want to know all about Nera's life in Mayview, everything Nera hadn't had time to go through yet in their correspondence.

Mother dipped her quill in ink and made notes as Nera recounted some of her older trials and triumphs from back when she'd just started out on her own. Easing births, setting bones, pulling teeth. More often than not, she'd managed to eke out a victory for life, and from the occasional defeat she'd made a point to learn what went wrong, to better be prepared for the next challenge.

Given a less-than-subtle prod from her mother, Nera mused that there was, indeed, a man in the village who'd been casting eyes at her. However, she was doing just fine on her own, and she'd kept away from such attentions thus far as she wasn't certain that was quite her thing. Mother laughed at that, telling the blushing Nera that she didn't have to have any one thing if she didn't so choose, or, indeed, any thing at all.

The two talked well into the night, taking a break only to go outside and see the midnight stars as they were on the darkest night of the year. Eventually the late hour got the better of them, and they fell asleep together in Mother's bed.

The next day it was time for Nera to leave, as it was not good for a medicine woman to stay away from her village for too long. The two exchanged hearty goodbyes, and promised to continue keeping Wisp busy.

Nera left for home, her step heavy only for the voluminous pages of medicinal lore her mother had bestowed on her, fresh out of the quill.

Three weeks after her visit, Nera woke up to a loud cawing from the door. Everything was dark, and Nera felt that she hadn't had a proper night's sleep. Wisp must've flown to her across the night. That was unusual, to say the least.

She rose to sit and fumbled for the lantern and tinderbox by her bedside. Getting a flame going was a moment's work. Then she dragged her feet to the door and opened it.

Wisp was standing on the porch, his head low, with a cylinder that must've been ten inches long beside him. There was no string, though the cylinder had a couple of clawholds.

"Oh, my. You've been brave," Nera said.

Wisp ruffled his feathers and stepped inside wearily, leaving the cylinder out on the porch.

"I'll take care of that for you," Nera said, picking up the package and closing the door. "You must be starving. Let me get you a little something before I open this."

Wisp cawed approvingly as Nera set some nuts and dried

berries on a plate in front of him. Then she sat on her desk and opened the cylinder in the light of the lantern.

Out popped a single scroll along with a black quill pen, similar to what her mother had used when Nera was visiting. She examined the quill in her hand. The feather had perfect vanes with a smooth shine to them. The tip was sharp, suitable for precision work. Such quills were often from crows.

"This yours?" Nera asked Wisp.

The familiar cawed and bobbed his head up and down.

"From a molting, I trust?" she continued. That was, after all, the usual way.

Wisp nodded again, then turned back to his nuts.

Nera flashed a brief smile. "A considerate gift, to be sure, but you wouldn't have had to fly all night to bring it," she said as she laid the pen down on the table and spread out the scroll.

Dear Nera,

I thank you for a truly blessed time these past few months. Our correspondence has been a wonderful way for me to reminisce, to take stock of my life through writing. I must confess I had an ulterior motive for this, but do not doubt my sincerity in everything I've written, for it was a necessity in fulfilling my other purpose as well. I'm proud of you, and though I taught you to be a medicine woman, I fear I may have concentrated on that overmuch, leaving you to teach yourself to be a proper human being. It is of some consolation that you've done a good job of it.

I have lived a good, long life, and I could feel it in my bones that this would be my last winter. So I poured out my soul through this here quill, to keep it when my body was done.

That time has come. Please take care of Wisp for me, and arrange a proper burial for my earthly remains. All of my wisdom, such as it is, is yours to find in my writings at home.

Or you may find it in your hand, as I am here for you, if you'll have me.

Love,

The letter ended without a signature.

After staring at the scroll for a few moments, Nera became aware of movement in her peripheral vision and turned to look. The quill was hovering over the inkwell in a quiet gesture of request, rotating as if suspended from above by a thread. Nera's mouth fell open.

Moving as if in a dream, she opened the inkwell. The pen carefully dipped in, swooped up to the letter and signed it: *"Raziela."* Mother's handwriting, no doubt about it.

Wisp hopped onto the table and nuzzled Nera. She pushed back softly, her eyes still on the hovering quill. Wisp hopped over her arm and nuzzled the quill, which caressed his feathers gently. Wisp tilted his head contentedly.

A single tear rolled down Nera's cheek.

"Welcome home, Mom."

Mikko Rauhala (they/them) is a Finnish speculative fiction writer who sometimes feels like the crowded center of a Venn diagram of all things weird. They often write their stories in both English and Finnish, which can get frustrating when there's no one else to blame for the occasional plot-relevant double entendre. Informed by their master's degree in intelligent systems, Rauhala is most at home in hard science fiction settings, but they're not exclusive and like to cross genres. Rauhala has dabbled in editing flash fiction for *The Self-Inflicted Relative* anthology, and some of their darker sci-fi can be found in the *Infinite Metropolis* short story and audio drama collection, co-authored with Edmund Schluessel. They can be reached at rauhala.org

Ink

E.D.E. Bell

You lean back against the vinyl seat and position your arm on the ledge. They told you they'd adjust you how they needed, but they probably don't have your bad back. So you get in a place you'll be able to hold.

Since this might take a while.

They're tapping out black ink into little plastic cans, like the ones you used to paint from when you were a child.

Their asymmetrical hair flops over as they lean across the stand. You can't help but think how cute they are, harmonizing the big, bold colors and fierce images tacked across their wall. Music with a smooth, rhythmic beat plays behind them. You wonder if they chose it for you.

They ask if you're ready.

That's a deeper answer, so you just blurp a little yep.

Again, they run a wipe across your arm. Cool, cleansing. Soft.

Soon, no one will wash this away.

They side-eye you, trying to verify that you really understand. With a shrug and a let's go, the buzzing needle makes contact with your aging skin.

You sink into the feeling. This is not pain. You've felt pain.

This is business. This is the hum of traffic, the flashing of a tunnel. This is life.

Quite a list, they say. Never like to pry, but if you want to tell me what it's for, we've got a few.

You close your eyes. You open them. There's a bright light, and deep beats, and someone outside is telling a sex joke.

These are all the things I was told not to say, you state. Things that are right. Things that are true. Things that I am.

Bit of an overreaction, they quip, then stop, like maybe they'd gone too far. Like maybe they were talking about themself. You feel that.

So you don't answer. You hold still, knowing each stroke will last a lifetime. What's left, anyway.

The pulsing beats are pleasant. They definitely picked this for you.

Try and relax, they say. This is going to take a while.

E.D.E. Bell (she/e) writes unique fantasy fiction that blends traditional and modern elements. A passionate vegan and enthusiastic denier of gender rules, she feels strongly about issues related to equality and compassion. After nearly two decades in technical intelligence, she now applies her magic to the creation of genre-bending fantasy fiction in Ferndale, Michigan, where she is proud to be part of the Detroit arts community. She loves cats and trees. She revels in garlic. You can follow her adventures at edebell.com.

The Drawing of a Sword

K. Alysee Simon

I slid my hand across the blank paper, pushing out any creases and brushing away any crumbs. The large parchment thinned in spots across the center. Soon, I'd need to replace it. Already this piece had served up six swords, two shields, and thirty-four arrows. It wouldn't survive much else before the cream surface tore under my pen's nib.

One more sword then, and hopefully I could retire for the day—if the commander allowed it. I stood from my stool and lifted my ink bottle, giving the contents a swirl. The red-brown ink swished against the glass. I breathed out slowly, preparing myself. It took months to learn how to work amidst the war camp's noise, to figure out how to ignore the clack of soldiers walking in armor, of orders shouted, of the roar of the nearby blacksmith's forge. War was never quiet.

Calm, I picked up my pen and dipped the tip into the ink before facing the parchment. One breath of anxiety rose in my chest as the blank expanse stared back at me. I didn't let it linger, forcing myself to start at the far edge, drawing a single curve from the left side, across the desk, to the right. I dipped for more ink, back to the parchment, drawing another line, completing the curve of the blade. Ink again, to etch out the fine lines of a hilt. Back and forth I went, to the ink, to the parchment, to the ink. I gave it depth, adding hatching across the blade before drawing a small jewel at the base of the hilt. The pen's nib scratched and scritched with each movement.

The motions pulsed through me like the beat of drum, and as I made the last mark, the tempo of my work ceased. I stepped back. The sword was more elegant than what I usually drew. War meant fast production, necessity only—a sharp blade, a strong grip, a balanced hilt. This piece was more.

"That's a bit much, don't you think?" Detta asked as she came up behind me.

"It will cut," I said simply. I ran my fingers over the coarse wood of my pen's barrel, my fingers catching in the notches where I'd bitten it, and one mark from when it got smashed between some rocks after I took a tumble. I needed to be more careful, because if another pen could be created in all the world like it, I knew not how.

"Is there any particular reason you're here?" I asked as I set aside my pen and turned to the parchment. Detta commanded over the army's archers, and strangely, also over me. We'd formed something close to friendship over the past two months—an understanding of where each of us stood.

She stood quietly waiting as I wiggled my fingers above the drawing's hilt and reached down. My hand slipped into the parchment and I gripped the sword, carefully pulling it from the sheet hilt first. The fine lines my pen made shook, vibrating with magic as slowly, inch by inch, the sword took solid form, slipping free until I held the entire blade out at my side.

This was the magic of my pen—the magic I was known across the kingdom for. It was the reason the Queen had me dragged from my home and stationed here, with orders to create until the war ended, or until I died.

Detta shook her head, and held out her hand to take the sword from me. I handed it over. "No particular reason," she said as she lifted it left and right before giving a casual swing. "Other than needing my daily dose of your bitterness." She flashed me a grin.

"No battles today?" I looked to the south, where somewhere beyond the rolling hills stood the army from the Southern Isles of Elotch. I had yet to lay eyes on them myself, and preferred to keep it that way. I'd heard enough stories about their soldiers riding into battle on the back of giant gear and clockwork wolves, they already filled my nightmares—and to think, their invasion could have been avoided if the Queen had simply apologized for the slight she'd shown the Elotch King at court last fall.

"No," she said, putting aside the sword, suddenly sober. She wore the leather armor she always kept on, even on battle-free days, as though she couldn't imagine the weight of breathing without it. "There are rumors that more ships have arrived on the coast, carrying more soldiers, and more of their mechanical wolves." She swept closer, a foot away, and slid her hand across the parchment which had indeed torn from the last sketch. "Most of the other commanders won't say it, but whispers have started spreading that this will be it. Our last stand." Her voice fell like the whispered scratch of my pen when I drew.

I took a step back, lost for words. I was no soldier of war. Years ago, I'd suffered an accident involving a horse and more ale than a youth of seventeen years should ever drink. It left me with a twisted leg, and the determination to become better with my hands than most were on their feet. Ten years of wood carving and blacksmithing and somehow, I created the pen—a creation I was never able to repeat again, no matter how I tried. My place was with it in my hand, and paper before me, drawing creations faster than a blacksmith could smith them.

If we were to lose, and the Elotchians to push into camp, I would run. There would be no last stand for me.

Detta must have seen the terror flash in my eyes, for she lifted her hand from the parchment and placed it on my shoulder. She left it there for a long moment before she pulled it away and moved back to her spot. "Have you ever thought of drawing something else?" she asked, her eyes falling on my pen where it rested beside my bottle of ink. "Maybe a magic staff that could kill a horde?"

I shook my head and rolled up the torn parchment, dumping it in a vase in the corner. "You know it's not so simple," I said, unrolling a fresh piece, weighting its corners with glass stones. "It only works when I draw something I could make without the pen's magic."

She rolled her shoulders before lifting a hand to push back her bangs. "And all you know is swords and shields."

"And horseshoes and helmets," I added.

"Is there nothing else you know how to make?" she muttered, but she was already headed out of the tent, to wherever it was commanders went to prepare for war.

"Maps," I called, unsure if she'd even hear me. "My father was a cartographer."

They came just before the sun rose in the sky, before the soldiers could break their fast with a meal, before most had even rolled from their sleeping mats and emptied their bladders. The warning came as a shrill wail of a horn, followed by the rumble of shouted orders. I woke with them. At first, I stood watching them prepare. Detta hurried by and I couldn't even get up the words to wish her health and strength.

The mechanical wolves came over the hilltops an hour later. They stood at the top, staring down at us, watching as our soldiers fell into ranks. A courtesy that they didn't come crashing down like a hammer on glass, smashing us to smithereens. I stood beside a few of the other blacksmiths, studying the indistinct black blob that was the far-off silhouette of their creations.

"This is it," the eldest of us said. "This is where it ends."

Anger flared in me at his words. I turned my gaze on him, my lip curling.

"Cay!" Detta called, catching me before the fire of my anger could catch hold of my tongue. "Get your pen. I want you on the front lines, drawing arrows."

"What?" I gasped. I'd never been called to do such work. After I'd been brought in, I'd been left to draw and create, alone in my tent. Never had I been forced to the front lines. But never had the front lines been a mere hundred feet from my tent.

"Hurry," she said, breathless with adrenaline and fear.

I hurried back to my tent, gathering a new piece of parchment, my ink, and my pen. I came back to find an archer I'd never met before waiting for me. He waved me along, hurrying me as fast as my limp could go. We stopped at the back of the front lines, the rows of our army's soldiers stretched out in the clearing before the camp. The horde stood hundreds of meters away, waiting as we organized—a respect their people showed in war.

Detta stood at the back, lines of her archers before her. She pointed to a spot at her side where a box had been set, a pile of stones atop it. I quickly sat and rolled the parchment out on the crate, uncorking my bottle of ink.

"This isn't what I signed up for," I said, my heart pounding with more force than I'd felt it exert before. I couldn't breathe, and yet I was breathing so fast I could barely do much else.

"You didn't sign up at all," Detta said, before she pulled on her helmet and picked up her bow. "Now start drawing."

I took in my blank parchment, my head spinning, ugly gasps of air catching in my throat. The horde on the hill began to move. First slowly, as though they too weren't sure of what they were about to do, and then suddenly like a dam breaking, they flew down the hill.

"Fire!" Detta called to her archers. They released their arrows, quickly reaching for more. She ordered them to fire again. I followed the arc of the arrows as they fell toward the advancing mass, their figures still too far out to yet feel like troops.

I always knew the war was real, and yet, until it stood right before me, I hadn't truly known its reality.

"Arrows! Cay, draw us arrows!" Detta hovered at my side, her face white with terror, her voice ragged from shouting. The archers around her reached for their quivers, pulling again from their stores, half their stash already depleted—not enough. There was no amount I could draw that would be enough.

The horns of warning sounded, their blare reaching deep within me and breaking through the ice holding me tight. I gave off one shiver before inking my pen. And then I drew.

I drew curved lines and broken ones. I hatched details and stippled shadows. I moved as fast as I could, my hand cramping as I held it over the paper, careful not to smudge the wet markings. The pen hummed in my fingers.

"Cay, what are you doing?" Detta shouted. The heat from her body burned at my back, her terror mixing in the air with that of all the other soldiers around us. My Kingdom's people. Many of whom were pulled from their homes unwillingly, just like me. All because our Queen wouldn't give a proper apology for a simple slight the Elotch King wouldn't let go.

I drew without looking up. I drew even as blood splattered across the parchment and Detta shouted at me for arrows, more arrows. I drew for what felt like hours, but couldn't have been more than a handful of minutes.

One more mark. I looked up before making it. The clockwork wolves descended toward us like an avalanche of moving metal, their gears clicking, the soldiers on their backs hollering war cries. Arrows flew from both sides, some finding their marks, others sinking into the ground or bouncing off shields. The distance between the two armies was closing.

I squeezed my pen tight. I'd first discovered its magic on accident, a sketch of a dagger coming off the parchment and into my hand. The week after was spent experimenting, learning the limits of what the pen could do—and what it could not.

I had always assumed the magic was tied to my own ability. That if I could make it at a forge, I could use the pen to draw it into creation.

I prayed I was wrong. I prayed it wasn't tied to my ability to create, but to my knowledge, to what I knew of blacksmithing—and map making.

Dipping the pen one last time into my ink, I drew the last line.

The pen snapped. It broke in two in my hand, the nib half tumbling to the ground, the other half falling to the parchment. It laid there, unmoving. I held my breath, my heart frozen in my chest as the ground trembled from the horde stampeding toward us.

It hadn't worked. Of course it hadn't. Detta screamed again for her archers to fire. Arrows sang through the air.

I studied the sketch, my hands numb. A coarse drawing of the battleground stared back at me, the lines rushed and rough, but solid. Until one disappeared, and then another, and another. The sketch faded away.

I looked up. All around us the ground continued to shake, but not from the stampede of mechanical wolves. The horde slowed. Wolves clanked and clacked as they skidded to stops. Our line of soldiers stumbled on their feet.

"What's going on?" Detta asked, looking to me.

"Magic," I muttered as the ground ripped open at the base of the hill, the chasm splitting too fast for anyone to react, metal wolves falling into it, filling the air with the scent of spilt oil as the earth continued to crumble beneath the enemy's army.

I had done it—saved our army, saved these soldiers, yet at the cost of others. So many others. They tumbled into the abyss I'd drawn, gone from our land, but also gone from theirs.

"I'm done," I said, bending to pick up the other half of my pen. The two halves fit together perfectly, but they felt wrong. Hollow and cold.

The ground finally stopped rumbling. The remainder of the horde stared across the chasm at us, so little of them left.

"Send a message to the Queen," I said, shoving my broken pen in my pocket. "Tell her I'm done making weapons. Tell her she needs to end this before we lose. Before we all lose."

K. Alysee Simon (she/her) is a librarian with a background in the arts, specifically ceramics. She came to librarian work and writing after graduation, and loves helping people, whether with words or finding information. When she's not reading, writing, or working, she enjoys playing video games, walking her dogs, or spending time with her significant other. For her, storytelling is about building worlds with endless possibilities, especially ones that have never existed before. She can be visited at ksimonfiction.wordpress.com.

Nothing to Write Home About

M. R. DeLuca

"Yes, Mom, I'll be finished sorting through Gram's stuff by tonight. Tomorrow morning, the latest. I'll let you know what was in Gram's secret room. No, I won't forget to pick up you and Dad at the airport. That happened only one time. I know you had to take a taxi fifty miles— Mom, I have to go. Say hi to Dad for me." Nestor hung up before his mother could say another word.

He hated to be rude, especially to his own family, but he had grown weary of everyone in his life treating him like he was an irresponsible child: his parents, his former (numerous) bosses, his ex- (also numerous) girlfriends. That is, everyone except Gram. She took him seriously. So seriously, in fact, that she'd entrusted him as the sole living keeper of her secrets.

And now she was gone.

Gram lived in a beautiful split-level in a desirable neighborhood. His family members were itching to put it on the market and split the proceeds, but—the will stipulated that Nestor, only Nestor, had to empty the contents first.

Which is how he found himself alone in the big, dusty old house.

He had no reason to say no. He was between jobs again, could really use the money from the house sale, and had promised Gram years prior that he, and nobody else, would empty the secret room. As flighty as people thought he was, he kept whatever promises he made.

So the executor handed him a pen-shaped skeleton key with a heart-shaped bow and explained that, per Gram's written instructions, the locked room should be entered last and alone.

After working almost non-stop for the better part of two days, Nestor was almost finished cleaning. Most of the things he had gone through so far were knickknacks or appliances, things he could discard without being slowed by sentimentality. But the smallest second-floor bedroom would surely take time.

He had never been in Gram's secret room.

Nobody had, in fact, except for her and Gramps. As family lore had it, as a young mother Gram one day said she had an important project to tackle and claimed the glorified closet. She never mentioned what she was doing all those hours, all those years, locked in that cramped little room, and all Gramps would say when their kids asked was, "Chasing immortality, how should I know? Go do your homework or something." But they told each other everything. Gramps knew what his wife was doing, and kept mum his whole life.

Nestor took a deep breath. This was it. He twisted the key in his hand. Gram had entrusted him with some, but not all, of the details he needed in understanding what he was about to see. Still questions, so many questions, left unanswered. When he pressed her, all she had mentioned was that jigsaw puzzles were more than the sum of their pieces, and patience precedes the full picture.

Nestor was more of a checkers kind of guy himself.

He paused just outside the faded door. He wanted to savor those last few moments of ignorance. Whatever lay behind the door, he needed to remember that Gram was a person like everyone else, and like everyone else, was entitled to her share of secrets.

He just hoped he could handle them.

He opened the door.

He surveyed the tiny room. When Gram had talked about dabbling in inventing, she wasn't kidding. The floor was littered with gears and wires and thingamabobs for which Nestor didn't know the names. The complicated machinery on the simple wooden desk, however, was neatly arranged, giving wide berth to a single fountain pen.

Nestor sighed in relief. He would marvel at some of the inventions and scrawled blueprints, maybe even be bemused by others, but the instructions were clear—to the trash heap they go. After emptying the cramped workspace, as Gram presumably wanted, and letting the lawyer know he was finished, he could finally return to doing what he did best: drifting through life.

"So you're Nestor. Edna has told me so much about you! She's right, you do need a haircut."

Nestor looked around. "Who said that?" He grabbed the pen from the desk, prepared to use it against the unseen intruder. Of course, he'd probably just toss it as a distraction and run, but the trespasser need not know that.

"Ow, stop squeezing me so tight! I know my daughter has taught you manners, so use them!"

Nestor loosened his grip, allowing the pen to slip out and levitate at eye level. He furrowed his brow. "I've heard your voice in home movies. You must be . . . Gramps?"

"Gramps? I like it! Short and snazzy. Say it again!"

"You're my . . . Gramps? As in, married to Gram?" So this was one of the . . . interesting inventions she warned he might find.

"I didn't introduce myself, did I? Darn it, I had years to practice this meeting, and I go and botch it. Let's not tell your grandma, okay?"

Nestor shook his head at the floating pen before him. "I'm sorry, but Gram died recently."

"I know! Isn't that great? Now we've both passed!"

This conversation was getting too morbid. "This conversation is getting too morbid."

"No, no, son, you have it all wrong. We've both passed . . . into these pens! Sentient little monsters, she calls us." He chuckled.

Monsters. Everything clicked. Nestor rubbed his temples and plopped in the desk chair. Gramps floated over. "Grams read the abridged version of *Frankenstein* to me as a kid. A lot. It wasn't just her favorite story, was it? It was an inspirational bible."

"What a smart boy! No wonder she entrusted you with this responsibility." Uh-oh. Nestor fought the urge to run. A simple promise was one thing. A responsibility? Now that was another ballfield. He still preferred checkers.

"I think you need to start from the beginning, Gramps."

"Gladly. You know, your grandma always told me I was a man of few words. Or was it that she wished I was? Well, I'll try to be brief.

"Gram had a true gift for inventing, and I mean once-in-a-generation talent. In another time and place, engineering schools would've showered her with scholarships and fancy equipment and whatever, but those opportunities weren't available to her in our day.

"Lack of outside support never stopped her, however. She continued innovating, privately, and I agreed to tell nobody, not even our children. We cleared out the smallest guest bedroom, and renovated it into a mini-laboratory that became her haven for decades.

"We took the secret of this lab's existence to our graves. Er, pens. I still don't understand half of her work, but I do know she was always trying to do important things, and made some real progress. Gram, who really was searching for immortality—I wasn't lying about that—found it. A glitchy form of it."

"Glitchy?"

"Hey, I like to be hip with the cool kids' lingo. And I know what a computer is, Gram made sure of that. Couldn't use the mouse, though, and dang it if those things mocked me until electronic styluses became all the rage. Ha! I can *transform* into a stylus pen at will. Who's laughing now, electronic rodents!"

"Gramps? You were talking about immortality?"

"Right. So these matching his-and-hers fountain pens we bought together on our honeymoon had the power to absorb our souls. Deep stuff, right? Gram discovered it after the kids moved out.

"One day I was using the pen I'm in now to do a crossword, and absentmindedly bit of a nice chunk of my candy bar. It lodged in my throat, and my breathing completely stopped. I found myself inside the pen, looking out at my body, yelling for Gram to administer first aid. It worked, and I returned to my fantastic earthly physique for many more years.

"I don't why or how these pens allow us to live forever. She performed experiments and, using mathematical methods, learned the pens only work on us. I told her it was the power of our everlasting love. She said it was a singularity in the space-time continuum that aligned with the stars, or something like that.

"She did her science-magic-whatever and programmed the pens to receive our minds and souls when we died. We can talk and move around as we wish, but I elected to stay indoors all these years. Your Gram never perfected teleportation, and I don't think the world is ready for a walking, talking pen yet. There'd be widespread panic. But not with robots. You young people love your robots, those big, boxy clunks over our fancy, fountain sleekness. It's downright discriminatory, I tell you! Anyhoo, that's it."

Nestor still had one question left. "Why couldn't she tell me all this earlier?"

"She didn't want to give you the whole story ahead of time, just in case all this didn't work. That way, you would've thought we just moved on, and couldn't blame yourself for us not 'making it' to the pens. She always cared about others' feelings more than her own, for better or for worse."

"Sounds like Gram. By the way . . . where is she? I don't see her pen on the desk."

"Have you given me great-grandchildren yet? How many kids you got by now? Six? Seven?"

"Gramps, I don't have even have one! Now where's Gram? It's been a long time since I've talked to her." Months, he was ashamed to admit.

"No great-grandchildren!" He scoffed. "Now I don't have to worry about what they'll call me. I was partial to Greatest Gramps or Super G . . . "

"Gramps! I mean no disrespect but. What. Happened. To. Gram."

Gramps started inching away. "Can't we talk about this later? I have to use the pens' room. 'When the ink doth flow, you've got to go,' as William Shakespen probably said."

Nestor raised an eyebrow. "Do you really have to go, Gramps, or are you just stalling?"

"Fine." He paused. "Gram left. We were arguing about who

sleeps on which side of the desk. We have our share of tiffs, like all couples do. Like when your Gram decided we needed to eat healthier, and she gave me veggie burgers every day. Boy, was she mad when she discovered I replaced the whole grain buns with sliced doughnuts! That was a bad idea. I should have used glazed, not sprinkles."

Nestor was growing impatient. "Gramps, I'm serious. Tell me where Gram went, or I will tear this house apart looking for her."

"There's no need," said a voice from the hall. "I'm right here."

Nestor jumped out of the chair. In the doorway floated a pen identical to the one before him. "Gram? Is that you?"

"Edna! I'm so happy you returned!"

She entered the room with a presence far greater than her size. "I was just downstairs, watching Nestor from afar. As for you, mister—I'll stay for good, too, as long as you promise to stop being so stubborn and ornery!"

"Never!"

Nestor dropped his face into his open palms.

Gram cackled. "There's my crabby Quinton! I've missed you, too!"

Nestor asked, "Do I want to know what just happened here?"

"Over fifty years of marriage, dear," said Gram. "And to a lifetime of many more."

"Enough with the mushiness! Now that Edna's returned, it's time to get down to business." He floated next to his wife. "Nestor, we can't live here after you sell the house, so we have another favor to ask you." Gramps took a deep breath. "We need you to bring us someplace we can spend eternity. Somewhere fun."

"Somewhere practical," Gram countered. "We're technologically advanced pens! We can't just fly around where we want, or we'll find ourselves captured and dissected node by node in a secret government lab. That's why we need someone we trust to transport us to our eternal hiding place. Now, if we were robots, they'd accept us everywhere."

"That's what I said! So we need somewhere less inhabited. Like a tropical island. Or the bayous of Pen-sacola?" Gramps chuckled.

"Quinton, mind your puns! This is serious. We're talking about our eternity here. We have to be realistic about Nestor finding us our forever home. We can't expect him to drop everything and run to Tahiti because you want to swim with dolphins. If he's going to help us relocate, it's going to have to be on his terms and with his input."

Nestor crossed his arms. "Gram? Gramps? This makes no sense. I didn't want to say anything earlier but—why me? Our family is huge, and full of accomplished people. It's one thing to clean a house; it's another to decide where you two are going to live forever."

"Because, Nestie"—few people could get away with using that nickname, and Gram was at the top of the list—"we can depend on you. I love my kids, but they're too unimaginative to handle this situation. You might not believe it yet, but you are a good person, and I know you'll do right by us. I truly believe that. I always have, and I always will."

That little seed of faith Gram had planted so many years ago had finally blossomed. She had believed in him when his own parents thought he was a failure. She was always the one telling him he could do it, he could commit, he could succeed, whether it was in school or work, regardless of his shoddy track record. Gram had such tremendous confidence in him that he had to reciprocate somehow. The woman had been sacrificing for everyone her whole life—it was her turn to be on the receiving end.

"You know what, Gram? I don't want the house sold. This is your and Gramps' home. You should live here."

"We can't do that," Gramps said sadly. "An eternally empty house would look suspicious, and we can't afford attention. Or the insurance."

Nestor knew exactly what he was going to do. "Then I'll live here. We'll be housemates. We'll set schedules and divvy up the rooms, so we'll still have privacy. We'll work it out."

"That's wonderful!" said Gram. Are you sure that's what you want? It's okay if you change your mind."

"I really hope you don't."

"Don't influence him, Quinton! He needs to make the best decision for himself."

Nestor felt giddy. A home, a place where he belonged, a chance to plant some roots. He couldn't take off at a moment's notice, but he didn't want to anymore. He wanted the obligation of family. He needed it. "I'm as sure as I've been of anything in my life."

"Get me some paper, Nestor." He obliged. She scribbled a quick will dated after the lawyer's version. "Take this to the lawyer."

Nestor grabbed the paper. "Gram, you forged a notary's signature!"

"Oh, hush. I'm a fabulous, immortal fountain pen and I can do whatever I want! What are they going to do, throw me in the pen-itentiary?"

Gramps roared. "There's my bride! Come here, my sweet."

The pens floated closer together. "Last chance to bow

out, Nestor. File those papers and the house can't be sold for a century," said Gram.

Nestor grinned. "I'm going. Be back later." For once, responsibility felt good.

"Be a dear and close the door on your way out, Nestie."

"Yeah, give us some privacy! We've got lots of canoodling to catch up on."

"Ew, Gramps," he said with a laugh.

"Now go on. Shoo!" said Gram.

As Nestor locked the front door, his cellphone rang. "Hello? I finished cleaning up, Mom. Listen, I need to run to the lawyer. I found some important documents that weren't filed. Yes, I did clear out Gram's secret room. The secret? Nothing to write home about, Mom—just some old tools, papers, and a couple of really wonderful fountain pens."

M. R. DeLuca is a short story writer with over a half-dozen publishing credits to her name. She is from New York and enjoys writing plot twists, humorous dialogue, and a brief author bio.

Write Me a Soul

Jennifer Lee Rossman

<u>*Page 1*</u>

You should have known better. No, scratch that. You did know better, but you wrote her into existence anyway, and now you have to deal with the consequences.

But how? How do you even begin to "deal with" a mistake of this magnitude?

Mistake. You shake your head. No, she is not a mistake. She is perfection, from her slicked-back hair the color of a black hole to her leather jacket to her pointed nose that's just a little crooked from where your pen slipped.

Maybe she's not what most people would think of when they imagine their perfect woman, but she's your perfect woman, a distillation of all those cartoon villains that gave you confusing feelings back when you were a little baby queer.

And she has fangs, because ... well, because some part of your subconscious apparently has a thing for fangs.

Hopefully she doesn't think you created her for any creepy reason. You don't expect anything from her, except maybe friendship if she's up for that.

You can't help but be proud of yourself for describing her so well, though, right down to the way she draws her mouth into a tight line when she's thinking. Every part of her, every movement is so real, you can hardly tell she's made of nothing but ink, ideas, and a little bit of magic.

But she can tell. She knows she doesn't have a soul.

You've spent all morning writing in your notebook, filling it with possible ways to help her. And because you've been writing with *that* pen, you can see every scenario unfolding in your mind like a second sight. It honestly makes your stomach queasy, having such power.

So. What do you do?

Break the pen (page 2)
Use the pen to try and help her (page 3)

<u>Page 2</u>

You know it's a bad idea, but you don't second-guess yourself. The pen puts up little resistance, snapping in your hand.

You expect ink to spill out, turn your skirt into a Rorschach test. (You would see sea monsters; you always do.) But the pen is magic.

Was magic.

You've never refilled it, never had to shake it or breathe on the tip to make it flow. And didn't it always have exactly the right color, whether you wanted black or blue or rainbow glitter? Maybe it shouldn't surprise you that the pen simply crumbles into ash and blows away on a breeze that comes from nowhere.

Your hands feel empty as your heart. It's gone. It's gone, and with it, all the beautiful mistakes you would have made in the future.

But you could have made good things, too. Wondrous machines to save lives, never-ending supplies of food and clothing.

Your eyes flick to her, and you feel her crushing disappointment. You should've tried to help her, not cut your losses and give up.

In the coming days and weeks, you try to make her happy. You play games, make her breakfast, anything you can think of to make her smile and show off those rows of pointed teeth.

She tells you she's all right, that she doesn't need to be happy, and you pretend to believe her because that's what friends do.

When she cries, her tears are like ink.

END

Page 3

"It's magic," you tell her, holding the pen in your hand for dear life.

You could tell her the story of how it came to be in your possession. The group home, the found family, the adopted bloodline and the "you're a wizard, Harry" jokes. But you think it's more important to show her.

You ask her what she wants you to write into existence.

"Flowers," she says after a moment, almost reluctantly. Like she doesn't want you to know she's soft inside.

"Flowers." You smile, grab a scrap of paper, and begin to write.

White anemones with black centers. Graceful white petals curling, cupping a lacy black eye. Bouquet spilling over a bride's hands, tied up with ribbons. Modern. Bold. Romance.

You've hardly finished your thought, and you already smell them. A second later, they appear next to you on the desk, the weight of all the flower heads slightly crushing the petals at the bottom.

With a soft gasp, she picks them up, marvels at them and buries her face in their aroma.

She has just one question. "Can you write me a soul?"

Confidently say yes (turn to page 4)
Say yes, uncertainly (turn to page 5)

<u>Page 4</u>

You open a new notebook. One of many blank notebooks you bought but never dared to use because it was just too pretty. Not worthy of whatever drivel you would put in it.

This, though. This is worthy. Hell, the notebook might not even be good enough. You're putting a soul inside of it; no notebook could be good enough, but this one will have to do.

On the first, crisp white page, you put the tip of the pen to paper.

Soul. Spirit. That indefinable spark of life. The fire burning in your heart. The 3-D glasses on your heart that makes the world real.

What are you writing?

You run your hands through your hair, chew on your lip. You can feel her watching you, her eyes glowering under heavily shaded lids.

But how do you write a *soul*?

You turn to a fresh page.

It is the light behind her eyes.

No. That's not right. To be honest, you don't even know if you believe in souls. You don't feel like you have a spark or a fire in you, at least not most of the time. If that's what a soul is, you only have one when you're with your loved ones.

You start to try again, but she senses your frustration and stops you. "It's not worth it," she says. "You're going to beat yourself up over this, and I'm fine without it."

You know she's not, but you don't want to get her hopes up.

Reluctantly, you set the pen down.

END

Page 5

Page after page of your beautiful notebook ends up crumpled on the floor. You struggle with describing a soul, because you don't really believe in one. It just seems too . . . fanciful. Magic.

Looking at the enchanted pen in your hand, you smirk.

"What's so funny?" she asks.

You start to tell her it's nothing, but then she touches your hand. A comforting, friendly gesture, it settles your mind for some reason. Puts you at ease. You haven't felt this good around someone since you left home, found your family.

"I was just thinking, I don't believe in souls. And yet here I have a magic pen that only works for certain people. The man who gave it to me, he's my brother now, he said only people with a certain kind of soul can write with this pen. Somehow I don't believe him."

"Souls . . . " She thoughtfully chews her bottom lip, somehow drawing no blood despite her razor teeth. "I think souls might be just our brains thinking about our brains. Consciousness. Brain waves, you know?"

She reaches for the pen but hesitates, looking to you for permission.

Your brother told you never to let anyone outside of the family touch it. That it's sacred, not for just anybody to use.

When you were writing out your options in your notebook, you saw one of the paths lead to this moment. And you didn't even hesitate; you only gave yourself one option.

Trust her (turn to page 6)

<u>*Page 6*</u>

She effortlessly writes a machine into existence. A small thing, with a screen and two electrodes. You hold your breath while she places one on her own temple, one on yours.

Two pixelated waves appear on the screen, perfectly in sync with each other.

"Souls," she begins, and somehow you mouth the words along with her because you know exactly what she's going to say. "Souls are just connections. Most people are born with at least one, and they come and go over time. I didn't have any because I'm made of paper and ink, but . . . but I think our brains fit with each other's."

You nod slowly. You didn't feel it at first, the connection. Not like with the rest of your family, where you just . . . clicked. But her ink was still wet. She didn't know who she was yet.

Now she's figuring it out, her brain is settling into a pattern, and it fits very well with yours.

For the first time in months, since you saw your family, you feel your heart beating in harmony, your breaths complementing hers. You feel that spark of life, the burning, the light.

Yes, you should have known better then to create life. But you're glad you did it anyway.

END

Jennifer Lee Rossman (she/her) is what you would get if Dr. Temperance Brennan from *Bones* was a Disney princess. She lives in a group home for disabled people in Binghamton, New York, and greatly enjoys beating her favorite staff member at Scrabble. She is the coeditor of *Space Opera Libretti*, and she tweets about gay stuff and dinosaurs @JenLRossman

CREATIVE
INK

Official Membership Offer

Writing is magic.
Voting is magic.
Community is magic.

Click your pen.
Do what you can. Your own way.
We're all here together.

You are—a good pen.
Your way will be right.
You are magic.

In acceptance of your membership,

Sign your name here: ________________________________

Content Notes

These content notes may reveal information about the plot of a story. They are provided here in case there are any elements you would like to avoid. They are for general reference and do not specify every element that might cause concern.

Throughout the collection, there are elements of sadness. Several stories acknowledge or demonstrate corporate, political, or cultural oppression including racism or colonization. Stories may reference historical events or war. They may reference general life trials, birth, or death. Stories may include family or relationship strife, including mentions of infidelity. Some stories hold moments of disrespect or deception. Magic may or may be perceived to influence events, sometimes without the clear consent of everyone affected. Stories may include cursing. Alcohol may be mentioned or used. There are several references to animal use including animals as food. If this general level of content would be troubling, we recommend you pre-screen or avoid reading the collection.

Specific additional notes:

Page 1, Penultimate - Issues of existence

Page 18, The Confessionist - Off-page mental anguish

Page 25, Mightier - Mild superhero violence

Page 32, Qalam - Mention of conquerors, fire, and destruction of religious texts, worry of stalking

Page 39, Inheritance - Death of grandmother, mention of depression, mention of difficult adoption

Page 50, The Taste of Words - Mild sexual flirtation, mention of blood and war

Page 65, The Cemetery Merchant - Mention of death of a spouse

Page 70, Love in the Library - Mention of homophobia

Page 79, Do Not Write to Wrong - Non-graphic mentions of war and gun violence against children, non-physically-painful attacks and bullying on children in school

Page 91, Invisible Ink - Invasive technology

Page 101, A Scrawl of Squid Ink - References to death and loss

Page 118, Today, I am a Fountain Pen - Mention of harm to a religious building and objects

Page 134, Material*Skin* - Loss, body and pain references, disembodiment, depression, smoking, gun mention, threat of death

Page 145, The Last of Your Kind - References to extinction

Page 147, Memory Malfunction - Invasive behavior toward disabled character

Page 162, Mystical Woo - Mention of 9-11

Page 174, Charcoals from an Unidentified Chicago Artist - References to fire and death

Page 180, Pointy Chances - Mild head bump and related joke

Page 196, Illumination - Fire, discussion of sin

Page 209, One Story, Two People - Off-page attempted assault, non-violent death

Page 221, Writ Large - Disrespect, loss of communication, brief mention of invasive technology in interrogation

Page 232, Rhapsody in D Minor - Mobility loss

Page 237, Written with Love - Temporary, non-violent mental coercion

Page 243, The Healer - Illness, mention of political violence

Page 248, Magical Markers - Hospital setting, cancer and death including children

Page 252, Rekindled - Mention of death and disease

Page 262, Ink - Mention of tattoo pain

Page 264, The Drawing of a Sword - Weapons, war, and non-graphic mass violence

Page 273, Nothing to Write Home About - Recent natural death of grandparent, lighthearted age and death humor

www.ingramcontent.com/pod-product-compliance
Lightning Source LLC
Chambersburg PA
CBHW051642180726
48284CB00006B/1830

9781945009600